Copyright

First Edition, November 2020

Copyright © 2020 by Anneke Boshoff

D1714099

Chapter 1

Brad Davis, the 25-year-old CEO of Davis International, sat at his desk looking out his office window. He had the perfect view of central park; this was the only view that could calm him.

He turned his chair back to his desk, the first thing he saw was the picture of him and his wife. He was married to Amelia Anderson. It wasn't your typical marriage; Amelia is one of his father's associate's daughter, this was an arranged marriage. Brad knew he would have to marry for the company one day, so now here he is married two years, now they want an heir to one day take over the company. Brad didn't want to have children with Amelia, but Brad didn't have a choice. The photo he has on his desk of him and his wife is just for appearance. They didn't want anyone to question their relationship, whatever that might be.

Brad lifted his head over to the door when there was a knock. "Come in." He calls out to the person knocking.

Damon, one of his best friends and also the head of his construction team, sticks his head through the door. "We're still on for Friday?" Damon questions. A smile formed on Brad's lips. Fridays were his night for relaxing. Brad and the boys would head to the beer garden, have some beers, and then head to the club to relax. Since Brad got married, he has not looked at another woman; even though he didn't like his wife, he didn't want to be disrespectful and have a girl on the side. He respected his marriage contract.

"You know I will be there. See you Friday." Brad stated as Damon nodded his head before heading out. Brad had to get ready for a meeting and needed to stop wondering what his life could have been like if he wasn't married or even if he was but actually liked his wife.

The rest of the week went by in a flash. He had one meeting after another. They also had an appointment for Saturday at the clinic to have IVF done.

Brad headed over to the bar to meet up with Damon and Conner like always. Conner is one of Brad's other friends, who is also his company's legal adviser.

They have been at the bar for a few hours, it was time for them to head out to the club. "Hey, What are you doing?" Damon tried to see what Brad was seeing. Brad sat at their table, looking at the bar through the bottom of his beer glass.

"Isn't she beautiful?" Brad uttered but kept looking through the glass. Damon followed his gaze, finally seeing who Brad has been staring at for the past hour.

At the bar stood a stunning petite brunette. Her skin glowed under the light, her hair was laying in loose curls over her shoulders, her smile could light up the whole room. She was the most beautiful woman Brad or Damon had ever seen.

Damon felt like he had to talk to her. "She is... I will get us the next round." Damon jumped up when Brad pulled him down to sit again. Brad stood up, brushing his hand down his trousers.

"I will go... It's my round anyway." Brad smirked as he walked over to the bar. Brad just had to talk to her. He knew he's married, but never before has any woman captivated him like this one, and he didn't even know what her name is. And a conversation with a beautiful woman was not against his and Amelia's agreement.

Damon watched as Brad strolled over to the bar. He felt a bit jealous as he wanted to be the one to go get the drinks for a chance to talk to the girl at the bar. He knows how Brad felt about his marriage, but there was nothing any of them could do.

******

"Could I have three beers, please?" Brad asked the barman as he stood next to the woman he watched for the past hour. Brad glanced at her, trying to get a better view of the woman that has him this enchanted. She locked eyes with him for a brief moment before looking away, her cheeks tinted light pink as she blushed. Brad thought that the pink on her cheeks made her more enchanting.

"Could I get you a drink?" Brad whispered to the woman next to him. He wasn't going to do anything against his agreement with Amelia. Brad just wanted to talk to this beautiful woman and get to know her. She woke feelings in him that he has never felt before.

She turned to Brad with a smile. She couldn't believe the sight next to her. Brad is a handsome guy. He was easily over 6ft tall, sandy blond hair with the most mesmerizing blue eyes. His left cheek had a slight dimple when he smiled, and she could get lost in his eyes.

"No, thank you... I am actually on my way out..." She grabbed her bag, ready to leave.   "Have a good evening." She jumped off the chair, and at that moment, Brad realized just how short she was. He was a good 6ft 5in, and she was maybe 5ft 5in. He loved how she would fit under his arm, where he would be able to protect her.

She walked out of the beer garden without looking back. If she did, she knew she would stay. She wanted to unwind after a terrible day at work. If only Brad had come up to her sooner, she would have let him buy her a drink. Right now, she needed to get home, she has an early morning, and she needs her rest.

The bartender gave Brad his beers, and he made his way over to his table. He could see the amusement on his friends' faces. They were total jerks.

"That was harsh to watch." Conner snickered, taking a sip of his drink. "What happened to the Davis charm?" Conner and Damon tried to hold back their laughter, but they were failing miserably.

Both their faces fell when they see the look in Brad's eyes. "He has to make a baby with someone he doesn't want to be with." The words come out of his mouth, but his friends don't want to believe it.

"Wait, are you serious?" Conner looked at Brad, confused. He told them about his father's demands, but they

4

were sure that he would find a way out of this. He didn't want children with Amelia. He didn't want to be bound to her in that way, and all of them thought that Amelia wasn't stable enough to have children.

"Yes, there is no way out of this. I have to give Amelia a baby." Brad took a sip of his beer.

"So, you are going to shoot into a cup tomorrow?" Damon raised his eyebrow at his friend. He has watched over the past two years how Brad has lost more and more of himself. He is not like he used to be, he is cold towards everyone, and tonight with that woman was the first time he almost saw the old Brad returning.

Brad smiled at Damon at the way he said it. "Yes, that is the only way she will have a baby that I am the father of. I just wished that I could have babies with someone I at least had a connection with." Brad took another long sip of his drink before he glanced at the exit the woman disappeared through. "Um... I'm going to head out. I have an early morning." Brad got up and grabbed his jacket, ready to leave.

"You want us to come with you?" Damon questioned, grabbing his jacket.

"No, you stay. At least one of us should get laid tonight. Austin can take me back. He's waiting at the SUV." Brad said his goodbye before heading out. All Brad could think about was what he had to do tomorrow.

*****

SIX WEEKS LATER

It has been six weeks since Brad and Amelia had gone for their IVF. When they had the IVF done, they were told that they could find out in a few weeks if she was pregnant. Three weeks later, she had done a test, and it came back positive. Today they are at the hospital for a scan to see how the baby is doing.

Brad, unfortunately, didn't feel the way he thought he would. He had always hoped to have a family one day, even if he was in an arranged marriage. He had thought that he would at least be a bit happy when he found out that she was pregnant, but to tell the truth, he did not feel anything except dread for the fact that he will be bound to Amelia forever.

"Good morning. I'm Dr. Barry and I will be you OB throughout your pregnancy." Dr. Barry greeted them both with a smile. Amelia gave her a nod, nervous about the scan. Amelia sat on the table when Dr. Barry motioned for her to lay down. "Now, let's see how your baby's doing." Dr. Barry lifts Amelia's top. "This might be cold." She said as she squirted some gel on her stomach. Brad was watching the screen intently, but not registering only when Amelia gasped does he snap out of his daze.

"Darling, look!" Amelia grabbed Brad's hand as she points to the screen. Brad's eyes grew wide. On the screen were two little heartbeats. Amelia smirked as she saw Brad's reaction.

Flashbacks

Day of the IVF

Amelia asked that Brad not be in the room while they do the IVF. Brad agreed, not that he wanted to be there after all, he had done his part. Austin, Brad's head of Security, made sure that the Doctor signs an NDA. They didn't want this to leak to anyone.

"Ma'am, you need to relax while we implant the fertilized egg." He helped her lay down before he turned back to the container with the eggs.

"Doctor, please can you implant two to three eggs. I want to make sure that at least one of them sticks." Amelia batted her eyelashes at the Doctor. She had her reasons for wanting two implanted; no one will ever know.

"Ma'am, I can't. Mr. Davis specifically told me to only put one in." The Doctor was a bit worried. He knows that Mr. Davis can be ruthless, and he didn't want to take the chance.

"He will never know. He wouldn't even care once he sees the babies on the screen." The Doctor nodded as he extracts three eggs to be implanted. If there would be questions asked, he would only say he placed one in. They have already screwed up anyway.

End of flashback

Today

"Congratulations... it's twins." Dr. Barry explained that the babies are doing good and that they and mommy are healthy. Brad nodded, not able to say anything. He felt sick. They agreed on one baby, how in the hell was she pregnant with twins.
After Amelia spoke to the Doctor about what she should do and not do during her pregnancy, she walked out the door. Dr. Barry assured her that she was in perfect health, and she didn't see any concern with the pregnancy.

"Dr. Barry, is the tour of the children's wing still set for next week?" Bard asked as he held the door to follow Amelia.

"Yes, you will be pleased to know that we have an incredibly talented pediatrician. She loves the kids and has this special bond with them, even the babies in the NICU."

"Wonderful, can't wait to meet her. I will see you next week." Brad said his goodbyes to Dr. Barry, then follows Amelia to the waiting car.

They walked to the car in silence, he had so many questions he needed answers to, but it would have to wait until they were in the car.

Amelia smiled at Brad as he got into the car behind her. "I can't believe we are having twins." Brad didn't say anything, just stared out of the window. "Brad, we are going to be a family." Amelia moved closer to him, placing her hand on his thigh. Brad turned, glaring at her.

"No, Amelia. I will be their father, and you will be their mother, that's it." Brad took her hand off his thigh and pushed it towards her. "It would do you good to remember not to touch me." She nodded. She had hoped that getting pregnant would make him see her differently.

*****

A week later, Brad sat in an SUV with Damon on their way to tour the children's wing at the hospital. Brad knew that the hospital needed funding, and this was his project. The children's wing was a soft spot for Brad. He wanted to help them.

Brad sat there, watching Damon as he scrolled through his phone. "Damon, do you think I'm a good man?" Damon snapped his head towards his life long friend. Damon didn't know what brought on this question.

"Brad... You are the most selfless, loving, and caring person I know. What's going on?" Damon turned his whole body to face Brad.

"If I am this great, then why am I not happy about my babies. Damon, I am going to be the father of two babies, and I don't care. I have always wanted a family, always wanted children, why am I not happy?" Brad leaned forward to rest his face in his hands. Brad could not understand what was wrong with him. He should be ecstatic about becoming a father in a few months.

Damon placed his hand on Brad's shoulder. "Because you have always been a dreamer, and you saw yourself fall in love, get married, and have a family with the woman you love. But instead of that happening, you got a company and an arranged marriage with a woman you can't stand. The fact that she's the mother of your children is blocking you from bonding with your babies." Damon wiped his other hand over his mouth. "Just remember that those babies are half you and half her."

"That's the problem. I don't want half, Amelia! Brad looks at Damon, shocked at what he just said.

Damon shook his head. He knows how Brad was feeling. "You have a few months to get used to the idea. One thing I do know is that once those babies are born, you will give them the world." Brad nodded, taking in Damon's words. He hoped that it would turn out like that once they are born.

They arrived at the hospital, Damon and Brad get out of the car. Brad took in the outside of the hospital. "Put repaint outside on the list, please!" Brad tapped his finger on a list Damon had in his hand of things they wanted to discuss with the pediatrician. Damon made a note of it. He was excited to handle something, dear to Brad.

The two of them walked into the hospital, making some more notes of what could be changed. The hospital was beautiful overall, the waiting area in the front needed some more seating, but Brad felt that it wasn't a priority with all the other waiting room.

"Mr. Davis, Mr. Black." Dr. Barry met them at the elevator. "It's good to see you again," She gave them her best smile. Brad knew what she was doing. He had seen it before. She was trying to convince him to invest in the hospital, but all he cared about was the children's wing. He felt that the kids could not take care of themselves, and they needed someone to stand up for them. Brad hoped that the new pediatrician was the one who would stand up for the children and babies.

"Good Morning." Brad and Damon say in unison.

Dr. Barry pressed the button for the elevator to open. "If you would please follow me, I would like to introduce you to our pediatrician. She will be taking you on the tour as she knows more of what they need." Dr. Barry pressed the button to the third floor.

The ride up to the third floor was quiet, but a comfortable silence. Brad tried to think of questions to ask once they met the pediatrician. The elevator pinged, and the doors open. Brad and Damon followed Dr. Barry over to a sealed door.

"This is the children's wing. Because of security threats before, we installed a security door that needs one of the doctor's that are permitted to enter this area's security cards to open the door." Dr. Barry slides her card through the slot, the door giving a green light as she opens it. They enter the area, and Brad takes in the entrance. He was impressed with the security measures.

"What type of security threats?" Brad asked as he gave Damon a concerned look.

"There was a bomb threat a few years ago, and also someone tried to steal a baby a few months ago." Dr. Barry motioned for them to follow her. Both Damon and Brad could only nod. They hoped that the children will be safe now.

Brad followed Dr. Barry further into the area when he suddenly froze when his eyes land on a beautiful brunette laughing with a nurse. He felt a flutter in his chest, something he has never felt before. He wanted to be the one she was laughing with, even though he didn't even know her.

"Dr. Bryan..." Dr. Barry called out. Brad's breath hitched as she turned around. Her dazzling blue eyes locking onto his, he felt the heat rising on his neck from the way she smiled at him.

Chapter 2

As soon as she sees them, Dr. Bryan made her way over to them. "Dr. Barry, what can I do for you?" Dr. Bryan smiled at the older Doctor before her, trying her best not to make eye contact with Brad. After all, this was the man she wanted to have a beer with but declined, not wanting to get into anything.

"Dr. Bryan, this is Mr. Davis. He is here for the tour of the children's ward for the funding. I take it that you will show him what we need and what we do around here." Dr. Barry gave her a wink. She knew that Dr. Bryan would tell Brad everything that is needed and how things work in the children's ward.

"Mr. Davis. It's a pleasure to meet you." Dr. Bryan held out her hand for him to shake. Brad took her hand, kissing the back of her hand, his lips lingering just a bit too long, never taking his eyes from her.

"The pleasure is all mine." Brad smiled before turning back to Dr. Barry. "Please call me Brad, and this is Damon." Brad motioned towards Damon, who just gives her a wave, trying to figure out where he has seen her before.

Dr. Barry explained that she needed to head out, having surgeries scheduled for today, but Dr. Bryan would take them on tour, seeing as this was her department. Dr. Barry couldn't help but notice the secret glances Brad and Dr. Bryan were giving each other. She just hoped that it was nothing.

"Right, we will start with the babies in the NICU, if that is alright with you. I have a few of them to check on and one to discharge." Dr. Bryan raised her eyebrow at the two men in front of her. They were clearly debating on their own about who knows what. They were clearly ignoring her with what they had going on. "Uh Um…" She cleared her throat as both men snap their heads towards her, feeling like they have just been caught doing something they were not supposed to.

Brad took a step forward, brushing his hand down his pants. "That would be perfect." Dr. Bryan smiled as she nodded for them to follow her. They walk towards the other side of the ward. "I see that you have put in a request for more beds in the NICU and also some new equipment." Brad held the request form in front of him as he points to a few points. Dr. Bryan was standing right next to him, looking at what he was saying. She wanted to make sure that those were all the requests that she had asked for.

"That's correct. In the last week, we had to transport three women in preterm labor to hospitals nearby. Because we couldn't accommodate their babies, and we lost one of the babies that were born while on their way to the other hospital…" Dr. Bryan looked down as she pulled on her white coat, trying to hide her emotions. "If we had more beds, the necessary staff, or just extra equipment to isolate them in a room, we could have been able to save that baby that day." Brad nodded as he took a few notes. He could see the passion Dr. Bryan had for her patients and for her department, and at this moment, he was happy that he decided to do the tour, to experience the environment for himself.

"How many babies come through here in a month or so?" Damon asked, not meeting anyone's eyes as he looks around the corridor. "What's in there?" He pointed to a door that had no sign on it.

Dr. Bryan smiled as she watched Damon. "To answer your first question, it's difficult to say. We may get ten babies or thirty babies. One baby could stay for three days while another could stay for three months. No one can choose when labor starts or when the baby would need to be in NICU. For instance, one lady came in at 35 weeks, her baby was born almost full term, and that baby ended up staying two weeks in NICU. Another lady came in at 33 weeks, her baby was released three days later. It all depends on the labor and the needs of the babies." Damon stared at her with so much adoration as she spoke about her passion. He could see the joy and pride radiating from her as she explained to them about the babies.

"Now, as for your second question. This is an unused room even though it is much larger than the NICU. I do hope that we could change it into a NICU as well. We could have the isolated babies in the old one, and for all the other, we could use this one." It was Brad's turn to stare at her as his mind went a mile an hour trying to find a way to make this happen.

"You mean like High Care NICU and normal NICU?" Brad questioned as she nodded, walking towards the door, opening it to show them the area.

"Yes… I know it would be costly to renovate a whole area into NICU, but I feel that it would be worth it in the end." She walked into the room, switching on the light. The room was much bigger than your standard room. It needed a coat of paint but still looked to be in good condition. "We could easily fit in 15 beds, with the equipment and everything…" Dr. Bryan looked down again, pulling on her white coat. Brad watched her closely as he noticed that this was something she did when she was feeling nervous. "I also know that if we do this, we will need to renovate the other one to have isolation cubicles." Brad nodded as he placed his hand on her arm to stop her from pulling on her coat. She looked up, locking eyes with Brad. She would lie to herself if she said that he wasn't handsome. Brad was well close to six-five. He had sandy blond hair that was styled perfectly. He has a chiseled jaw that made him look even more handsome than he was. She couldn't tell if he was built or not, but by how his dress shirt hugged his body, she would guess that he was fit and had the perfect body.

"You're right, it will be costly…" She nodded, looking down again. Brad placed his forefinger and thumb under her chin, lifting her face to look at him again. His heart fluttered as her bright blue eyes met his. He has never felt a spark between him and a woman before. "But it's not impossible. That's why I am here, and right now, I feel that the hospital needs more beds for the NICU, and the fact that you already thought about how to do this, make my job a lot easier." He smiled, seeing the light pink shade on her cheeks.

"I can see this happening…" Damon turned around, seeing Brad and Dr. Bryan just staring at each other. Damon felt a twitch in his heart. Brad had never look at anyone the way he was looking at her. He wished at that moment that Brad wasn't married and expecting children with his wife. "Uh Um, Brad…" Damon cleared his throat, pulling Brad back to reality.

"I think so too, Damon. Now let's go see the babies." Brad felt his eyes burning being caught staring at another woman by his best friend. Dr. Bryan nodded as she leads them out of the room towards the door on the other side.

"I need you both to put this on!" She handed them blue scrubs and caps. "If you are feeling under the weather or just recovering from something, I would have to ask you not to go in. These babies are fragile and can't come in contact with any germs right now." She eyed Damon and Brad, both shaking their heads in understanding. "Great, then you need to follow me." She took a few drops of the disinfectant at the door, putting it on her hands and motioning for the guys to do the same. Brad and Damon followed her, doing everything she does. She pressed the button, waiting for the nurse to open the door for her.

They all walked in together, the nurses greeted them as they stand with their respected patients. Dr. Bryan walked over to the first bed taking his chart and looking over it. A small smile forms on her lips as she read over his progress from last night.

"This is Conner. He was born at 32 weeks, he has been in the NICU for two weeks. He might be here for another week or so." Dr. Bryan bends down, taking Conner's hands to see if he has gained some strength in his arms. "Hey, Sweetie, it's time for your physio." She motioned for the lady to come closer and start with his physio. Dr. Bryan and the guys move on to the next baby. Brad's heart sinks as he saw a small baby in an incubator.

"She's so small." He rests his hand against the glass, staring at the baby.

"She was born at 25 weeks and has been here for a month already getting stronger with each passing day." Dr. Bryan took her file to go over her vitals and see how she did during the night. Brad watched her as she moved. He could feel the butterflies in his stomach, but he knew that he should forget about it. He might not have been married for love; he was still a married man. A nurse walked over to Dr. Bryan, handing her a tube with milk. "Brad, would you like to feed her?" Dr. Bryan held out the tube, and Brad nodded excitedly.

Brad froze as he took the tube from her. "You will show me what to do, Right?" He looked at her with concern as he stepped up next to her. He just realized that he didn't know what to do. Dr. Bryan handed him some disinfectant, he rubbed his hands with it before she passed him some gloves.

"Don't worry, I will help you. All you need to do is put your hands inside the incubator through these holes, then you take the tube." He nodded as he does what she said. "Now you take the tube in your hand and attach it to the feeding tube, and hold it up." Brad smiled as he does as he is told, seeing the milk start becoming less. Dr. Bryan made some notes on the baby's chart while keeping an eye on how Brad was doing. It wasn't long before the tube was empty.

"Is that it?" Brad asked as he looked at the tube and the baby, unsure how she could eat that little.

"Yes, that's it. She is still small and only needs 15ml every three hours for now." Dr. Bryan smiled as she turned the baby on her side, giving her a few light taps on her back before letting her settle in.

They walked from baby to baby, Dr. Bryan telling them about each baby. Damon and Brad were hanging on her lips as she spoke about each baby with so much passion. Dr. Bryan treated each baby as if they were her own. She had so much love for the work she did.

"Why is this one dressed?" Brad raised his eyebrow at her as she smiled, picking up the little boy.

"This is Cornell, and he is going home today. He is just waiting for his mommy to arrive." She snuggled the boy in her arms. "Do you want to hold him?" Brad nodded, holding out his hands. He wasn't expecting his day to be this full of love and affection or that he would learn this much about what goes on in the Children's ward. Dr. Bryan shook her head, motioning to the sanitizer. Brad smiled as he took some before she handed him the little boy. Damon watched them. He has never seen Brad like this, Brad was having fun, and it was all because of this Doctor.

A nurse came walking up to Dr. Bryan, whispering something to her. Damon saw the way her demeanor changed at whatever the nurse told her. "Please stay with Cornell. I will be right back!" She took Brad by the arm, letting him sit down with his back towards the glass room the nurse came from. She motioned for Damon to stand next to Brad. She then turned around, walking towards the same glass room.

"What do you think that's about?" Brad and Damon turned to see Dr. Bryan talking to a lady before the lady sank into the chair, covering her face with her hands. Dr. Bryan turned towards the machine switching it off, the nurse closing the curtains in the room.

"Not sure, but it can't be good," Brad said as they both watch on. They could see the lady crying into her hands. It wasn't long before Dr. Bryan appeared, handing her a bundle of blankets. Brad hung his head, realizing what just happened. He looked down at the baby in his arms, glad that this baby gets to go home. Damon rubbed his hand over his mouth as he tried his best to hide the sadness. He knew that working with these babies isn't always a happy ending.

Dr. Bryan came out of the glass room, walking towards the men. She took Cornell from Brad, laying him back in his crib. She then talked briefly to the nurse before turning back to Brad and Damon.

"Let's go through the rest of the Children's ward." Her voice was soft as she tried to contain her emotions. She turned, not waiting for their answer, walking out of the NICU with them following her. Brad wanted to make sure that she was alright. He just didn't know how to approach the topic. He wasn't supposed to see what was happening. That was the reason she had him sit with his back towards the glass room.

They walked around the children's ward. Dr. Bryan introduced a few of the patients. Telling Brad and Damon more about them and what they needed. She told Brad that if they could just get the NICU for now, that would be perfect. They could hold off on the other requests she has for a while. She explained that the NICU and cancer ward was her top priority, only because those were the ones with the need for better equipment and more space.

After taking the tour and learning everything there was to learn about the Children's ward, they went down to the cafeteria for a late lunch. Brad wanted to speak with her some more, but truthfully he wasn't ready to let her go just yet.

"You aren't from New York. What made you decide to come here?" Brad asked as he took a seat across from her, and Damon taking a seat next to him.

"No, I'm from Boston. I got an offer and wanted a new start. This was perfect, and I loved the pediatric program the hospital had." She took a bite of her salad. Brad nodded, taking in her words. She could have gone anywhere in the world, but she chose to come here.

"I'm glad you chose this hospital." Damon smiled as he took a sip of his water.

"Thanks, this is my passion. I love working with kids." Brad smiled at her as she said that. He saw the passion she had for her job more than once today. Dr. Bryan was radiant as she showed them everything. She made him want to help the kids, to make their stay in the hospital as comfortable as possible. And she is the reason he wants to make sure that her requests get approved.

They talked and laughed over lunch. Damon and Brad telling her some of the things they used to get up to. She told them about her life in Boston, and they learned that she is actually from Europe, but she doesn't have an accent. She had applied for her permanent residency but was told that it could take a while.

Damon could see this significant change in Brad, he was relaxed, and he couldn't keep his eyes off Dr. Bryan. Damon knew that this would hurt Brad in the end, knowing he would never be able to act on his feelings. He would just have to admire her from afar because he was a married man.

"Dr. Bryan, it was a privilege to be able to be on this tour with you, to learn what goes on behind the doors of the children's ward. Thank you so much for your time." Brad held out his hand for her to take. Brad feels a spark as soon as her small hand touches his hand.

"Please call me Erina, and the pleasure is all mine. I am glad that I could share this with both of you." She shook Brad's hand before shaking Damon's next before they turned to leave.

Erina watched as Brad and Damon leave. She smiled when Brad turned around, locking eyes with her. She felt a flutter in her chest as he smiled at her giving her a small wave. He was so much different than what she thought he would be. When she heard that she needed to provide the CEO of Davis International a tour of the Children's ward, she was expecting some a grumpy old man that would find fault with everything, but instead, this tall, handsome blond guy showed up.

"That was unexpected." Damon clapped Brad on the shoulder as he opened the door of the SUV.

"Yes… That was. I want to do everything I can to get this approved. The Children's ward is for our future. We need to help the kids the best we can." Brad got into the car, followed by Damon.

"Then we got our work cut out for us. I will let the others know to meet us at the office." Damon took out his phone, sending a text to Mike, Mia, and Conner. He knew the team would be able to make this happen.

*****

18

The next few weeks, Brad and the other worked on the proposals to have the Children's ward approved funds. Mia and Conner agreed to hold a charity ball to try and raise some of the funds. Damon and Mike were getting items to sell at an auction to bring more funds in. They wanted to have a silent auction at the charity ball, Brad felt that this would help to have more of the requests approved. He did have the final say, but he didn't want to go against the board, this being the reason he decided that after the charity ball, he would donate whatever was still outstanding to have the renovations done from his private account.

For the past few weeks, Brad has also tried his best to avoid Amelia, knowing that she would berate him for giving money away like this. Mia and Brad sat at his desk in his home office, going over some arrangements. Mia watched as Brad went over the final guest list smiling all the time, which wasn't typical for Brad. Mia is one of Brad's best friends. She has known him basically her whole life. Their parents were best friends until his father became power-hungry and wanted everything his way.

"What has gotten into you?" Mia raised her eyebrow at Brad as he lifted his head smiling. It was actually freaking her out seeing him this happy.

"I have no idea what you are talking about." He looked back down, noticing a name next to Erina's. He smiled, knowing Conner was doing this for him.

Mia smirked as she watched him again. "Is the guest list to your liking?" Brad only nodded as he hands her the list back.

"I approve. We can go ahead." Mia took the document just as the door to his office burst open. Amelia rushed in as blood covered her hands and the front of her dress.

"Help..." She looked at Brad, frightened. He jumped up from his chair with such force sending it slamming into the wall.

"What happened?" Brad asked just as Mia rushed past Amelia to get Austin, Brad's head of Security. Brad picked

Amelia up, running with her out of the door to where they had a car waiting for them.

"I… I felt dizzy and fell. I… I… don't know if the babies got hurt." She buried her face in Brad's chest as she smirked, knowing Amelia had Brad right where she wanted him. She knew that once something happened to these babies, Brad would be putty in her hands, and he would do anything to keep them safe.

Brad ran down the stairs at the front of his mansion. "Don't worry, we will get you to the hospital." Amelia had her arms wrapped tightly around Brad's neck, not wanting to let him go.

Brad helped Amelia into the SUV getting in behind her. Austin pulled away as soon as he was sure all the doors were closed. After a short drive, they made it to the hospital with Dr. Barry and Dr. Bryan waiting for them as the SUV pulled up.

Dr. Bryan wasn't sure who it was, just that it was a VIP patient, and they needed to do everything to make sure she and the babies were safe.

As soon as the SUV came to a stop, Brad jumped out, not giving Austin a chance to open the door for him. Brad helped Amelia out before helping her onto the gurney. Dr. Bryan felt her heart skip a beat as she saw Brad's pregnant wife in front of her. Dr. Bryan knew that Brad was married because he told her that much, but he said they didn't have a relationship and lived separate lives. And yet here he is with her, and she is very much pregnant. Brad met Erina's eyes, and he could see the realization in them and a hint of hurt.

"Let's get her into the emergency room," Dr. Barry called out as she pushed Amelia into a room. Dr. Bryan turned towards Brad and Austin with a file in her hands. It didn't matter how she felt. His babies were her patients now.

"Mr. Davis. I just need some information before I go in there." She looked into the file, not meeting Brad's eyes. She motioned for him to sit, still not meeting his gaze.

"Mrs. Davis is about fifteen weeks with twins, is that correct?" Dr. Bryan finally looked up at Brad, who was just staring at her. "Sir… I need to know. If something goes wrong, I won't be able to help at all."

"Yes, if I have my dates correct. That's how far she is." Brad lets out a breath he didn't know he was holding.

"Do you know what happened?" She again doesn't look up at him as she made some notes in the file. She felt stupid for everything that happened every time they met to go over the ball's details or just met to have fun. She shouldn't have trusted him when he said that his wife was nothing to him.

"I am not sure. She said she felt dizzy and then fainted. She must have had something in her hand that could have cut her." Brad sat forward, rubbing his hand over his face. He needed to talk to Erina.

"Let me go see what needs to be done." She closed the file and looked at Brad with a severe expression. "I am going to be honest with you, if she does go into labor and we can't stop it, the babies will not survive. It will be considered a miscarriage." She turned, walking to the door before she turns back to Brad again. "I would suggest that you take care of your wife." With that, she walked out the door as Brad hung his head. He wanted to explain everything to her. She needed to know that what happened between them wasn't just him wanting to forget his wife. His mind drifted off to all the times he had spent with Erina.

The first time was the day of the tour. Brad was waiting for her to get off her shift. He couldn't get her out of his mind. He wasn't going to let anything happen between them. He just wanted to spend time with her. She agreed that she would go out to drinks with him when she met him after her shift.

After that, he had spent more and more time with her. He couldn't get enough of her, or rather wanting to see her all the time. He would meet her for breakfast if she worked the night shift or for dinner if she worked during the day. He would spend the day with her if she had a day off. He knew it was wrong to spend more time with another woman and not with his wife, but he only wanted someone to talk to, and she was it. He was doing all of this with only Damon and Conner knowing about it. That was why Conner was going to the ball with Erina, then she would be near Brad without causing a scandal.

With all the time Brad has spent with Erina, he felt more alive and happier than he has ever felt in his life. Brad was brought out of his thoughts when Damon and Conner came into the room.

"I just saw Erina, and she's pissed." Damon raised his eyebrow as he sees the look in Brad's eyes.

"I need to talk to her. She needs to know that Amelia doesn't mean anything to me. And that I didn't just use her." Brad ran his hand through his already disheveled hair.

"Nothing happened between you. You only spend time together. I don't think she's upset with you." Conner took a seat next to Brad. Giving him a reassuring smile. Brad looked between the two of them, if only they knew the half of it. They know everything he wanted them to know.

"If only... I am pretty sure she's pissed at me, and she has a right to be. I never told her about the pregnancy." Damon stood there shocked, and then anger filled him.

"You idiot, what the fuck did you do? Please tell me you didn't sleep with her." Damon paced up and down in front of Brad, mumbling to himself, trying to figure out what the hell Brad did.

Brad jumps up, placing his hands on Damon's shoulder. "I didn't sleep with her... I almost did... But I stopped myself from ever going that far with her. We haven't even kissed." Brad took a deep breath, trying to calm his racing heart. "I did something I wasn't supposed to do... I fell in love with her." Conner and Damon gasped as Brad confessed his feelings for Erina.

"Why, Brad? You know you can't give her anything... You know you are married and not getting out of that marriage... Why would you do that?" Damon's voice was laced with anger. He couldn't believe that Brad would do something like that. He knew that letting Brad spend time with Erina would end in one or both of their hearts breaking. Brad lets go of Damon's shoulder. He walked back to his seat as he slummed into the chair, defeated. Damon saw the hurt and guilt in his best friend's eyes. "Shit… man, I'm sorry. This can't be easy for you." Damon took a seat on the other side of Brad, him and Conner sharing a knowing look, both of them knowing they needed to fix this.

"You said you almost slept with her? When was this?" Conner asked in a calm and collected voice. He wasn't going to judge his friend. Brad has never been happy, not like he is when he is around Erina.

"It was last night…"

"Wait, what?" Damon narrowed his eyes at Brad. "At my damn house…." Damon got up and walked to the door. He couldn't believe that Brad would do that at his house.

"Damon…" Brad got up to follow him when he bumped right into Erina. He wrapped his arms around her waist to keep her from falling. "I'm sorry I didn't see you." He looked down at her, seeing the unshed tears in her dazzling blue eyes.

Dr. Bryan pushed away from Brad brushing her hand over her coat jacket. "That's clear. I need to speak to you." She motioned to the waiting room with her head. They went into the waiting room together, and Conner was still waiting for Brad. Erina walked over to Conner, giving him a hug. "It's good to see you." Brad watched their interaction, feeling a tad bit jealous.

"Erina, it's always a pleasure." Conner motioned for her to sit. He wanted to talk to her and find out how she was doing. After hearing Brad's confession, he knew there were feelings involved for both of them. "How are you feeling?"

"This is not about me. I will be alright. I knew he's married. I should have never let it go that far." Her voice was laced with sadness and guilt.

23

"Please let me explain.." Brad walked closer to Erina but stopped when she held her hand up. She couldn't let him near her at all, not now.

"Mr. Davis. I need to talk to you about your wife." Erina gave Brad a stern look, not letting him see what she was feeling. "I don't believe that this was an accident. Either someone tried to hurt her, or she did this to herself.

Chapter 3

"What do you mean? She would never do that. She was the one that wanted the babies. She would never put them in danger." Brad started pacing in front of Conner and Erina. He had lost count of how many times he has run his hand through his hair.

"Brad, just hear her out." Conner tried to calm him down, motioning for Erina to go ahead. "She doesn't have a reason to lie to you."

"The way that she was cut shows that it was not an accident." Dr. Bryan took out a document from Amelia's file just when Dr. Barry walked into the room. Dr. Barry nodded, motioning for Dr. Bryan to go on. "Here, you will see where she was cut; now if it was an accident, the cut wouldn't have been this clean. This is a cut that was planned. Even the angle of the cut is not correct. If it was an accident, it would have been straight in, and not only superficial like this one." Dr. Bryan showed them all the ways it could have gone with how Amelia explained it happened, and none explained the way the cut was made or the angle it was in, or the area it was made. "Whoever did this knew that they would not hurt the babies if they did it like this." Dr. Bryan watched Brad's jaw clench, Conner standing on the other side of him shaking his head.

"Mr. Davis, if I may." Brad nodded, telling her to continue. "I think Mrs. Davis did this to get attention. She has cried in there that if you weren't so busy and home more, she wouldn't have tried to do everything herself, and then she wouldn't have fallen. She needs you more than ever now. She's hormonal and emotional. Being pregnant with twins takes a lot from the mother." Dr. Barry gave Brad an apologetic look. Brad frowned, taking in her words. He locked eyes with Dr. Bryan for a moment before shaking his head.

"Amelia would never do that. I know her well enough to know she wouldn't put the heir in any danger. It doesn't matter how I feel about her; she wouldn't do this. She wanted these babies." Brad stood up straight as he spoke to the two doctors in front of him. Conner shook his head, not sure why Brad didn't want to believe them.

"I just had to come and tell you what our findings were." Dr. Bryan gave him a nod before walking out of the room. Yes, she felt guilty for falling in love with a married man, but he told her they had an arranged marriage and that she meant nothing to him. She still felt guilty for letting things go that far; he's married. She had decided to take a step back and not be alone with him again. He needed to focus on his wife and their babies. It didn't matter how hard that would be for her.

"Sir, you can take your wife home when you are ready. She and the babies are doing good." Dr. Barry smiled as she handed him an ultrasound picture showing both babies next to each other.

"Thank you…. I will be out shortly to take her home." Brad smiled at Dr. Barry, looking down at the photo in his hands.

"Brad…. Are those them?" Conner pointed to the photo in his hands. Brad nodded, just staring at them. Brad had no connection to these babies, none at all. Yes, he was scared when he saw the blood all over the front of Amelia's dress. He was worried they would have to go through this again, and he would not be able to. Not with his feelings towards Erina, he wouldn't commit like this with Amelia again.

"Conner, I need to talk to Erina." Brad gave him a pleading look, silently asking him to help him. Conner noticed that Brad had no connection to the babies. He wasn't acting like the excited father to be.

"Fine, I will go find her. But if you upset her in any way or lie to her more than you already have. I will be the one committing murder, even before Damon gets a chance." Conner raised his eyebrow at Brad, waiting for him to tell him that he would be honest with Erina. Conner liked her. She wasn't like the girls he was used to meeting. She treated all of them as regular guys and not like they were billionaires. She was also the only one that dared call out Damon's bullshit. Hanging out with her was like a breath of fresh air. In the last few weeks, they had spent time together, he had grown close to her as a friend.

"I won't. I want to tell Erina everything and hope that she will listen to me. I didn't lie to her; I just never told her about the babies. I need to tell her everything. I need her in my life, even if it is just as a friend." Brad rubbed his hands down his face trying to hide the tears threatening to spill. He knew that he's married, and if he could, he would want to get out of this marriage, but that was not an option. Brad just couldn't lose Erina. Since she came along, he felt more alive. It was as if she was breathing life into him. He needed more of her. He needed to keep her in his life.

Conner gave him a nod walking out of the waiting room. He headed to a nurse's station to find Erina. The nurse told him that she was in the NICU, and she would ask someone to get her.

Erina walked over to where Conner was waiting for her. She raised her brow, not knowing what this could be about. They had already arranged their fake date for the charity ball, so she didn't think there was anything else to talk about.

"Erina, I know you are busy, but Brad would like to have a word with you." Conner could see the hesitation in her eyes. He stood there with his hands in his pocket, knowing he needed to get her to speak to Brad even if he thought Brad didn't deserve it at the moment. Conner knew what his friend had been through, and he had seen a different side of Brad since he has been spending time with Erina, and he wanted that for Brad. He would help him however, he could. "I know you're upset with him and feel guilty. But please give him a chance to explain everything to you."

"Fine, I will hear him out, but you don't leave the room. You stay in that room with Brad and me." She raised her brow, waiting for him to answer. She was not going to be alone with

Brad. She didn't trust herself alone with Brad, she had never felt this way about anyone, and the fact that he is married hurts her more than she ever thought.

"I will stay in the room at all times." Conner racked his fingers through his hair, knowing Brad will not like this, but he has a chance to explain everything to her, with him in the room whether he liked it or not.

"Give me a few minutes. I just need to see one of the babies that have just been admitted to NICU. I will be out as soon as the baby is stable." Conner nodded, heading back towards the waiting room. Erina heading back to the NICU. She had twins to admit and knew it would take a while. They were born at 30 weeks, and the one was weaker than the other one. She needed to attend to them. Brad could wait.

*****

After Erina was done with her rounds, Conner and she made their way down to the waiting room to see Brad. They walked in, seeing this defeated look on his face, but as soon as he saw Erina, his face lights up.

"Thank you for coming." He smiled as he motioned for her to sit down. Conner sitting in the corner, not saying anything. Brad raised his brow in confusion, not sure why Conner was sitting down.

Erina saw the confusion on Brad's face. "I'm here to listen to you, but I asked Conner to stay." She pulled on the white coat like she did so many times before. Brad felt guilty that he was making her nervous, that she didn't want to be alone with him. That was the last thing he ever wanted to do.

"I need to explain what happened." Brad took a deep breath. "I got married to Amelia two years ago after my father convinced me that it was the best for the company. He wanted us to merge with her parent's company. I have no connection or feelings for her." Erina looked down, hearing that they were married for two years already. She knew that arranged marriages sometimes end up with the couple falling in love with each other.

"Brad, you cannot spend two years with someone and not care about them. You cannot get her pregnant and not care about her. This wasn't a one night stand that just happened. You are married to her, and she's having your babies. This doesn't seem like an arranged marriage anymore." Erina swallowed the lump in her throat, forcing it down. She was not going to breakdown in front of him. He didn't deserve to see her tears.

"Just let me explain...... She was my father's choice, and I just wanted to take over his company. I knew that I would be able to make the company a better place. Since I have taken over, the company has been more involved with the community, and we have expanded to other parts of the world." He looked up, meeting her eyes, then Conner's eyes.

"I have never been intimate with Amelia, not even on our wedding night. I have never shared a room with her. We live two separate lives." Erina shook her head, feeling the anger build up in her. "Erina, I swear to you.... My father was pressuring us for an heir, he wanted to secure our bloodline, and I had to listen to him. We went for IVF, and that how she's pregnant" Brad rubbed his hands together to stop them from shaking. He has never felt like this about anyone in all his life. He wasn't sure what this was; all he knows is that he can't lose her.

"Brad, you cheated on your wife.... I did the one thing I promised myself I would never do. Because you told me that you felt nothing for your wife, that it was political. And now I find out you have twins on the way." She stood up, pacing in front of him. "I should never have let this happen. You need to give your all to your wife and babies. I will not be that woman."

"What, woman?" Brad got up to stand in front of her.

"The woman that breaks up a marriage, the woman that takes away those babies father. We will be professional from now on. What happened between us can never happen again. I will not let it happen again." She turned her back to Brad.

29

Conner was able to see the hurt on her face, the tears welling up in her eyes, and the hurt in Brad's eyes even though he tried to hide it.

"Erina.... Please just listen to me. Amelia and I might be married on paper, but that's where it ends. We can still be together in away." Erina flipped around, and before she even registered what she was doing, the palm of her hand connected Brad's cheek. Brad stood there, shocked at what had just happened.

"How dare you.... I made a mistake, but it will not happen again. Take your wife home, Mr. Davis!" She turned around, storming out of the room. Brad wanted to follow, but Conner stopped him. Erina was hurt, and Conner could see it.

"Give her time to calm down. Damon and I will talk to her, explain to her." Conner gave his shoulder a reassuring squeeze.

"I screwed up big time. How am I going to get through this without Erina?" Brad pressed his palms of his hands to his eyes, trying to hide the tears threatening to spill. "I just told her she could be my dirty secret. And she is so much more than that."

"You deserved that slap. No one wants to hear that they can be your mistress. I will talk to her. Take Amelia home and make sure she doesn't try something again." Conner patted Brad's back as they walked towards the door.

*****

It was the night of the Charity Ball, Brad didn't want to be there. He was looking forward to it, but he wasn't so sure he wanted to be there after the talk he had with Erina. But he's the CEO and didn't have the luxury of not going to the event. He straightened himself to his full length, putting on his stoic expression. He will get through the night and not show anyone how he was really feeling.

Amelia stood in her room looking over herself, she had a prominent baby bump, and her dress showed her 17 weeks bump perfectly. She was dressed in a long tight-fitting red dress. She knew red was Mia's color and that this Charity ball was planned by Mia and Conner. She wanted to get under Mia's skin, knowing if she could do that, her plan would be in full motion. Soon Brad won't be able to stay away from her.

*****

Brad stood with Amelia greeting the guest as they arrived. He told Conner and Mia that they would welcome the guest to show their support for the cause. Brad felt his anger boiling inside him, seeing Amelia in the red dress. She didn't even like red. He wasn't sure what she was playing at, but he was going to find out.

"Don't your wife look beautiful tonight?" Amelia asked as she tightened her grip on Brad's arm.

"Why are you wearing red?" Brad smiled, not showing his anger, but she could hear it in his voice.

"Because I want my husband to show me the same affection as he shows every other lady that crosses his path. I'm your wife, and it will do you good to remember it." She digs her nails into his arm. Brad winched at the pain as he shoots her a look.

"You aren't my wife; you are just the woman I am married to." Brad turned to greet the next guest, that being Ashley and Petra.

"Mr. And Mrs. Davis." They both greeted them before giving each other a confused look. Red did not look good on Amelia.

"Thank you for being here." Brad kissed the back of their hands, he wanted to greet everyone the same, for when Erina arrived and he kissed her hand, it wouldn't be suspicious. Amelia gave them a nod standing with her arm still in the nook of Brad's arm and her other one resting on her tummy. She saw Mia and

Damon enter with Conner and the Doctor right behind them. Amelia smirked, seeing Mia's face. She turned Brad's face towards her, kissing him on the lips. Brad stood there, shocked, unable to move. Erina stopped feeling her heart beating out of her chest. Her hold on Conner's arm tightened. He looked down at her, seeing the hurt for only a brief moment before she was blank again.

"It is going to be alright!" Conner whispered into her ear. She nodded, giving him half a smile as they step forward.

Damon just gave Brad a nod, not even acknowledging Amelia. He had this bad feeling about her ever since Conner had told him what Erina had told him and Brad. Yes, he was still upset with Brad and Erina for what they did, but he knew they were both feeling crappy about it already. He wasn't going to make them feel even worse than they already did.

"Brad… And spouse…" Mia smirked at Brad but just glared at Amelia. Brad kissed the back of Mia's hand, smirking as she kept glaring at Amelia. Mia and Damon headed into the ballroom, waiting for Conner and Erina inside.

"Mr. And Mrs. Davis." Conner greeted them, Erina following with a small wave. Brad kept his gaze locked on hers as he kissed the back of her hand, his lips lingering slightly longer on her hand than the others, hoping it would go unnoticed by everyone, but Amelia saw it and the look in Brad's eyes.

As soon as Conner and Erina were out of earshot, Amelia turned to Brad before pulling him to a secluded area.

"How could you embarrass me like that. You were eye fucking the doctor in front of everyone." She jabbed Brad's chest with her finger with each word. Brad grabbed her hands to stop her.

"I only greeted them like everyone else. Dr. Bryan is here with Conner. You know I don't love you. I will never love you." Brad spat out, letting go of Amelia's hands.

"You will not treat me like this. I am pregnant with your children. You will respect me and treat me like your wife." She took a step closer to him, her eyes narrowed. "Or you will be sorry."

"Do…. Not... Threaten... Me," Brad spat out through gritted teeth, his hands bowling into fists. Amelia smirks at him putting her hand on his chest, moving closer to him.

"I own you now…. How do you think the press and board members will feel when they find out that because of their king abusing his Mrs. Davis, she lost the heirs?" Brad's eyes widen in shock. She wouldn't, would she? "I thought so…. Now be a good husband and come show everyone, including that doctor, you love me." She grabbed his hand, pulling him towards the ballroom doors waiting to be announced.

Brad stood there waiting next to her, Erina's words running through his mind. *"It wasn't an accident."* Dr. Barry's words following right after it *"She has cried in there that if you weren't so busy and home more, she wouldn't have tried to do everything herself and then she wouldn't have fallen."* She did this to herself; she did this to have a hold on me. *Fuck I'm screwed.* Brad closed his eyes, hearing the Harold announce them. He tried to calm his breathing and slow down his heartbeat.

"Mr. Brad Davis and Mrs. Amelia Davis." The Harold called out. Amelia smiled, walking into the room with confidence. Amelia gazed around the room, her eyes landing on Mia, Damon, Conner, and Dr. Bryan standing by the bar, Mia glaring at Amelia as Brad lead her to the center of the dance floor.

"Would you like to dance?" Conner held his hand out to Erina, who nodded, taking his hand. Damon and Mia shared a look before following them, Damon didn't want to dance, but he wanted to be there for Brad and Erina.

Conner and Erina moved around the dance floor. They were moving entirely in sync. Brad glanced over, seeing Conner twirling Erina, as she gave him a deep laugh. He felt the twitch in his heart, watching her laugh with someone else. Even though he knew that Conner and Erina were only friends, he wasn't the one who made her laugh like that.

"Look at me!" He snapped out of his daze as Amelia spoke, pulling him closer to her. He turned his head, trying to look at Amelia, but he felt sick looking at her. "Don't forget what I told you." She glared at him before seeing Damon and Mia over his shoulder, both looking at Brad and her.

"Amelia, I will never give into you. I will fight you on this!" He spins her out before pulling her back in. As soon as she is back in his arms, she grabbed him at the back of his neck, pulling his face towards hers, capturing his lips in a passionate kiss. Brad tried to break free but was afraid that it would cause a scene if he pushed her away.

Chapter 4

Brad felt sick to his stomach as he felt Amelia's tongue enter his mouth, her hands in his hair. He wanted it to stop; he wanted her to stop. He needed to get away from her; he needed fresh air. Brad could faintly hear a few gasps, but one stood out to him. He was sure that was Erina, and at that moment, there wasn't anything he wanted more than to run to her and kiss her the way Amelia was kissing him right now.

"I need some air..." Erina watched Brad and Amelia in a heated kiss not far from her. She watched as Brad stood there, frozen with shock and something else on his face, but she couldn't take it anymore.

"I will come with you." Conner took her around the waist leading her out to the balcony, Damon seeing them leave, whispering to Mia before following Conner and Erina.
Erina paced up and down; she didn't know why this upset her this much. She had told Brad to pay attention to his wife, and that is what was happening. Maybe it was because it didn't look like Brad wanted it. It looked as if Brad felt violated in some way. Was everything he has been telling her genuine? Did he really not care about her?

"Bryan...." She snapped her head up, hearing Damon's voice seeing him and Conner looking at her with concern in their eyes. For some reason, Damon called her by her last name, and she liked it. This was her and Damon's thing.

"I'm fine, guys. It was just too stuffy in there." She waved off their concern before walking over to the railing. She stood there looking out over the gardens.

"If you were fine, we wouldn't be concerned. Tell us what you are feeling." Conner stood next to her, his hand resting comforting on her shoulder.

"He… He lied to me again... Look at them." She waved her hand at where Amelia and Brad were. Conner looked over to where she was pointing. He knew what she was talking about, he was in the waiting room when Brad told her about his marriage to Amelia, and a bit more than a week later, here Brad was locked in a kiss with Amelia.

"Bryan, that is not coming from Brad. She is manipulating the situation." Damon walked over, standing next to her, rubbing his hand on her back up and down.

"It doesn't matter. Brad…. He's Married…. To her and she's…. having his babies. There can never be more than friendship between us." Her breath hitches as she tries to speak. Who was she kidding? She had fallen head over heels for Brad, and this was breaking her heart.

Conner was about to say something when the balcony doors opened. They all looked up, seeing Brad in the door.

"Just great." Erina huffed throwing her hands up in the air, glaring at Brad. She stepped away from Damon and Conner before shaking her head. Damon could see the hurt in her eyes and her trying to keep it together.

"Let's go get something to drink." Damon grabbed her hand as they pushed past Brad without saying a word. She lowered her head as they walked past Brad. Mia, who was not far behind Brad and saw Damon walking to the bar with Erina.

Brad felt his heart sink, watching her leave with Damon. There was nothing he could do to stop them, he didn't want to cause a scene, but he wanted to get away from Amelia. He knew this is hurting Erina just as much as it is hurting him.

"How's she doing?" Brad asked just above a whisper, the uncertainty evident in his voice. Conner looked at Mia as she raised her shoulders, not knowing what to say.

"She's alright. I don't think you should push it. Damon and I will talk to her and explain to her what's going on…."

Conner brushed his hand over his face before locking eyes with Brad.

"I just wouldn't get my hopes up. Just be there for her as a friend and let her be your friend. She won't have anything more with you while you are married." Conner gave him an apologetic look before walking past him and Mia. Her eyes are growing wide in realization, not having been sure why Brad was acting like this, but after hearing Conner talk about her, she had figured it out.

"What the hell Brad...... You're in love with the doctor." Mia stood in front of Brad, glaring at him. "Does Amelia know?" She started pacing in front of Brad. "How long has this been going on? Why don't I know about it? Shit...... Brad, we have to find a way out of this marriage for you." Mia turned around, smiling at her friend's stun expression. She would do anything to see him as happy as he has been the last few weeks.

"You're not upset.... I know I should have told you.... But I didn't want Amelia to know, and now she does." Brad took a seat on one of the chairs, Mia sitting next to him.

"Hell no, I like the doctor.... She a feisty one." She rested her hand on Brad's arm as he glanced at her.

"Thanks, Mia.... I will tell you everything." Brad placed his hand on top of hers as he started telling Mia everything. How he met Erina at the bar not knowing who she was and a few weeks later he met her at the hospital. How they started seeing each other and one thing led to another. He told her how she found out that Amelia was pregnant, and she said to him that she couldn't be more with him than their doctor. He told her how she had avoided him for the past few weeks since finding out, and what he hears about her is what Conner or Damon tell him.

"Well, can you blame her? You basically told her she could be your dirty secret, and she does not look like that type. She doesn't need a man to keep her happy, and she doesn't need to settle being someone's secret. Just saying." Mia turned towards the bar seeing Erina laugh with Conner and Damon. "Do you want my advice?" She cocked her eyebrow at Brad.

"You're going to give it, even if I don't want it." Brad chuckled as she gave him a mock shocked expression.

"Give her time…. Be there for her and spend time with her when she's with the others. But don't let your wife get to her. She doesn't strike me as the type that will take lightly to it if Amelia has anything to say to her."

"So, you're telling me to treat her like I treat you." Mia nodded, finally happy Brad got what she was trying to tell him. They laughed and chatted for a while before they head back inside.

*****

A few days after the charity ball and Erina was meeting Damon and Conner at the beer garden for their weekly hangout. Erina entered the beer garden seeing her friends in the back of the room.

She walked over to them, smiling. She needed it today. She was having a tough day at the hospital, almost losing the twins that were born at 30 weeks.

"Hey, guys…." She gave them both a hug. Before sitting down, Damon slid her beer over to her. She took her first sip savoring the taste of cherry dancing on her tongue. They knew her too well. Ever since they came to this beer garden, Erina fell in love with their cherry beer, and the guys knew it.

"How has your week been? I haven't seen you since the ball." Conner asked as he took a sip of his beer.

"It has been good. I have had a busy week at the hospital. I… Uh um…..." She took another sip of her beer. "I almost lost the twins today." She looked down as Conner and Damon gave her hand a little squeeze.

"Are you alright?" Damon asked as he gave her a one-arm hug.

"Yeah, I'm fine. Now, what have you two been up to?" Conner looked at her, wanting to say something but not sure if he should.

"Erina, we need to talk to you about Brad." Damon just blurted out, rubbing his hand on the back of his neck to try and hide his nervousness.

"I don't want to talk about him." She shook her head. It's not that she didn't want to talk about him, she wanted to, but she also tried to forget him. She needed to, for her own heart and safety.

"You don't have to talk. Just listen to us for a moment." Conner raised his eyebrow, silently asking her to give them a chance.

She lets out an exhausted sigh, looking deep into her glass, watching the bubbles burst at the top. She looked up, meeting Conner's eyes. "Fine.... I will.... I will listen, but it won't change anything."

"What Brad told you that day in the hospital was the truth. He is in a political marriage with Amelia, and they did have IVF done because Brad doesn't want to do or touch Amelia." Conner looked back at Damon, asking him to help him.

"I know he told you that you could still be together, and it might have come out wrong....." Damon rubbed his hand over his face. "Brad didn't mean that you should be his mistress.... He just wanted you to know that Amelia doesn't care if he sees someone else as long as it doesn't cause a scandal."

"Guys, this is all good and well, but he is married and having babies with her. Even if he doesn't love her or want to be married to her, he is. She doesn't look like she's alright with him seeing other people. It looks like she cares about him and wants him to pay more attention to her." She lets out a breath she didn't know she was holding. "He needs to focus on his wife. I will be their doctor or not theirs; I will be the babies doctor. I will be civil with him and her when I see them because they are my patients' parents. But that is it.... There can never be anything between us, not while he is married. I will not destroy a family because I fell in lo...." She cut herself off, realizing what she was about to say. She closed her eyes, trying not to let them see the tears that have welled up in her eyes. Conner and Damon shared a look. They had a feeling that there were more feelings involved between Erina and Brad, but to hear her almost say it just confirmed it had them worried about them.

"Bryan…. I know it must be hard. We will support you in whatever you want to do." Damon rubbed his hand up and down her back, trying to comfort her.

They decide to change the subject seeing how hard it was for her to talk about it. They spoke about what they all did since the charity ball, Damon telling her that they would start with the renovations in the next week or so. She was excited to have the NICU upgraded but knew there would be complications until it's done.

After a few drinks, they decided that it was time to call it a night. Damon was offering to go with Erina and make sure that she had arrived home unharmed. Conner had to go, having an early morning. He knew that Erina would be alright and safe with Damon.

*****

A few days later, Mia sat on her bed, watching her boyfriend get dressed for work. Mia had been dating one of Brad's guards for the past eight months. At first, she tried to hide her feelings for him, but he crept into her heart with his snarky attitude and not even being a bit afraid of her. Once they started dating, she informed Brad, and he was more than happy about it.

"I will see what I can find out today. I feel like Amelia is hiding something." Brett leaned down, kissing Mia.

"Just be careful and let me know as soon as you have something." She pulled him down on top of her, kissing him deeply.

"Babe, I have to go. See you tonight" He kissed her one last time before heading to the door. He stopped at the door turning towards her with a smile.

"I love you…." He winked as he walked out, not giving her a chance to respond.

"I love you too." She muttered as he closed the door. She had only hoped that he heard her. She had this sinking feeling that something wasn't right, but she couldn't put her finger on it. After a quick shower and getting dress, Mia headed out to the office. She worked at Davis International as one of the accounting managers. She wasn't looking forward to today as Amelia wanted to meet with her to make arrangements for some tea party she wanted to have with her high society friends. Mia was irritated that she had to help Amelia with this. It was something her assistant could do. She didn't need the approval of the accounting manager.

Mia knocked on Amelia's office door, waiting for her to call her in before she entered the room. She saw Amelia sitting at her desk with her hand resting on her baby bump, a smirk on her face.

"Mia, it's so good of you to join me," Amelia smirked as she gets up, moving closer to Mia. The look in Amelia's eyes made Mia feel uneasy. There was something about Amelia that wasn't right. And that sinking feeling she had this morning just intensified.

*****

Brad was heading to his office with Conner to discuss his options on a trade agreement that needed to be done within the next few weeks.

"Do you think you will have time for a round of golf this week?" Conner asked as they walk down the hall.

"Yes…. I will make time. I need a distraction…... I have been stuck…..." Brad froze as he heard Amelia scream. He looked in Conner's direction before they ran to her office. Brad flung the door open, seeing Amelia on the floor covering her face as Mia stood towering over her with this bewildered look on her face.

"Mia…." Brad shouted as he kneeled next to Amelia, trying to help her up. "What are you doing?"

"I didn't do anything…. She would have been in a worse shape if I wanted to do anything to her." Mia scoffed, looking at Brad, pleading with him to believe her.

"Get Out Now…." He shouted as Amelia gripped the lapels of his suit jacket, shaking with fear. He wrapped his arm around Amelia, trying to calm her down.

"I will be right out." Brad mouthed to Conner and Mia as they nod and leave the room.

"Brad…. I…. I was so scared. She said she was going to hurt the babies. She pushed me down…. And just before you came in, she was about to pull a dagger on me." Amelia said in a hoarse voice, trying to catch her breath. Brad cupped her face making her look at him as he wiped the tears with his thumbs.

"Don't worry. You are safe now. Do you need to see the doctor?" Brad asks as he helps Amelia to sit down on the sofa.

"No, I'm fine. Mia didn't hurt me. Thank you for being there for me. I don't want Mia anywhere near me again. I don't know what she will do if you aren't here. You know she has a bad temper." Amelia looked up at him with tears in her eyes. She looked genuinely scared, and he knew what he had to do, no matter how hard it would be.

"I will take care of it. Mia won't come near you again." Brad moved away to get a glass of water for Amelia. He returned, giving it to her. "I will be back later to check on you; for now, I will have Austin stay with you." Brad turned, walking to the door, his heart hammering in his chest as he walks out. He told Austin to stay there and not let anyone into the office, and if Amelia were to leave, to call him immediately. Austin nodded, taking his place at Amelia's door, as Brad walked to his office, knowing that Conner and Mia will be there.

Walking into his office, Brad walked over to his bar cart, pouring himself a finger of scotch. He downed his glass before turning to look at Mia, shaking his head.

"Mia…. I asked you all to support me in this. I told you what was going on…... All I asked was for you not to provoke Amelia…." Brad looked at her with a defeated look in his eyes.

"Brad…. I…." He held up his hand, stopping her from saying anything.

"I don't want to hear it…. I don't want to know what happened. All I know is that Amelia was on the floor, and you were standing over her…." Brad rubbed his hand over his face trying to wipe away the tiredness, It was still early, but he had a headache that wouldn't go away. "Mia, unfortunately, I will have to ask you not to come to this floor or anywhere near Amelia until further notice." Brad looked down, trying to keep himself the stoic CEO he has to be.

"Br…." Conner tried to protest but cut himself off as he saw the look in Brad's eyes. He turned to Mia. "I think it's best if you leave now." Conner gave Mia an apologetic look.

"I don't know what she has done to you, but this." She motioned her hand towards Brad.   "Is not the Brad I use to know. All I can say is I hope my friend returns to his normal self soon or even to the person you are when Erina is around." Mia walked out of his office, slamming the door behind her.

Brad sank into the chair next to him. He dropped his head into his hands as his elbows rest on his knees. "What am I going to do?" Brad asked not to anyone specifically.

"We will get through this. You still have Damon and me in your corner, and Mia won't write you off just yet." Brad nodded, giving Conner a small smile. He wanted this to be over. Brad wanted the babies to be born and then get what he needed against Amelia to divorce her. For now, he still had his friends, but he was pretty sure it wouldn't last too long.

*****

Mia walked over to her car, seething at what just happened in Brad's office. She knew Amelia had planned it, and she knew that she was provoking her, knowing just what to say

43

to get her rallied up. How did Amelia know about her and Brett in the first place?

Mia was brought out of her daze when her phone buzzed. She took out her cellphone, smiling when she saw Brett's name on her phone. Opening it up, she read the message.

I got the info, meet me at our special place........ Love you xxxx

She smiled at his message, typing her reply to him, before getting into her car. She drove off to their special place to wait for him. She knew that what he has will be able to get Brad free from Amelia.

Arriving at their place, Mia started a fire in the fireplace while waiting for Brett to come, knowing he would be a few hours before he would arrive. She laid down on the sofa in front of the fireplace, waiting for Brett to arrive.

Mia's eyes fluttered open as the sunlight filtered through the blinds. Rubbing her eyes, she looked around the room only to see that the fire burned out, and Brett was still not there. She must have fallen asleep in the time she was waiting. Mia took her phone, dialing Brett's number only to get his voice mail. She started to worry, seeing the time, it was already 7:30 am, and he was supposed to be here last night already.

Mia knew that the only one she could phone to find out was Damon. She couldn't even call Austin because of what happened with Amelia. Dialing Damon's number, she was relieved when he answered on the third ring.

"Mia…." Damon's groggy voice came over the phone.

"Damon, could you please find out if Brett came back to Brad's last night. He was supposed to meet me, and he hasn't!" She tried to keep her voice as calm as possible. Brad had been the only one Mia ever thought she would love until Brett showed up, and the thought of losing him was freaking her out.

"Let me find out for you." She heard Damon move on the other side of the line asking someone about Brett, and then it was quiet. She waited for Damon to come back on. She could hear faint noises, which was the only way she knew that the phone had not been dropped. "Mia, no one has seen him since yesterday."

"Damon, I think somethings wrong." Her voice cracked.

"Just keep calm. I'm going to see what I can find out, and I will let you know." Damon's voice was calm and soothing. Mia thanked him before putting the phone down. She knew that something had happened.

Damon walked over to where Austin and Brad were standing. Austin had a grieve expression on his face. He heard Brad mention Mia's name and Austin nodding before walking away.

*****

Amelia sat on her bed, rubbing her hand over her tummy as the babies moved. "I need a way for your father to touch me. If he feels you moving, he will fall in love with you and maybe with me as well." She whispered to herself, lost in the feel of them moving.

While she was sitting on the bed, there was a lite tap on the door. She called for them to enter, seeing one of her maids entering.

"Ma'am, I was to tell you the package has been dealt with," Amelia smirked before nodding and waving the girl away.

She got up from her bed, walking over to her window, happy with what had just happened. "One down and a few more to go." She smiles, running her hand over her tummy.

*****

Austin arrived at Mia's, walking towards her door. He felt the burning inside his chest, remembering the day he had to do this same walk towards Damon's parent's house. Since she was a child, he had known Mia and had never seen her this happy with anyone, not even Brad.

He knocked on the door as a servant answered it and took him towards Mia's study. As he knocked on the door, he could feel his chest tightening even more and his heart hammering inside his chest. He heard her faint voice calling for him to enter.

"Austin…. Tell me you have some news…..." Her face fell as she saw the look in his eyes. "No…... No…. do not say it." Mia felt the sting in her eyes as Austin walked over to her. She knew that if he said it, it would make it real.

"I'm sorry, Mia…. He was found in an ally early this morning." Austin gave her a knowing look as she sat down with her face in her hands. "It seems as though he was mugged. He had no belongings with him."

"He was murdered…." She lifted her head, locking eyes with Austin. He could see the fire burning in the redhead's eyes, and it scared him. "And I am going to make the one pay that took him from me." Austin could see the fire in her eyes, and he knew she was right. Brett had been murdered; he just didn't know why or by who.

*****

A few months later, Mia still didn't have a lead to who had murdered Brett, and she hasn't spoken or seen Brad since the day of Brett's funeral. She didn't even talk to him at Brett's funeral because Amelia was next to him, and she was clinging to him as if she couldn't walk by herself.

For the past few months, Conner and Damon had seen how Brad had become less and less like himself. He looked like the fire in him had been extinguished. Brad would run to Amelia whenever she would call him. He had started spending less time with them and more time with her. There was even talk of her moving into his room at some point, and that had them worried. They knew that Brad did not love her, and the man before them was a shell of the man he used to be.

Conner and Damon had decided to take him away for the weekend, Amelia was healthy, and the babies were still a few weeks away. Amelia didn't like the idea of Brad leaving the country. Conner used the excuses of a trade deal that needed to happen this weekend, which would greatly benefit Davis International. After agreeing that they needed to do this for the company. Amelia had asked them to please return as soon as they are done.

"I can't believe she let you go," Damon said, excited as they all get into the SUV.

"I think I should stay. Amelia might need something." Brad said hesitantly. He has tried to do whatever Amelia asked of him, to keep her happy even though it was killing him.

"No, Brad…. There is a mansion full of staff, and the doctors are on call. She will be alright." Conner closed the door telling Austin to drive before Brad can decide to get out.

*****

Early Sunday morning, Amelia stood in the bathroom, not feeling well. She had called Dr. Barry, telling her she felt sick, and Dr. Barry told her to come in as soon as possible. Amelia was almost 35 weeks pregnant, and Dr. Barry was worried that something would happen to the babies, and truthfully, she didn't want to have them born. Amelia finally had Brad right where she wanted him. She just had to get rid of Conner and Damon like she did Mia.

Amelia walked towards the door when she felt water running down her legs. She screamed for her guard that came running inside—ordering him to phone Brad and get her to the hospital. He rushed out, getting another guard, to get her to the hospital.

As they arrived at the hospital, Dr. Barry and Dr. Bryan were waiting for her outside. Amelia had tears as the contractions were intense, and she couldn't get a hold of Brad. His phone went over to voice mail instantly.

Dr. Barry explained to Amelia that they would have to deliver the babies via emergency c-section immediately. They couldn't wait for Brad as one of the babies was in distress. Amelia agreed, and they wheeled her to the OR.

"Mrs. Davis, I know we only spoke a few times, but I will take good care of your babies. If there are any questions, I will gladly answer them for you." Dr. Bryan smiled down at Amelia try to reassure her. She has seen what having preterm babies does to some mothers.

"Will they be alright?" Amelia said just above a whisper.

"I am going to do everything I can for them. Babies born at 35 weeks have a high survival rate. We will know more once they are born." Amelia nodded as they enter the OR.

After Amelia was put under, it was only a few minutes before the little boy was born, and right after him, his little sister was born. Dr. Bryan took them and cleaned them up before moving them to the NICU to start assessing them. They both got an 8/10 on their Apgar test, they had a bit of difficulty breathing, and she wanted to get them to the NICU as soon as possible. She didn't want to take any chances.

*****

Brad laid in a lounge chair with Conner on the beach while Damon swam in the waves. Austin came running up to him and Conner.

"Sir, The twins came early!" Brad shot up as his face fell, hearing the news.

Chapter 5

Brad walked up the hospital's stairs, his feet were moving, but he felt as though time had slowed down. Ever since discovering that Amelia had gone into labor, he felt like things were going in slow motion. All Brad wanted was to make sure Amelia and the babies were doing alright. He might have had a few other thoughts, but then the guilt would eat him up inside, and he would go back to hoping they are all alright.

Once Brad got inside the hospital, he was met by the head nurse who took him to Amelia's room, where Dr. Barry was waiting for him when he came into the room. Amelia had given birth to the twins more than twelve hours ago. Brad was shuddering to think of how she will react to him not being there. She had made it clear that she will not take it lightly if he were to miss their children's birth.

Walking into her room, he saw her lying there, still sleeping. He had expected to feel something towards her seeing her like this, but there was nothing. He didn't feel a thing. All he saw was the woman he had married for political reasons, he had believed everyone who told him that he would eventually learn to love her, but that was never going to happen.

"Mr. Davis." Dr. Barry whispered as she walked up to him. "She is resting for now, but you can stay."

"Could I see the babies?" Brad asked, looking away from Amelia. He didn't want to see her. He saw that she was alright, and that was all that mattered at the moment. He didn't need to stay and play the caring husband part.

"Sure, let me take you there." She motioned for him to follow her. "Now, even though they were born prematurely, they are in good hands. Sir...." Dr. Barry turned to look at him as they wait for the elevator to arrive. "I think that Mrs. Davis might have done something to make the twins come earlier. I know it's a far fetched idea, but we found a high amount of Pitocin in her system." Brad's eyes widen with what she has just said. Surely Amelia wouldn't have gone that far.

"She... what?" Brad braced himself against the wall as Austin rushed to keep him from falling over. He felt his breathing become fast, and his heart was pounding in his ears.

"The amount was more than what was needed. She could have killed herself or the babies. Dr. Bryan will be able to update you on how the babies are doing." Dr. Barry motioned for Brad to enter the elevator. Austin, Brad, and Dr. Barry stood in the elevator, trying to process what Dr. Barry had just told them.

Once they arrived at the children's ward, Dr. Barry buzzed them in, walking towards the NICU. "Now, sir, you will be able to go in and out of NICU as you please, but unfortunately, we cannot let others enter only parents and grandparents." Brad nodded with his hands in his pocket, feeling unsure of what to do. He has been in the NICU before but having the babies there felt different. Even if he didn't have a bond with them, he never wanted any harm to come to them. Brad took some anti-bacterial soap at the door after putting on the scrubs before pressing the button to have himself buzzed in by the nurse. As he walked in, the nurse pointed towards the isolation room, and his heart sank, knowing that babies in isolation needed more help.

He walked over to isolation seeing the two small beds next to each other. As he got closer, that's when he saw her. Erina was standing with one of the babies in her arms. He couldn't help but admired how she held the little one close to her as she spoke sweetly to the baby.

Brad stood in the door watching her with his baby, and at that moment, he wanted nothing more than to have her be the mother of the twins, even though he knew that it was impossible and that their mother would soon be able to come and see them.

Erina stood with the baby in her hand, and when she looked up, she saw Brad at the door watching her. She tried to read him to see how he felt, but he stood there with a blank face just watching her.

"Hey, I didn't know that you had arrived. You should come closer to see your babies. They need their father and mother." She motioned for him to come closer. She needed him to bond with the babies before Amelia came and needed all the attention. She knew that Brad never once bonded with the babies during the pregnancy, and she needed him to do that now. They needed at least one parent in their corner.

"I just arrived. How are they doing?" He stood next to her watching the one baby sleeping in the incubator. She turned towards him, giving him a reassuring smile. She knew how difficult it could be to have a baby in the NICU. She has seen parents come and go.

"They are doing good. Do you want to hold her, and then I can update you on the babies?" He nodded as she handed him the little girl. She showed him how to hold her with all the wires and tubes that are connected to her.

"Now your daughter over here is doing extremely well. She's just on normal oxygen and only on 40%." She pointed to a few places on the monitor explaining everything to Brad. He smiled as he took everything in, she told him, before looking down at the little girl in his hands. She was so small and fragile, he brushed his thumb over her small cheek, and his heart instantly melted when she opened her eyes, looking up at him. She had the brightest blue eyes he had ever seen. Right there, Brad knew that he would do anything to keep these babies safe. He would give them the world if he could.

"And my son? How is he doing?" Brad looked up, meeting Erina's eyes while holding his daughter a bit tighter in his arms, where he knew she would be safe.

"He has neonatal pneumonia, which is not uncommon in preterm babies. We have him on antibiotics to fight the infection. We also have him on a ventilator." Erina could see the look of dread on Brad's face. She reached out, giving his arm a little squeeze trying to reassure him. "Brad, all that this means is that he needs time to grow stronger. The slightest his body has to work because of the pneumonia It could be feeding, crying, or even just breathing, he tires out and stops breathing. We are only helping him to grow stronger, and once he is strong enough, he will be able to breathe on his own." Brad nodded as he locked eyes with her. He stood there, just staring at her.

After explaining everything she was about to do to his son, she helped Brad sit down to hold his daughter while she worked on his son. "It will help if you take off your shirt. Skin to skin kangaroo style works wonders for preterm babies." Brad raised his brow at her as she chuckles.

"You just want to get me out of my clothes." He laughed as he felt lighter with her than he has felt in the past few months.

"Nope…. But I think your daughter will be happy with it." She turned around to take a blanket out of the cupboard. When she turned, she saw Brad had put his daughter in her crib as he took his shirt off, she tried not to stare at him, but she was failing miserably. He was more toned and built than what she remembered. He picked her up again, cradling her in his arms.

"What do I do now?" Brad asked with a smile as she took the baby from him. Turning her to lay with her chest against Brad's bare chest, Erina's fingers brushing against his chest made his heart flutter from her touch, remembering the feeling he always got when she touched him.

"Now, all you do is sit back and hold your daughter." She covered the baby with the blanket before taking Brad's hand, putting it on her back. "You need to loosen up. She can feel that you are nervous. She loves you and doesn't want you to be perfect or the CEO of a company. She wants her daddy." Brad nodded, relaxing a bit more, looking down at the little girl on his chest. His little girl.

Erina turned to work on the little boy. She needed to draw blood to make sure that his infection has gone down. She also needed to check his tubes and feed him while Brad was with his daughter. She was going to give him the bottle to feed her as soon as the milk was ready.

A nurse came in with two bottles giving them to Erina. Erina turned to see Brad looking at her with hopeful eyes. "Would you like to feed her?" Erina held the bottle up for Brad as he nodded, feeling his chest about to burst from his heart growing in size.

"I would love to." Erina nodded as she gave him the bottle showing him how to hold the baby and hold the bottle. Brad gave his daughter the bottle and smiled as she started to drink.

"That's it; you are doing good for a first-time dad. Now when you are done, you can change her nappy." Brad's eyes shot up with horror as he looks at her, unsure of what to say or do.

"I think I'm not ready to do that. Maybe you can show me." He smirked as she laughed, shaking her head. She turned back towards the little boy, checking how he digested his milk.

"Why are you doing that?" Brad raised his eyebrow, watching what Erina was doing as she pulled some fluid from his stomach.

"I'm making sure he can digest his food as he should. He can't cry or let us know he is in discomfort. This is the only way to see if he is eating enough or overeating." She saw the concern all over Brad's face. She stood in front of him after she was finished with the baby. "Hey, I will make sure they are taken care of. I will not do anything that doesn't need to be done. He is a strong little boy, and soon you will be able to hold him just like you are holding his sister." She gave him a reassuring smile, feeling her heart twitch, knowing that once Amelia comes to see the babies everything will change.

"I know you will look after them. Thank you so much for being here." He reached out to squeeze her hand. He wanted her to know how much he appreciated her. Not just as a doctor but also as a friend.

*****

Amelia stood outside the NICU after walking out. She couldn't believe what she saw. Brad was openly flirting with the doctor. She couldn't accept that he would do that with their daughter in his hands. How could he humiliate her like this, showing affection towards Dr. Bryan in the open?

She walked back towards her room to get her phone. She would make sure that they will remember who she is and who Brad's wife is. He will do good to remember that those babies are hers and his.

She took her phone out of her bag, slowly sitting down on her bed, feeling the pain from the incision shooting through her lower half. She dialed the number waiting for the person to answer.

"Do you have someone in mind?" They answer, getting right to the point.

"Yes, DR. Bryan...." Was the only thing she said.

"I will handle it." They ended the call, Amelia letting out a relieved sigh.

She smiled, getting up to go back to NICU. She will make sure to show Dr. Bryan that Brad is her husband and make Brad remembered who his Mrs. Davis is. She walked towards the NICU. The nurses nodded as Amelia walked past them. She had some pain but wasn't going to be weak and show them she was in pain.

Arriving at the NICU, she got dressed in the scrubs handed to her before entering the room. She watched as Dr. Bryan stood next to Brad, she was talking to him, and he was staring at her with a look she has never seen from him. She walked over to them, Dr. Bryan noticing her first.

"Mrs. Davis, it's good to see you walking already." She smiled as Amelia nodded at her giving her a smirk as she walked over to Brad, pulling him into a deep kiss. His eyes grew wide, looking at Dr. Bryan with shock in his eyes, half pleading with her to do something. Brad froze in her arms, knowing she was just doing this to prove a point.

"Darling, I missed you so much. Look at our perfect babies we made together." She cooed at him, keeping her arms wrapped around him.

"Amelia, how are you feeling?" Brad said with a bit of a bite in his tone. Moving her to sit in the chair, he was sitting a little while ago. "You need to take it easy. You just had surgery." He kept thinking that she has done this. She had put the babies in harm's way to get him back.

"I'm fine, now that you are back. We can finally bond as a family." She smiled, holding onto his hand. "Dr. Bryan, how're our babies doing?"

"They are doing exceptionally well. Your son is keeping down his feed, and his infection has gone down a bit. We might be starting to nurse him off the ventilator soon. If he does good, he can go over to the nasal intake like his sister." Dr. Bryan brushed her finger over his cheek as she told Amelia how he is doing. Amelia glared at her, shaking her head.

"I would appreciate it if you would be professional with my children and not treat them like commoner babies. I don't want you touching them unless it's to give them medical attention." Amelia spat out as Dr. Bryan took a step back, raising her hands in defense.

"Yes, of course, Mrs. Davis. I apologize for my behavior." Erina took a step away from the beds. Her hands clap in front of her. "Now, as for your daughter, we will be lowering her oxygen flow gradually from the next feed to see how she does. If all goes well, she might be taken off oxygen completely within a day or two." Amelia nodded, never taking her eyes off Dr. Bryan. She was too confident and didn't seem bothered by her.

"Thank you, Dr. Bryan. I have meant to ask why are the babies in isolation?" Brad asked in a calm voice, pulling his hand out of Amelia's hand.

"Because of who you are. We wanted to give you some privacy, we can't give you the whole NICU, so isolation was the best we could do." She walked over to the monitor looking at it, making sure that they are both stable. "Now, you are more than welcome to stay with the babies. I have to check on my other patients, but if you need anything, call or press that button." She pointed to the button next to their beds. "And someone will be with you." Dr. Bryan nodded her head at Brad and Amelia before turning to go to the other babies.

Brad watched as she leaves before turning towards Amelia, narrowing his eyes at her. "Was that necessary, she's a wonderful doctor, and she bonds with her patients...." Amelia held her hand up to him, stopping him from speaking.

"Brad, I don't care what type of doctor she is. If she flirts with my husband. I will be rude to her. She needs to know her place, and she needs to know that you and the babies are mine." Amelia glared at him as he shook his head with a smirk on his face.

"Amelia, your manipulation is over. I will get rid of you one way or another." Brad squared his shoulders, letting her know he was serious. She lets out a laugh that made the hairs at the back of his neck raise.

"Don't be ridiculous. You won't get rid of me. I am the mother of the heirs to your precious company. The shareholders will never forgive you if something happens to them or me." She got up, running her perfect manicure nail down his chest, grabbing hold of his belt pulling him closer. "Our next baby will be conceived naturally." She whispers in his ear as he pulls away.

"Over my dead body." Brad walked out the door, not wanting to be in the same room as Amelia. He said his goodbye to Dr. Bryan before heading out. Walking to the front of the hospital, Brad took out his phone to phone Conner.

"Brad, how are the babies doing?"

"Hey, they are perfect and doing good. I held my daughter most of the morning." Brad smiled into the phone as he told Conner all about the babies and how they were doing. He told him about how Erina was with the babies and everything she had shown him.

"That's wonderful. Now I take it you did not phone me just because you wanted to talk about the twins." Conner had a teasing tone to his voice, Brad laughing at his friend's silliness.

"I need to meet you. I want out of this sham marriage of mine. I need you to help me." Brad got into the SUV, still talking to Conner.

"It's about time. I will meet you at Damon's house as that is the only place we know won't be bugged." Conner walked out to get into his car to drive to Damon's, knowing Damon was at home and he would also be able to help.

"I will meet you there. I will bring dinner." Brad smiled, feeling like he will be free of Amelia soon. He would talk to the guys and then go back to the hospital to see his children, and he will avoid Amelia as much as possible.

*****

A few days later, Erina was jogging through Central Park during her morning run, only needing to be at the hospital at noon. She loved just spending her free time in the park or with Conner and Damon. Both of them are becoming good friends of hers. Yes, she did miss Brad, but what Amelia said and did that day just reminded her that Brad was out of the question.

She ran across the street on her way back to her apartment, when suddenly someone grabbed her arm, pushing her up against the wall. She felt the burn on her face as the person scrapped her face against the brick wall.

"Please.... Just let.... Me go...." She pleaded as she felt him hold her arm against her back, his other hand roaming her front. Her body stiffens as she feels his rough hands all over her. She didn't want his hands on her.

"I don't mean you, harm sweetheart. I only have a message for you." He kissed the side of her neck as she tried to shake him off her. She felt the fear in her but refused to give up; she would not give in to this guy.

She pushed against the wall with her one hand, only to be slammed back against the wall again. She felt the sting in her hand and arm as his grip tightened.

"Now listen to me…. You will stay away from Mr. Davis. If he comes near you, you leave without a word. If you ever come near him again or if you ever tell him about this, a few scraps will be the least of your worries." The guy growled into her ear, feeling her body shake as he roamed his hands over her body again, if only he had more time. "You can be glad I don't have time. I would have loved to destroy this sweet body of yours." He pushed her against the wall again, disappearing down the street.

Erina walked over to her apartment, her body shaking as she tries to calm herself. Opening her door, she walked right to her phone, dialing the only number she knew she could trust.

"Hey, everything alright?" His voice came over the phone a bit groggy.

"I…. I need your help." Her voice shook as she spoke to him.

"I'm on my way…." She could hear the concern in his voice, hearing some shuffling around the room as she presumed he just woke up. "Just hang tight. I'm on my way."

"Thanks." She hung up, sitting down on her sofa, her legs pulled up against her chest as she rested her head on her knees, the tears streaming down her face, thinking about everything that could have happened. She thought of everything he could have done to her. What bothered her was that he only gave her a warning before he disappeared, telling her that he didn't have time to do more.

She sat there for a few minutes when there was a knock on her door. She lifted her head, knowing it was him.

"Erina...." She heard his voice through the door. She got up to open the door for him to come in.

"Hey.... Thanks for coming." She turned her back on him, walking to the sofa. He looked at her, concerned, as he closed the door behind him. He walked over to her, taking a seat next to her.

"What happened to you?" He asked as he hooked his finger under her chin, lifting her face to meet his. "Erina, who did this to you?" He gasped seeing the scrap marks on her face, brushing his hand over her cheek softly, before pulling her into a hug. He wanted to keep her safe, to comfort her, and let her know that he would always be there for her, no matter what. She was like the sister he never had, and didn't want to see her get hurt.

She shook her head, moving out of his embrace. She looked down at her hands, feeling the tears running down her cheeks even more. "Someone wants me to stay away from Brad and to walk the other way if he approaches me. If not, this won't be the worst that happens to me." He lets out a sigh rubbing his hand down his face. "Conner, you cannot tell him. I know who sent him, and I do not want to get...." Conner interrupted her before she could say anything else.

"I will not tell him.... And I know who might be behind it. I think we should find a way to keep you safe. They know where you live. I would like you to come to stay with me.... or.... or Damon for a few weeks. I have a whole mansion, and you won't even know I'm there." He smiled as she chuckled at how nervous he is.

"I will be fine.... I can stay with one of my friends from the hospital. But thank you for the offer, even for offering on behalf of Damon." Conner nodded as he saw the smile in her eyes. He didn't want her to stay with someone he couldn't trust, and he knows that Brad would want her with either him or Damon.

Conner asked her more about her attacker, trying to find out who it might be. He knew who would have sent the person, but if he could find out who it was, he might be able to have him arrested without Brad knowing about it. Erina explained everything that happened to her and how scared she was thinking about what might have happened.

After talking for a while, Erina told Conner that she needed to get ready for work. He offered to stay and make sure that she would get to work safely, knowing that the twins are still in the hospital, which placed her in danger. She agreed to let him take her to work and pick her up after her shift.

*****

A few weeks after the twins were born, it was time for them to go home. Erina was standing with one of the nurses going over the twins' paperwork.

"Dr. Bryan, do you think we should voice our concern about Mrs. Davis and the twins to Mr. Davis?" The nurse asked as she looked at Dr. Bryan with concern.

"We can't say anything. My job is to look after them if they are admitted to the hospital. But this, we don't have proof except what we saw." Erina turned, heading back to the twins to give Brad and Amelia the papers.

Chapter 6

Two weeks after the twins left the hospital, Erina met Damon and Conner for their weekly get together at the beer garden. Erina took a seat next to Conner, groaning as she rests her head on her arms.

"Rough week?" Conner chuckled, shaking his head taking Erina in. She had bags under her eyes, clearly visible that she hasn't slept in a while.

"Week..... Month..... I haven't slept since moving in with Joanne. She and her boyfriend are rough. If they aren't fighting, then they are well-doing something else, and they are loud." Erina groaned as Damon laughed, causing her to give him a knowing look.

"Our offer is still on the table. I'm never at my house. I can't leave Brad at his house alone with that witch. And Conner has his whole mansion to himself." Erina shook her head, taking a sip of her beer, considering what Damon just told her.

"If I do this.... I want to pay for rent. And only until we find the one behind the threats." Conner and Damon nodded, agreeing with what she said. Truth be told, both of them would feel better if she was with either of them.

"Alright, we will agree to this, but where will you be moving into?" Damon gave her a knowing look. He knew she was closer to Conner than him. He wouldn't mind giving up his house to her.

"Since your house is closer to the hospital, I would love to move in there. Not that there is something wrong with your mansion Conner, it's just time-wise Damon's would be the best." Erina locked eyes with Conner, giving him an apologetic look. She didn't want to hurt Conner's feelings, but she had to think about the time it would take her to get to the hospital in an emergency.

"I understand; time-wise it is for the best. And you will have the protection of Damon and Austin. That would make me feel better." Conner gave Erina a one-armed hug, the three of them clinging their glasses together.

The rest of the night, they spoke about what they were doing the past week. Damon was telling them about how Brad was doing with the babies. Brad and Amelia have set up a schedule when he has his time with the babies and when she has her time with them. Erina disagreed with that, stating that the babies needed both their mom and dad.

Conner had told them how he and Brad had been working on getting him out of the marriage. But they couldn't find anything as of yet. He knew that Brad would want Erina to know that he is working on getting out of the marriage, even though she didn't want to see Brad at the moment. He knew she still cared about Brad. He could see it every time Brad's name was mentioned or every time she saw him.

Damon and Erina discussed her moving in. Damon told her that he would help her move her things into the master bedroom, but she didn't want the master bedroom telling him the guest room would be acceptable that it was only temporary.

*****

The day after Damon and Erina was at the beer garden with Conner, they were standing in his house. Damon had a beautiful three-bedroom home with two bathrooms. It wasn't a very over the top place, but it complimented Damon perfectly. Erina had a few boxes and bags with her clothes. She didn't bring too many things, not wanting to stay too long. She had hoped that the threat towards her would be forgotten soon.

"Is that all?" Damon asked as he carried the boxes into the house, Erina following him with two smaller boxes.

"Yes…. I will only be here a while. I still have my place and will be going back there when this cools down." She smiled as she sets down the boxes in the room Damon showed her. Her room was down the hall from his, with a room between him and her. Damon walked in after her, setting the other boxes down next to the window.

Damon stood against the door, watching as Erina packed some of her things away. "I will be here tonight and tomorrow, so how about I make us some dinner." She looked up from her bag as she took out some of her shirts to put away.

"That sounds great…. I might get used to that." Damon laughed as he turned to walk out. Both of them stopping at the top of the stairs when the door opens and Conner came walking in.

"Hey…. I brought some pizza…." He nodded at them as he walked in, putting the pizza on the table before turning back towards them, rubbing his hand on the back of his neck, and carefully choosing his next words. "Uh um…. you need to see this…." Conner walked towards the television switching it on. Damon and Erina were walking over towards the sofa.

Erina froze once Brad's face came on the screen. She shook her head, sitting next to Conner on the sofa. They watched as Brad stood in front of the cameras smiling as he held up his hand to get the crowd to calm down. She knew that Brad had to make a statement about the twins seeing as he is a tycoon in the business world.

Good day. It is with pleasure that I introduce you to heirs to Davis International. We waited to introduce them to you because they had to grow stronger. Without further a due, please welcome Geoffrey Constantine Nathaniel Davis and Regina Annabelle Davis.

Brad stepped aside as Amelia walked up to him with both babies in her arms. She handed Nate to him as she stood with Belle, her smile blooming as she hooked her arm through his. He looked down at her, and in an instant, Erina saw it, for the first time since she has seen Amelia and Brad together. Everything Brad, Conner, and Damon told her, and she never wanted to listen or believe them. And now she saw it.

"Brad doesn't love her...." Erina jumped up, pointing to the screen, where Brad stood with Nate in his arms, his smile never reaching his eyes. "That.... That's his diplomatic smile. I have seen his happy smile, his in love smile, and I have been blind. I have never seen any of those smiles towards Amelia." She started pacing in front of Damon and Conner, both of them smiling, happy that she has finally seen the light. "I have been so stupid." She stopped and looked at her two friends. Her smile faltered as she realized why she didn't want to believe anyone. "But that doesn't matter.... He is still her husband.... and the father to her children." She looked down, trying to hide the tears that are about to spill over.

"Bryan.... He might be married, but he is not her husband. There is still hope." Damon gave her a hopeful look. She nodded, feeling a little bit of hope. She knew she should just let him go and move on. There were other guys out there, even if they weren't Brad. She couldn't wait forever for him.

*****

A few days after the announcement, Brad sat in his office, feeling tired from not sleeping with the twins being a little difficult. Brad was worried about Nate as he would not sleep and kept on crying. Brad wiped his hand down his face, trying to rid himself of the tired feeling. He took his phone and for the first time that day he smiled. He had a photo of Erina standing with Belle just before they were discharged. After checking his emails, he placed the phone back down and turned back to his work.

Brad was busy going over some paperwork when there was an urgent knock on the door. Brad called for them to enter, seeing Austin and one of the nannies enter. Brad has been working in his home office since the twins were released from the hospital. He didn't want to be too far away from them.

"Sir.... We need you to come to the nursery urgently." Austin bowed while talking. Brad jumped up, sending his chair against the back wall, following Austin and the Nanny out of his office, heading towards the nursery.

Coming around the corner, Brad picked up his pace, hearing Amelia shouting, glass breaking, and the babies crying. He started to run towards the door when he heard Nate screaming, feeling like his heart was beating out of his chest. Brad wanted to get to the babies as soon as possible. He wanted to make sure that his children were safe. Not sure why they were crying or why Amelia was shouting the way she was.

Brad burst through the door, his eyes landing on Nate in Amelia's hands as she held onto him. "Just shut up....." She shouted, feeling frustrated. Brad walked over to her slowly, not wanting her to do anything to Nate.

"Amelia.... Let me take him." Brad's voice was calm, even though he was a nervous wreck inside. He held out his hands towards Amelia as she locked eyes with him. His eyes widening, seeing this wild, uncontrolled look in her eyes.

"He.... He won't shut up." Her hands were tightening around his little arms as she held him away from her. Brad stepped closer, taking Nate out of her hands by force, bringing the baby to his chest as he cradled him, trying his best to calm him down. Brad looked over the side where the crib was seeing Belle sleeping soundly.

"Austin, get the SUV ready and phone Dr. Bryan and Dr. Barry," Brad whispered to Austin as he rocked Nate against his chest. "Amelia, you need to see the doctor. Let's go." He motioned to two guards to escort her out to the SUV as he grabbed Nate's bag from one of the nannies. "Please watch Belle. I'm just going to take him to have him checked out." The

Nanny nodded as Brad turned to head out the door, already phoning Damon to tell him he is heading to the hospital.

*****

Erina laid on the couch watching a movie, having a day off from the hospital, when her phone rang. Even though she was off, they knew they could always call her if there were an emergency.

"Dr. Bryan…." She answered, but before she could say more, she heard Austin's urgent voice.

"Erina…. You need to meet us at the hospital. Nate doesn't want to stop crying. It doesn't matter what Brad tries to do." Erina shot up off the couch grabbing her keys running towards the door while Austin was talking.

"Austin…. I'm leaving the house right now. Tell Brad to keep him upright and not to let him sleep. He needs to stay awake. Crying is good."

"I will do that. See you at the hospital." Austin ended the call. Erina locked the door behind her as she runs to her car, driving off towards the hospital. It was days like today that Erina was happy that she was staying at Damon's house. It was only a few minutes away from the hospital.

Erina parked on her spot, putting on the coat and grabbing her equipment from her car. Before running to the front of the hospital, being met by Dr. Barry.

"Were you also called?" Erina looked over at Dr. Barry as she paced up and down.

"Yes, Mr. Davis wants me to check on Mrs. Davis. Not sure what happened." They both turned as they saw the SUV stopping before them. Erina's eyes grew wide as she hears Little Nate even through the closed doors.

Austin jumped out, opening the door for Brad with the baby. Brad got out, running up to Erina, holding Nate close to him. She could see the worry on Brad's face. His blue eyes were even bluer with the unshed tears.

"You have to help him." Erina took Nate carefully as she and Brad ran inside. Amelia was getting out of the SUV just as Brad and Erina entered the door. She brushed past Dr. Barry, following Brad. Austin shared a look with Dr. Barry as they followed Amelia.

Erina took Nate into an emergency room, asking Brad to wait in the waiting room while she did the examination. He didn't want to leave him, but he knew that Erina would take care of him.

*****

Brad paced up and down in the private waiting area, a thousand thoughts going through his mind as he tried to figure out what was wrong with Nate. The door to the waiting room opened, causing Brad to stop and see who was coming in.

"What the hell? The first trouble we have, you run to her." Amelia waved her arms around as she walked closer to Brad, pushing him against the wall. "You will never take my child from me again." Brad took hold of her arms, pushing her back as he looked up at Conner and Damon entering. Amelia snapped her head over to them, smirking. "Thanks for coming."

"Brad, what happened?" Damon narrowed his eyes at Amelia. He knew what she was doing and wanted to save his friend and the babies. He didn't know how to do that at the moment.

"I'm not sure yet. He's in with Dr. Bryan, and we are waiting for an update." Brad sat down at one of the chairs, hanging his head in his hands Damon and Conner sitting down next to him.

Amelia gave them all a look before she stormed out of the room. She had this feeling that Damon knew something with the way he looked at her. She just wasn't sure what he knew; she just had that feeling.

*****

67

Erina stood by Nate's bed, looking over his vitals. She had asked a nurse to call Brad for her. She didn't want to leave Nate's side, still concerned with his oxygen level and the crying. Erina had ordered an MRI and full blood work. She was waiting for Brad to come to let him know that she wanted to admit Nate, what she was about to tell him she knew was going to kill him nearly. She knew that Brad would do anything for his children.

Erina was standing with her back towards the door when it suddenly opened. She didn't turn around immediately as she was busy setting up a drip for Nate.

"Excuse me?" Amelia cleared her throat, not getting the response from Erina she wanted. Amelia had come to see how Nate was doing after leaving Brad with Damon and Conner. She tried to get to Dr. Bryan before Brad had a chance to talk to her. She was not going to have Erina feed lies to Brad.

Erina turned around, seeing Amelia standing in the door. "Mrs. Davis..." Erina said, half shocked to see Amelia. Erina stood half in front of Nate. "Sorry, I was just busy getting everything ready."

"How is he doing." Amelia gave her a heartbroken look, silently asking her to tell her that he will be alright.

"Ma'am, he.... he is not in the best shape." Erina motioned for her to come closer. "I am worried about his blood oxygen level; it is lower than normal. I would like to admit him to make sure that he gets the care that he needs." Erina took his chart to show Amelia, but she held up her hand.

"I'm sorry, doctor. But do you think that I am not capable of looking after my child? He will get the care that he needs back home." She said through gritted teeth.

"Ma'am, that is not what I meant. Nate is a very sick little boy. I am waiting for the MRI results. He is in a lot of pain, which is what's causing the excessive crying. I would not recommend you taking him...."

"He is my son. I will not let you use him to try and get to my husband. We are going home right now. And you do not need to speak to my husband." Amelia walked over to Nate, picking up his fragile little body, cradling him close to her. "Now, are there something I should sign."

"Ma'am, please…. If he doesn't get the medical care that is needed….. He… will… die." Erina was sure to slowly say the last part, hoping that Amelia would see that Nate needs to stay.

"This will not work. Look at him. He is calm and relaxed." Amelia lifts Nate a bit before walking to the door. "I will make sure you are replaced." Amelia walked out of the room, leaving Erina dumbfounded with how irresponsible Amelia could be with her own child.

Walking out of the emergency room, Erina saw Amelia talking and smiling to Brad as she hands him the baby. Erina walked over to Brad, wanting to tell him that she does not recommend Nate go home, Amelia seeing her approach.

"Dr. Bryan said that Nate needs some rest, and he will be fine. We can go home." She motioned for Brad to leave as she turned back towards the head of the hospital. "I want you to find a new pediatrician for the hospital. I do not trust the current one. She wants to milk us for money, and she is putting the babies in harm's way with unnecessary medication and treatments." She glared at Erina, saying the words, the head of the hospital looked between Amelia and Erina.

"Of course, Mrs. Davis. I will get right to it." He turned to head back to his office. Erina hung her head, knowing it will be too late for the babies. Conner stood by the door, seeing what happened between Amelia, the director, and Erina. He knew there was more to this than what Amelia was telling them. He could see it on Erina's face. He would have to mention this to Brad, fully knowing that Erina wouldn't do it.

*****

A few days after they returned from the hospital. Brad was sitting in the nursery with Belle and Nate sleeping on his chest. He was still worried about Nate. Nate had trouble sucking on his bottle, he had been drowsy most times, and if he wasn't sleeping, he was crying his little head off. There was just something that was bothering him about how Nate was, but every time he would ask Amelia what Erina said, she would only say that she said there was nothing wrong he just had some colic.

Brad got up as one of the nannies took Belle to put her in her crib, and Brad took Nate to put him in his crib. It was almost time for Amelia's time with the babies. Brad had also wanted to see if he could contact Erina and find out what was going on with his son.

The day at the hospital, Brad wanted Amelia to be checked out as well. He had a feeling that she had postpartum depression. He wanted her to be in with Dr. Barry while he sorted Nate out, but once again, things didn't happen the way he wanted it to happen.

After saying good night to his two little ones, he walked out towards his office, taking out his phone dialing Erina's number. It was ringing for a while before someone answered.

"Hallo…." The male voice came over the phone.

"Hallo…. who is this." Brad felt his chest become tight. Why would a guy be answering her phone? He didn't know why, but he was jealous even though he had no right to be jealous.

"This is Christian. Are you looking for Erina?"

"Yes, please, I need to ask her something." Brad tried to hide the hurt in his voice.

"Let me just find out if she's done. She was in the shower." Brad could hear the man walking, his heartbreaking, hearing that there was some other man with her while she was in the shower. He could only imagine what they were doing before she went to take a shower, for the phone to ring as long as it did. "Erina, there's phone for you."

"Just take a message. I will call them back." Brad could hear the joy in her voice.

"You know what, it's fine. I will phone Erina later. It's not that important." Who was he kidding? It was crucial. He just didn't want to ruin her time with this guy. He had lost her, he should have done something about his scam of a marriage a long time ago, and now it's too late.

"If you are sure. I can get her to call you when she gets out?"

"No, I will speak to her later. Thank you." Brad hung up, sinking into his chair after he finally made it to his office. He closed his eyes as he let his head fall back against the chair, a tear running down the side of his face. When did his life get this complicated? When did he become this broken man he was right now? He was fine with the arranged marriage until Erina walked into his life. This was all that drifted through his mind.

Brad walked down the hall to the nursery the next morning on his way to see the twins before his day started. This was his routine every morning. Sometimes, Amelia would be in with them when he got there, but she wasn't most of the time. He walked into the room, greeting the nannies, not seeing Amelia anywhere. "Did they have a good night?" Brad asked as he saw they are both still sleeping.

"We won't know, sir. Mrs.Davis made us leave. Nate was difficult, and then he just stopped crying. She must have gotten him to calm down." The one Nanny said as she stood by the table, busy getting their morning feed ready. Brad's eyes grew wide as he felt his stomach drop. He turned, walking towards Nate's crib as his heart was beating out of his chest, he instantly knew that something was wrong.

"How long ago did you get here?" He asked as he tried to get to the crib, but it felt as if he was not moving.

"Not long ago...." She froze, seeing Brad's face, letting the bottle crash to the floor.

Chapter 7

Erina just laid down on the bed, having worked an 18-hour shift already. She was exhausted, just wanting to lay down for a few minutes. She rolled onto her side, just closing her eyes for a moment when Christian came rushing into the room.

"Dr. Bryan...." He stopped noticing her groan before opening her eyes. "They need you at the emergency room, the Davis family have an emergency, but they don't know what it is. They are paging all the possible doctors." Christian walked over to the fridge, grabbing a bottle of water for himself and for Erina. Tossing hers to her as she caught it.

"Thanks, let's go then. I could only hope that it's not one of the babies." She smiled as she and Christian walked out of the attending's lounge. Christian was the trauma doctor on call. He was mostly working when Erina worked due to his wife being Erina's right-hand nurse.

"I'm not sure, the call was very vague, and they just said we needed to be alert." He took some scrubs handing Erina some as well.

"I have a bad feeling." Christian nodded, knowing why Erina was feeling like this. His wife had told him about the outburst Amelia had towards Erina and the fact that she took the baby against medical advice.

*****

Brad stood next to Nate's crib, his heart pounding out of his chest as the worry and fear got the best of him. He leaned down and picked up his fragile little boy. "Austin...." He shouted. His voice had an urgent tone to it as it boomed through the nursery. He ran out of the nursery with Nate in his arms once again. But this time, it was so much different, Nate was barely breathing, and he was already turning a pale greyish color. Brad knew that they had limited time to get him to the hospital.

"Mr. Dav..." Austin froze as he saw Nate in Brad's arms. He now understood why Brad's tone was so urgent. He turned on his heel, shouting orders into his earpiece. He and Brad ran towards one of the SUV's waiting out front.

"Austin, step on it...." Brad's voice cracked as he laid Nate down on his thighs, trying to rub his chest as firmly as he could, making sure not to hurt him. "You need to wake up, open your eyes for daddy. Let me see your beautiful blue eyes." Brad pleaded with Nate to hold on. He needed his son to wake up.

"We are almost there. The doctors are waiting for us." Austin looked in the rearview mirror seeing the glistering in Brad's eyes as he just nodded.

*****

Along with two other doctors, Erina and Christian were standing by the entrance at the back of the hospital, waiting for the Davis motor to arrive. Erina was feeling anxious, she was praying that it was something else, but Nate kept popping into her mind.

"Here they are?" Christian said as he stepped closer to the SUV. Before he could open the door, it flung open Brad jumping out, locking eyes with Erina, and at that moment, she knew that this isn't good. She rushed forward without giving him a chance to say anything.

"We need to get him to an emergency room stat." She held out her hands to take Nate from Brad, tears forming in her eyes as she blinked to keep them from spilling over. "Follow me." She turned, running into the hospital with Brad, Christian, and Austin on her heel.

Entering the private room, she slowly placed Nate on the bed, starting to work on him. She hooked him up to some oxygen, ordering Christian to get a drip ready while she did the rest of the exam.

"We need to move fast. Can you tell me what happened?" Erina asked Brad, not taking her eyes off Nate the whole time.

"I'm not sure. Amelia was with them last night. The nanny said he was crying and then stopped." Erina snapped her head to look at Brad, the look of dread on her face.

"What time was that?" She took some epinephrine to administer it to Nate, Erina, and Christian, calling out orders and procedures they needed to do to stabilize Nate. They had incubated Nate after he still didn't want to breathe even after receiving oxygen. She was still working on him when she heard Brad let out a breath.

"I'm not sure. It was Amelia's time with the kids. I went to get some sleep. I haven't slept much since he came back home a few days ago." Brad shook his head, the guilt taking over. If only he went to check on them during the night. If only he had told Amelia, he would stay with them. If only Erina wasn't with someone else when he phoned, then he could have spoken to her about what was really wrong with his son. "I should have stayed with him."

Erina took her light to check his pupils. Christian gave her a look, silently telling her they needed to get Brad and Austin out of the room. She gave him a nod as he turned towards Brad.

"Mr. Davis, I'm Dr. Lambert." He held out his hand to Brad. They shook hands before he motioned to the door. "We need you to step out for just a bit. We need to do what we can for your son." Brad turned, seeing Erina's worried face, knowing she would have asked him if she wasn't busy trying to save his son. Brad gave Christian a nod, motioning for Austin that they should step out. He wasn't going to move too far away from the door. He wanted to be here when Erina came out of that room with news.

Erina and Christian went back to working on Nate. He was listening to his breathing while she checked if he had any brain-damaged.

"Christian…. Look at this." Christian stood next to Erina as she lifted Nate's eyelid shining her light into it. "There is no response…." Christian shook his head, they had Nate attached to machines as soon as they saw that he wasn't responding to the oxygen they were giving him, and in that time, he must have lost his will to fight.

"Erina…. He is brain dead…." He looked over to her, seeing the will to fight for this little boy. "There is nothing we can do for him." Erina nodded, putting her hand on top of Nate's tiny body.

"I'm…. So sorry." She leaned down, whispering to Nate, if only she had made sure he stayed in the hospital the day Amelia took him. If only she had reached out and spoke to Brad about his condition even though the head of the hospital told her to leave it. If only she did more, she could have saved this little boy. Nate was only seven weeks old. He should have been safe in the arms of his father or mother and not on a hospital bed after being abused.

Christian placed his hand on her shoulder, giving it a comforting squeeze. "Do you want me to speak to Mr. Davis?" He asked her as she shifted to look at him. He could see this was hard for her. He had heard the rumors going around, but Erina was his friend, and he would always be there for her.

"No…. I need to do it." She gave him a sad smile as she walked towards the door, ready to provide Brad with the news. She had told one of the nurses to keep an eye on Nate until they returned. She wasn't sure how he would handle it. She understood that he doesn't love Amelia, but he does love the babies. They were his, and she could see that they meant everything to him.

75

Walking out of the room with Christian on her heel, she saw Brad standing by the window looking out over the garden at the back of the hospital. Austin saw Erina approaching. Seeing the look on her face, he tapped Brad on his shoulder.

Erina was fighting the emotions inside her. The first rule of becoming a doctor is being strong for your patient and their family. Walking closer to Brad, she felt her heart racing. She stuck her hands in the pockets of her coat to hide them shaking. She wasn't going to be able to stay strong and not breakdown in front of Brad, not if he started crying.

"Mr. Davis…. We need to talk…." She motioned for Brad to enter a private room near where they were standing. Christian went with her just to be there in case he had to step in and tell Brad. Brad nodded, walking into the room with Erina and Christian behind him. Austin waiting by the door.

"How is he?" Brad's voice cracked as he tried to keep his emotion from spilling over.

"Sir…. Nate has been through a lot of trauma, a lot more than his little body could handle." Brad's gasped, hearing the words come out of Erina's mouth. Who would want to hurt a baby? "Sir, we did everything we could…."

"No….. He's…. He's just …. No, don't say it…." Brad begged her. He had training in dealing with difficult situations, but never in his life has he thought he would lose his child. Erina blinked back the tears trying to stay the effective, stoic doctor she needed to be.

"I'm so sorry…. Nate is brain dead…." Brad got up from the chair, walking over to the other side of the room. Before they could do anything, Brad's fist came back, punching a hole in the wall, the blood streaming down his hand. "Austin…." Erina yelled as she walked over to Brad.

"No…. Just get away from me!" Brad pushed Erina away, Christian catching her just in time before she fell to the ground. Austin came running into the room, holding Brad back, trying to get him to calm down. He looked over to Erina to make sure she was alright. Brad's body shook in Austin's arms as he let go of the hurt breaking him apart. "I…. I should have stayed with him." Brad sobbed into Austin's shoulder as he tried to comfort his boss and friend. He has seen Brad grow up and seeing him this hurt and broken had Austin all emotional. He had never seen Brad like this, not even when his mom died.

Austin locked eyes with Erina, "Call Conner and Damon." He mouthed to her while he allowed Brad to let go of his pain. She nodded, taking out her phone. She knew they would be there for Brad. She knew they were his support system.

*****

Amelia walked into the nursery later that afternoon, seeing the nanny with Belle, she nodded walking over to the crib, not seeing Nate.

"Where is Nate?" Amelia narrowed her eyes at the nanny.

"Mr. Davis took him to the hospital, ma'am." Amelia froze, swallowing hard, as she remembered the night before.

Amelia paced up and down in front of the cribs. Nate had been crying for the past hour and a half, she had told the nannies to leave her alone, but the one was still in the room, making sure that Amelia had everything she needed.

Amelia was thinking of a way to get Brad to actually spend a night with her. The babies were 7 weeks old, and she had gotten the all-clear from the doctor. Most men would be excited once their wives were cleared, but not Brad. He doesn't even greet her properly. He tries to get and stay as far as possible away from her.

"Maybe if I only hurt you a little, your father will stay with us and then eventually fall asleep with me in his arms, and he will see that I am not as bad. He will see that I actually love him and want more than what he is giving me. It has always been your father. He just never saw me like that. But I made sure that once you…" She leaned down, picking up Nate holding him

away from her. "Now if you would just shut up…. I can't think with you crying all the time." She saw the nanny walking out the door. She goes to lock the door to make sure no one comes in when she's trying to work on a plan to get Brad to give himself to her.

Amelia stood with Nate in her arms. He was still screaming his little head off. She held him up to her eye level shaking him roughly. "I'm your mother. Listen to me. You are just like your father." She shouted before pulling him back to her chest, rocking him. Belle was a quiet baby, not needing as much attention as Nate needed. He wanted to be in their arms the whole time, and Brad always gave in to him holding him or sleeping with him on his chest.

"Finally…." Amelia smirked, seeing Nate's eyes close. She walked over, putting him in his crib, not paying attention to him at that moment. She didn't know why she needed to have babies to get Brad to give her more attention. She gave him the family he wanted, and still, he didn't want her. She ruined her body for him and his children, just like her mother told her to do. The guilt of what she had done crossed her mind for a brief moment. "He will never find out."

Amelia was brought back from her thoughts as Belle started crying. She looked at the nanny, shaking her head. "I need to get to the hospital." Amelia turned around, walking out the door of the nursery heading to the hospital. She wanted to get to the hospital. She couldn't leave Brad alone with Erina for too long.

*****

Damon and Conner came running into the private room where Brad was sitting. Christian was sitting next to Brad, tending to his hand, Erina wanted to, but Brad didn't want her near him. He was upset and hurt with losing his son, but he was hurt with knowing Erina is with someone else. Conner saw Erina standing against the wall. She still had a few tears running down her cheeks.

"Brad..." Damon said, not sure how to approach him. Not sure what was going on, Erina only said that Brad needed them and that she couldn't get near him.

"I.... I failed him." Brad hung his head as the tears streamed down his face. Damon crouched down before Brad to be on his eye level. He has only seen Brad being like this once.

"Who did you fail?" Damon looked from Brad to Erina. She just shook her head as she pushed herself away from the wall. Conner standing next to her, he pulled her into a hug, letting her know he is there for her.

"Nate...." Brad's voice broke as he looked up, seeing Erina's eyes well up again. "Why don't you tell them." Brad pointed at her with his other hand. Christian was finishing up with the one that Brad put through the wall.

Conner and Damon turned towards Erina. "We did everything we could. Nate was not strong enough. He is brain dead.... the machines are what's keeping him alive at the moment." Erina turned towards Brad. "Sir, I'm sorry to say, but you need to make a choice about unplugging the machines." Brad shook his head. He didn't want to do it.

"Brad, I'm so sorry." Conner took a step towards him. Just as Christian was done with Brad's hand, he moved to let Conner take his seat. Conner silently thanking him as he stepped away.

"Now, sir, I will give you something for the pain, and the stitches need to be removed in about 10 days." Christian cleaned up the things he used before walking over to Erina.
She smiled at him as he stood next to her. She was thankful that she had him with her today. "I'm going to check on Nate." She walked to the door, turning around. "Christian, please stay with them." Erina tried to whisper, but Brad heard her. He arched his brow, looking between her and Christian. She turned and walked out, closing the door behind her.

"You're Christian?" Brad walked over to him. Christian was as tall as Brad, with dark hair and blue eyes. Brad gave him a nod, remembering him answering Erina's phone the previous night.

"That's correct, I'm Dr. Christian Lambert. Is there a problem, sir?" Christian didn't know what his name had to do with any of it. Yes, he and Erina should have been using their surnames and not their first names when talking to each other, but they were really good friends, and his wife was one of her best friends.

"No, I spoke to you yesterday when I tried to phone Dr. Bryan." Christian smiled, now knowing what this was about and why Brad didn't want Erina near him. Brad was jealous even though he had just lost his son.

"I remember. Erina was in the attending's lounge. Her phone was on the table. She had to take a shower because a baby threw up on her. And I mean everywhere." Damon gagged hearing that. "And it was at that time that someone phoned to speak to her." Brad looked at him confused, yes he was hurting because of his son. But he didn't understand where this was going.

"So you and Erina aren't dating?" Brad asked before he could stop himself. Christian chuckled, shaking his head as he fished out a ring attached to a chain around his neck to show Brad.

"No, I'm married. My wife is her head nurse, and we have become friends." Brad felt the blush creeping on his cheeks. "Sir, I think you should see your son. Let Dr. Bryan explain to you what is happening." Brad nodded as they all made their way to the room where Nate was in. Brad slowed his steps the closer he got to the room. He felt his heart sink to his feet. His eyes were burning with tears wanting to spill. He swallowed as they stop outside of Nate's room, Austin opening the door for them to enter.

Brad walked in, seeing Erina working on Nate's chart. She looked up, seeing Brad enter the room. "You can hold him if you want." She stepped up next to Brad as he responded to her with a slight nod. He was too scared to say anything, afraid that his voice would betray him. She motioned for Brad to sit down at the end of the bed before picking up Nate, carefully handing him to Brad. He held him against his chest like so many times before. He looked down at the sleeping form of his son, but this was not his son anymore. This was just the shell of who his son use to be.

"I want…. I want to let him go." Brad swallowed back the lump, his voice cracking as the tears ran down his cheeks. She nodded as she took the documents walking closer to Brad.

"I just need you to sign this for me. You can hold him while I remove everything." She held the documents for Brad to sign, Conner and Damon standing behind him. Both with lumps in their throats. They have seen Brad grow close to the babies. There were nights that Damon had to spend in the nursery with Brad if it was his turn with the babies at night.

"I'm going to start with removing the ventilator, and then I am going to switch off the machines. You can hold him, and I will be here if you need anything." Brad nodded, moving him a bit away from his chest, letting her take out the ventilator. She removed all the pipes and wires. "I gave him something for the pain. He is not feeling any pain." Again Brad only nodded, the tears now flowing down his cheeks as he watched the life drain out of his baby's body.

"My sweet little boy…. I will always love you…. You have no more pain…." Brad leaned down, kissing the top of his head. Holding him even closer to his chest.

Erina stood in front of Brad, she knew he needed this time, but she wondered why Amelia wasn't there. Brad was making all these choices on his own. She took her stethoscope to listen to Nate's heart, noting the time on his chart. She didn't want to call the time of death in front of Brad. Wanting to give Brad more time with him.

*****

Amelia ran up the hospital's stairs. She knew that Damon and Conner were there, seeing their cars parked out front. She also knew that she had to play this right, and then Brad will be hers forever.

The nurse at the front desk told her that a doctor will be right with her, that they were busy with Nate, and someone would be out as soon as they are done.

"Don't give me that crap. My husband is with my son, and I want to see them now." Amelia shouted, wanting to get to Brad. She didn't care what happened to the child. He was collateral anyway.

After a short while and a few calls, the nurse took her to the room Nate was in. It had been a few hours since Erina had unplugged the machines when Amelia showed up.
Amelia walked into the room. She froze when she saw Erina standing with her back to the door with Brad's head on her shoulder. His one arm wrapped around her waist. Amelia slammed the door close, making Brad and Erina jump apart.

"Amelia…." Brad narrowed his eyes, the anger boiling inside him.

Chapter 8

Amelia looked from Brad to Erina. She could see the anger in Brad's eyes. Closing her eyes for a moment, she looked at him, tears welling up in her eyes.

"Where's ….. Where's Nate…… Where's my baby?" Amelia chocked out, reaching out to Brad with her trembling hands. Brad took a step back, making sure Amelia doesn't touch him. Erina stepped closer to Amelia, seeing the pain in her eyes.

"Mrs. Davis." Erina held her hands up, motioning to a chair. "Please take a seat." Amelia looked at her before taking the seat.

"You know damn well where your child is." Brad's voice vibrated in the small room. His anger could be felt with the bitterness in his voice. His eyes locked on Amelia, trying to read her.

"I don't know…. When I got to the nursery, they told me that you took him." Amelia's body trembled as she talked, trying to keep her emotions in. She could feel her chest tightening, feeling like she couldn't breathe. "Please…. Brad…. He's my baby." Her breath hitched as she tries to catch her breath, the tears stream down her face. Erina gave Brad a look to tell him to calm down and help Amelia calm down and remember what they talked about.

"Amelia, I'm sorry…. I was emotional…." He crouched in front of Amelia taking her hands. He tried not to let her see how much he despised it or her. "When I got to Nate, he wasn't doing good. We rushed him to the hospital." Brad looked back towards Erina, silently asking her to go on.

"When Nate got here, he was barely hanging on.... we did everything we could.... I'm so sorry. Unfortunately, Nate didn't make it." Erina looked down as she saw Amelia grabbed onto Brad's shirt pulling him closer to her resting her face against his chest. Brad tensed at Amelia's closeness, wanting to push her away from him but knowing he had to play his part.

"No.... No.... My Baby...." Amelia cried while trying to get as close as possible to Brad, but she could feel Brad's body stiffen at her touch. Suddenly she pushed him back, glaring at him.   "You or the nanny did this. She was the last one with him, and you brought him to the hospital." She stood pushing Brad back, making him fall to the ground with a thud, before walking towards Erina, stopping right in front of her. "You were all a part of this." She turned, eyes blazing with fire as she stared at Brad. "You killed our son just to get closer to her...." Erina's eyes shot towards Brad. She knew she had to do something before the rest of the hospital heard this. This could cause a scandal that would impact Davis International, and Brad could not afford a scandal right now.

"Amelia.... pull yourself together." Brad got up off the floor, stalking closer to her, his hands pulled into a tight fist, his jaw clenching. "I brought him to the hospital because he needed medical attention. If I wanted to see Dr. Bryan, I would just come to see her. But I don't do it, because my children need me. I would never endanger them, let alone kill them." Amelia took a step back, looking from Brad to Erina. She has seen Brad upset, but this was pure anger, and this was towards her.

"Br.... Brad, if it wasn't you and it wasn't me. Then who?" She turned to look at Erina. She was going to make sure Erina would not get near Brad again. "Who would want to hurt an innocent baby?" Amelia broke down again, Brad stepping up to her, rubbing her back.

"Mrs. Davis, would you like to see him?" Erina asked, taking a step closer. Amelia nodded, walking to the door with

Erina. "Lydia will take you to where he is. Mr. Davis just needs to sign a few documents, and then we will arrange for an autopsy. That way, we will be able to see when the prince was hurt and what caused his death." Amelia snapped her head over to Erina, hearing about the autopsy.

"Autopsy?" Amelia raised her brow. "Do you really need to do it? Hasn't my son been through enough?"

"Unfortunately, Mr. Davis has asked for it, so it needs to be done. And even if he didn't, we would still have done it because his death was due to abuse. The authorities would want an autopsy report. The hospital needs to give you some answers." Erina smiled as Amelia only nodded deep in thought. Erina watched as Amelia walked down the hall. She was concerned with the way Amelia asked about the autopsy. She felt like she shouldn't have said that much about it.

Brad walked out of the room, wanting to see if Amelia has left already. He needed to talk to everyone about what happened with Amelia. They were all so sure that they would be able to prove that it was her, but with the way she acted, they will have a bit of a problem. He thought back to just after Nate died.

"Brad.... I need to take him." Erina placed her hand comfortingly on his arm. Brad looked up, the tears still flowing down his face. "I know it's difficult. But I need to let them take him to be cleaned." Brad nodded, not handing him over, still clutching his little body against his chest, he knew the time would come, but he wasn't ready to say goodbye.

Brad.... You need to let her take him." Damon said in a low voice, resting his hand on Brad's shoulder. Damon motioned for Erina to take Nate from Brad. She moved forward, putting her one hand on Nate's head and her other under his back, never taking her eyes off Brad. As she lifted Nate out of Brad's arms, his arms fell back down to his sides. She turned, handing Nate to Christian, telling him to take him and get everything ready. Christian nodded, walking out with Nate. Brad knew that this would be the last time he would see his son.

"Sir, do you want to head back to the house?" Austin asked, feeling his heartbreak for his friend. He knew Brad wouldn't want to see Amelia at this moment, not with what has happened to Nate.

"No.... I need to know what we can do. Conner?" Brad turned towards Conner. "This is enough for me to get a divorce, right?" Brad gave Conner this hopeful look. Erina stood there watching the men, feeling that this is not really her place.

"I will leave you to it then." She turned to leave when Brad grabbed her hand lightly, pulling her next to him. He looked back at Conner, still waiting for his answer, never letting go of Erina's hand.

Conner considered the best way to answer Brad's question without giving him too much hope. "If we can prove that she was the one that caused Nate's death, then you have reason to charge her and divorce her. But we need proof." Brad nodded, feeling his heart racing. He wanted Erina to hear this. He had every intention of trying and showing her that they could be something once his divorce was over.

"Then we need a plan." Austin smiled while Damon nodded. They will need a great plan to be able to prove it. "Dr. Bryan, is there anything you can do to help us?" Austin, Damon, and Conner turned to look at Erina, Brad already looking up at her, still holding her hand in his.

"As a matter of fact, there is. We can perform an autopsy. That way, we will be able to see what caused his death, and when the injury was caused. But you have to know it will only be an estimated time." Erina pulled her hand out of Brad's, taking a step away from him before turning back to him. "I will be back." Brad locked eyes with her, instantly feeling calm. Erina walked out of the room for a moment.

"We need to have the autopsy done. We need that as proof." Conner broke the silence in the room while they wait for Erina to come back. They all nod, understanding that if they don't get it, Brad can't prove anything.

Erina walked into the room with Nate's chart in her hands, walking to the stand between Brad and Conner. She opened the file, reading some of Christian's notes, she knew what her notes said, but she needed to make sure that Christian's were the same.

"Right now, if I am correct, Nate died due to shaken baby syndrome." Brad looked at her with a raised brow. Erina told him about the first time they brought Nate into the hospital and what Amelia did. She also told him about why she didn't say anything and that even just mentioning it to them placed her career in jeopardy. Brad stood up from the bed he was sitting on, pacing the room. He knew something about that day wasn't right. He knew that something happened, but he wasn't sure what it was.

"Please pull those records for me. We can have them on file and use them against Amelia as well." Conner met Brad's eye to make sure he didn't overstep. Brad gave Conner a grin in return, telling him that what he is doing is perfect. "Now Brad.... You will have to take a step back to keep yourself safe. Austin, Damon, Erina, and I will handle it from here."

"No, I don't want Erina in danger." Brad let out the words before he was able to even register them. All he knew was that he didn't want to lose Erina or cause her any pain at all. "Brad, they need me. I am the only one that could get to his files and charts without looking suspicious. I will be safe." Brad lifts his hand cupping her cheek, his thumb brushed along her cheek, as he tried to find the words.

After a while, Brad finally agreed to let them do it. They also told him to be there for Amelia and to make her think that she is winning. Brad didn't like that, but to get her for this. He needed to do what was asked of him.

A nurse bumped into Brad, bringing him back from his thoughts. He walked over to Erina by the nurse's station, ready to sign the documents that needed to be signed. Erina and one of the pathologists that were going to do the autopsy. They wanted to make sure that it was done right. Austin would guard them to make sure that everything was done correctly.

After a while, Brad left the hospital with Amelia. She was still in a state about losing her son. Erina stood next to Conner, watching as Brad walked out the hospital's back door, his arm around Amelia's waist as she clutched onto Brad's side.

*****

It was a few days after the death of the young Nate. Brad had given a statement and told them that he would give them answers as soon as he had answers. Everyone wanted the one that caused the death of a baby to be prosecuted for their crimes.

Erina and the pathologist walked down the hall with Austin trailing after them. Brad had postponed the funeral until after the autopsy was done. He wanted answers as soon as possible. He couldn't be with Amelia knowing this might be all due to her.

"Austin... you are more than welcome to stand inside. You do not need to wait outside." Erina turned towards Austin, he smirked knowing what she was doing.

"Thank you, Dr. Bryan. I will be in the corner." She nodded as they walk into the room. Erina stopped looking at the pathologist with a concerned look on her face as he shrugged his shoulder. The coroner stood before them with this confused look on his face.

"Can I help you?" He asked as he goes through his list of what he needs to do today.

"We are here to do the autopsy of Nate Davis." Erina stepped forward, walking towards the table that Nate was supposed to be on.

"Nate Davis was already taken. The release for his body was signed, and he is at the funeral home awaiting the funeral at the moment. It was stated that Mr. Davis decided not to have the autopsy done." The coroner looked between them as they all stare at him in disbelief.

*****

Brad walked into his office with Conner after a board meeting concerning the falling stock. Brad felt defeated like there was nothing he could do.

"I have to finalize the funeral. The board feels that we need to put him to rest. Hopefully, our stock would stabilize after his funeral." Brad sat down in his chair, running his hand down his face. Conner taking a seat on the other side of Brad's desk. He looked at his life long friend, wishing there was something he could do for him.

Brad's eyes shot over to his phone when it started to ring, Conner looking up at him both seeing Austin's name flashing on the screen. Conner knew they couldn't be done just yet.

"Austin....." Brad answered, waiting for his guard to speak.

"Sir, we have a problem. Nate's body has been taken...."

"WHAT...." Brad shouted, getting up from his chair. Conner moved back, turning to see Brad pacing in front of his window.

Conner wasn't able to hear what Austin was saying. He could only assume by the look on Brad's face that it was not good at all. Brad shook his head, letting out a low growl, his hand balling into a fist. His whole body was shaking with anger.

"Who gave the authorization for that. I want those documents." Brad said in an authoritative voice. Even Conner felt a shiver run down his spine with the tone Brad's voice took. Brad ended the call throwing his phone down on the table next to him. He reached out his hands to place them against the wall, hanging his head between his arms, his breath ragged as he tries to calm down.

"Brad, what is it?" Conner asked, half uncertain if he should say anything. He rubbed his hands on his thighs, observing Brad. Brad turned around with this dark look on his face.

"Someone stopped the autopsy. Nate has been taken from the hospital, and the funeral has been arranged." Brad said slowly before he and Conner shared a look.

"Amelia…." They both said in unison. Brad ran out of his office with Conner close on his heel. He got to the front room, and like they thought, there was a small casket with flowers and a picture of Nate. Everything was ready for the funeral.

Amelia walked in deep in thought. When she saw Brad, her eyes grew wide, stopping as she tried to think of something to do.

"Amelia, did you have Nate moved before the autopsy was done?" Brad glared at her when he felt Conner's hand on his shoulder. He instantly knew he needed to approach this differently.

"Morning, Brad. Yes, I did. I want to put this behind me and focus on my husband and daughter. I felt the autopsy wouldn't bring my son back." She looked down at her feet, willing herself to form a few tears.

"I need to give answers, and without an autopsy, I can not do that. The police are also waiting for the autopsy." Amelia took a few steps closer to Brad, giving him a sad smile. Brad considered her for a moment, feeling that he could not stand this anymore.

"I'm sorry, I just felt like he has been through enough and that I want to get this over with." Amelia touched Brad's arm, resting her head on his shoulder. He felt the chill run down his spine, wanting to pull her off him. Every time Amelia touched him, it felt as if his skin turned ice cold.

"It's done now. There is nothing I can do about it. We need to announce the funeral."

"I have already sent out a statement. It is tomorrow. I should have spoken to you about it. I am sorry." Amelia said in a soft voice, not meeting Brad's eyes.

Conner stood behind them, he heard everything, and he could not believe it. This made him believe that Amelia was definitely hiding something, and they were much closer to find out what. They just needed to find out how first.

*****

Three weeks after the funeral, Brad and Damon were sitting in the nursery. Belle was lying on her play mat, making cute baby sounds at the toys above her. Brad was lying on the sofa, watching her, and Damon sat on the chair on the other side.

"You look tired?" Damon said as he takes a sip of his whiskey.

"I Am." He ran his hand through his hair. "I have been with Belle day and night. I have even been with her when Amelia is with her, and then I am too scared to fall asleep. Not sure what Amelia would do to Belle or me." Damon chuckled as Brad gave him a look that could kill him.

"Sorry…." He held up his hands in defense. Damon watched Belle kicking as she tried to talk to the toys. He smiled as he just thought of something. "I have an idea." Brad lifted his head, looking at Damon.

"Please tell me this will be something that will let me sleep," Brad said. His eyes tired. They just wanted to close.

"What if I look after Belle tonight. I will take her to my house…. Before you give me that look. Erina is staying with me. She will be there to help if anything happens." Brad jumped up, smiling at Damon. Brad wasn't sure why Erina was living with Damon, but knowing she would watch his daughter was good enough for him.

"That's it…." Brad exclaimed as he walked to the changing table. Packing a few things for Belle. Damon got up, walking over to Brad.

"What's it?" Damon handed some diapers to Brad. While Brad took out some clothes and two blankets from her dresser, putting them in her bag.

"I will tell you once I have everything arranged. Thanks for offering to watch Bella tonight. I might just get some sleep. I am going to lock my door and make sure Amelia can't get to me." Brad smirked, walking over to the kitchen, taking some bottles and formula. Taking out the one can of formula, Brad saw a bottle of pills, not knowing what it is for. He took the bottle to have a closer look. Not seeing any harm as it was still closed, he placed it back where he found it, making a note to speak to Erina about the pills when he got a chance.

Damon picked up Belle, placing her in her carrier. Brad handing her bag to Damon again, thanking him for looking after her for the night. Damon walked out of the room with Brad. He watched as Brad went into his room. He waited to hear Brad lock the door before taking Belle and walking to the front of the house.

*****

Erina stood in the kitchen, busy preparing dinner for her and Damon. It was her turn as she was home before him. He had let her know that he would be spending the night at the house because Brad needed some rest. She heard the front door open, not paying much attention, she knew Damon would come to greet her once he was ready.

"Let's go see what Erina is doing." She heard him talk to someone. She lifted her head as he walked in with Belle in his arms. "She's making dinner." He lifted Belle to see what Erina is doing.

"Damon, did you steal Belle?" Erina walked over to him, Damon handing Belle to her.

"Is that what you think of me?" He smirked, walking to the stove to see what she was making. "Brad needs sleep, and I offered to watch her. He jumped at the idea once I told him you were here. So I guess you are watching her." He raised his brow in a knowing look.

"Uncle Damon is seeing things again. Your father is probably just happy to sleep a bit." She looked down at Belle before walking to tell Damon what still needs to be done with dinner. "Now you can finish dinner, and us ladies will go take a

92

bath." Erina turned, walking out of the kitchen to give Belle a bath. Damon taking out his phone to send Brad a text, just to let him know Belle was in good hands.

After dinner, Damon stood up to clean the kitchen while Erina made a bottle for Belle, letting it cool down. After she was done, she turned to help Damon with the kitchen. Erina took the bottle after she had helped Damon, and the bottle had cooled down.

"I am going to put Belle to bed. Will it be alright if she sleeps in my room, or do you want her to sleep with you." Erina turned to look at Damon, she knew he wanted her to look after Belle, but she also knew that he would look after her if she had to go to the hospital.

"She can sleep with you. Just call if you need any help." He smiled as she nodded, walking towards the stairs, heading to her room.

*****

A few days later, Amelia walked down the hall on her way to the nursery. She was feeling happy with how things were turning out. Walking into the nursery, she could see that Belle was still asleep, and the nannies were nowhere to be seen. She walked over to the cupboard, taking out some pills from the bottle, crushing them, before putting them inside Belle's milk.

"What did you just put in the milk?" Amelia froze, hearing an unfamiliar voice behind her. She slowly turned, seeing a man standing by Belle's dresser.

"Who are you?" She saunters towards the door just as Brad walked into the nursery with a smile on his face.

"Ah, good you are here." He smiled at Amelia before walking over to the man shaking his hand. "Amelia, this is Dr. Christian Lambert. He will live here in case Belle might need medical attention urgently. His room, for now, is right there." He pointed to the adjoining door in the nursery.

Chapter 9

Amelia stared at Brad before looking back at the doctor. She didn't like the fact that a doctor was living in her home. "Why do we need a doctor to live here?" She asked, looking down at the bottle in her hand.

"I feel that it would be what's best for Belle. We still don't know why Nate died, and I still believe that if Nate got medical attention sooner, he might have survived." Brad walked over to Belle as she starts fussing. He picked her up, laying her in his arm as he held out his hand for the bottle Amelia was holding. She looked down at the bottle then over to Christian before handing Brad the bottle.

"Mr. Davis, I saw Mrs. Davis put something in the milk. I would suggest getting a fresh bottle." Christian took a step closer, trying to stop Brad from giving the milk to Belle.
Brad looked at Amelia with a raised eyebrow. "Care to explain?" He asked, rocking Belle gently. She was hungry, but he didn't want to give her something that could harm her.

"I was advised by Dr. Bryan to add some vitamins to her first feed for the day. And that is what I was adding to her milk." Amelia brushed her hands against the front of her dress. Christian looked at Amelia, trying to figure out why she would act this nervous if it was really just some vitamins. "Dr. Lambert, would you say that my daughter needs some vitamins?" Brad asked, pulling Christian's gaze back to him.

"Yes, sir. We do advise the parents that all preterm babies need some vitamins." Christian walked over to the crib, where his phone was lying. He picked it up before he turned back towards Brad. "If I were you, I would speak to Dr. Bryan about this. If she prescribed some vitamins, this would be all sorted out."

Amelia glared at Christian as he spoke. She was getting fed up with him. He was only there for an hour, and she already wanted him gone. She would have to find a way to get rid of him sooner rather than later. All three of them snapped their heads to the door as the nanny walked in, greeting Brad and Amelia with a smile, before walking over to the dresser to get Belle's things ready for a bath.

"Thank you, Dr. Lambert. I have something else I need to discuss with Dr. Bryan. I will also ask her about this." Brad smiled, handing the bottle to the nanny, asking her to make a new bottle for Belle.

"Do you really not trust me?" Amelia asked with half a bite in her tone. Brad turned, walking up to her, looking at her with this blank stare.

"I am doing what is best for our daughter, she is now the heir, and I need to keep her safe." Amelia nodded, feeling her heart race with Brad being this close to her. She leaned into him just as he took a step back from her, handing Belle to the nanny, who had the new bottle for her. "I have a meeting to get to. Amelia, you need to plan the spring festival, and Dr. Lambert, if you need anything, give me a call." Christian nodded before he looked down at his phone again. Amelia stood there, watching as Brad walked out the door. Not looking back once before closing the door.

I need to do something. If we can be together only once, maybe Brad will see that we are meant to be. She thought to herself. She turns, looking between Christian, who was busy on his phone, and the nanny who was busy with Belle.

"I have to go. I will see you all later." She turned, heading to the door before she turned back and looked at Christian. "And Dr. Lambert, don't dare touch my daughter without me being present." Christian lifted his head with a smirk, knowing Amelia can't do anything to him. Brad had given him the authority to do what he saw fit to keep Belle healthy.

"You'll have to take that up with Mr. Davis, ma'am." Christian turned back to his phone. He was trying to find the vitamins that Erina told Amelia to give. Amelia never mentioned a name, and he was doing research on vitamins for babies.

*****

Two days later, Brad sat at his desk, drumming his finger on his desk, deep in thought. Christian had asked him if he could have a few hours to himself to pick up some boxes for his wife that was also moving in. Brad agreed, asking him to join him as soon as he was done.

Belle was with Amelia and the nanny, knowing that the nanny would look after Belle. Brad had wanted to speak to Erina about the pills he found hidden behind Belle's milk formula and also about the vitamins she told Amelia to give to Belle, but the past two days, he has been busy with meetings and his preparations for the trade deal he wanted with France.

Brad took his phone, dialing Erina's number. It ran for a few times before he heard Damon's voice on the other end.

"Hey, Brad…. Bryan is just cleaning her hands." Damon said. Brad could hear a shuffling in the background.

"Hey, I just need to ask her something." Brad felt a tiny bit jealous. It wasn't that he thought Damon and Erina had something going on. It was just that he wanted to be the one to share a house with her. The one to make dinner with her and to have her there every day. Even though he knew that Damon stayed with him most of the time.

"Sure. Wait, let me put you on speaker for her." Brad heard Damon tell Erina something.

"Morning Brad…. Is everything alright?" Brad heard Erina's voice come over the phone. His heart fluttered, hearing her voice. Even though they never really had something real, he still got butterflies when he heard her voice or sees her.

"Morning, I just need to ask you about some medication I found in the nursery and about the vitamins you told Amelia to give Belle."

"You can ask me anything. You know I want to help, however possible." Erina turned her attention to the phone. "Before we go on, I never gave Amelia any vitamins for Belle. We never even discussed Belle at all."

Brad swallowed, feeling his mouth become dry at the realization that it might not have been vitamins. "Erina.... I found some pills hidden behind Belle's formula. Can you tell me what it is? I am sending the picture to Damon's phone." Brad pressed a few buttons, hearing the ping over the phone. Then he heard Erina gasp.

"That's.... Tylenol...." Brad heard Erina telling Damon to get her a book from her medicine bag. "Just hold on a bit." She was quiet for a moment. "Brad, could you see if any of the pills have been used."

"No, I didn't check. It was a sealed bottle." Brad lets out a deep breath trying to calm himself. With the way Erina sounded, he felt that this was not going to be good at all.

"Brad.... those pills are hazardous for a baby. You need to get those out of the nursery asap. I will phone Christian. He needs to take a blood sample from Belle and get it to me urgently." Erina lets out a staggering breath feeling her heartbeat out of her chest.

"Damn.... I left Amelia alone with Belle. Christian went to get some of his wife's boxes." Brad slammed his hand down on the desk, calling for Austin while still having Erina on the line. He needed a reason to get Belle to Erina. "I am bringing her to you right now."

"Brad, take her to the hospital. I will meet you there." Erina said before both of them hang up the phone. Brad turned to Austin, telling him to get the SUV ready and tell Conner to meet them at the hospital. He needed this as proof that Amelia had harmed the children.

Brad walked out of his office. He told his assistant to move all his appointments for the rest of the day. Brad didn't have anything that needed his attention right away. He walked into the nursery, seeing Amelia standing by the counter, preparing a bottle for Belle. Brad smiled, walking over to Belle, where she laid in her baby swing. He picked her up, whispering to the nanny to get a bag ready for her.

"Brad, this is my time with her, unless you want to spend it with her and me." Amelia cooed as she walked over to Brad with the bottle she just made.

"I actually want to give you some time to relax. There is an urgent matter for me to attend to at Conner's office, and he asked me to bring Belle along. He hasn't seen her this whole week." Amelia raised her brow at Brad.

"She can't go. She hasn't been feeling well. We just had to change her because she threw up all over everything." Amelia reached out to take her from Brad, but he moved away. "And she looks a bit yellowish to me. I am waiting for your doctor to come back and check her. What does it help that you hired a doctor, but he isn't here when we need him?" Amelia took a step closer, again reaching out to take Belle.

"Don't worry, I will ask Dr. Lambert to meet me at Conner's. You need to rest. As for him not being here, I told him he could take a few hours off. Next week you have to watch her while I am in Paris for the trade deal." Brad waved off Amelia taking the bag from the nanny. "I will see you later today or tomorrow." He walked out of the room, checking the bag to see if the nanny did what he asked her to do. He smiled as he saw the pills wrapped in a plastic bag. He had asked her to grab the drugs while he was busy distracting Amelia but to use a plastic bag and not touch it.

*****

Erina paced up and down in her office, Damon sitting by her desk watching her. She was going through papers trying to find information on the medication that was given to Belle. If it was given to her. Erina had never been in a situation like this before. She never dealt with a parent trying to kill their own child or purposely trying to harm them.

"Bryan, you need to stop. We don't even know if Belle was given anything. You need to calm down." Damon got up, walking over to her, taking her hands in his looking into her eyes. "You got this." Damon pulled her into a hug just as the door open, Brad standing there with Belle in his arms. Damon pulled away, Erina walking over to Brad, her eyes going wide, taking in Belle's appearance.

"How long has she been like this." She asked, Brad not paying attention, his gaze still locked on Damon. "Brad...." Erina said a bit louder, putting her hand on his arm.

"Sorry, she was fine when I left her this morning. But Amelia said she has been throwing up and not feeling well." Brad turned his attention to Erina as she took Belle out of his hands. "I don't know if this will help." He took the bottle Amelia prepared out of the bag. "Amelia made this just before I came into the nursery." Erina nodded, motioning for Brad to come closer. Damon stood there against the wall, Austin standing next to him. They both knew what Brad was thinking of seeing Erina in Damon's arms.

"I need you to put your hand right here." She took Brad's hand, putting it on top of Belle's chest, taking the bottle from his other hand. She took a sample tube, taking a sample of the milk.

"I will have the lab test the milk with her blood sample." Brad nodded, not meeting her eyes. He just wanted his daughter to be alright.

Erina told him to hold on to Belle while she took the blood sample. Brad held Belle close to him. Erina took one of her feet, pressing the needle into the vein slowly, Belle not even making a sound. "You're good at that. I don't think I have heard my kids cry once when you had to give them an injection or take their blood." Brad smiled down at Erina.

"It takes years of practice, and I have a steady hand." She beamed up at him, feeling the same flutter she always felt when they were together. "Now I going to send this to the lab, but I am admitting Belle, her color has me worried." She turned to walk towards the door, heading out to have her nurse take the blood and milk for testing.

"Can you please take this to the lab? I need the results urgently." The nurse nodded, Austin going with her to make sure that nothing is tampered with.

*****

Amelia walked down the corridor towards Brad's office. After Brad left, she knew that Brad would eventually take Belle to the hospital to be checked out, with Belle being as sick as she was. She wanted to make sure that when he got back, she would be able to get what she wants from him.

Walking into his office, she took out a plastic bag with white powder in it she poured it into his favorite scotch. When he gets back, she knew that he would head to his office first to have a drink before heading up to his room.

"When he drinks this, I will come in, and he will make love to me like a husband and wife should." She said to herself, rubbing her hands together. She placed everything back like it used to be before she walked out of the office, making sure no one saw her.

She walked back to her quarters, telling one of the guards to let her know as soon as Brad returns. She wasn't going to let this opportunity pass her by. She wanted to make sure that she will never lose Brad. He was hers and would always be.

*****

It had been a few hours since Erina admitted Belle. She had the staff bring a cot and machines into her office until they could have a private room ready for them. Brad sat by her crib, holding her tiny hand. He felt powerless to help his daughter, he had already lost his son, and now his daughter was getting worse.

"Brad.... You need to take a break. I will stay here with her." Damon placed his hand on Brad's shoulder. He was concerned about his friend. Not wanting him to push them all away. Conner and Erina were going over some paperwork that he could use to build a case against Amelia. They needed to put in the paperwork to have the divorce finalized.

"I'm Fine.... my daughter needs me." Brad shook his head, closing his eyes as a tear slips down his cheek. He knew he was rude and unfair towards everyone, but he felt guilty for failing his kids.

Erina looked up from her papers when the nurse entered with the test results, handing them to Erina before walking out. Austin stood by the door watching as Erina went over the results, looking up; she met his eyes. He subtly nodded at her.

"Uh um...." Erina cleared her throat, making Brad look at her with concern. "Belle has an extremely high amount of acetaminophen in her bloodstream...."

"Wait, what? What does that mean?" Brad got up, moving closer to Erina. "How did Christian miss this."

"It means that your daughter has been drugged for weeks. And I don't think Christian saw the symptoms. I have a feeling that the dose that she received increased on times that he wasn't near her." Erina motioned for him to sit down, taking a seat next to him. "Belle is in total liver failure. She needs a transplant as soon as possible." Brad hung his head, his hands shaking with anger and sadness.

"How.... How does.... this happen..." He looked at Erina. She could see the tears in his eyes as he tries to keep them back. She reached out to squeeze his hand. When she tried to pull back, Brad's grip tightened, lacing his fingers with hers.

Holding his hand, she looked down at the page again. "I am so sorry...." She sat up straighter trying to compose herself, still holding his hand. She felt that if this will make him feel better, then she would give him that. "Belle needs a liver transplant as soon as possible." Brad squeezed her hand, feeling his chest tighten. He clawed at his throat, feeling like he can't breathe. Damon stepped forward just as Erina let go of Brad's hand, taking his face in her hands, turning him to look at her. She could see the fear in his eyes. His breathing was shallow and fast. "Brad, you need to breathe." She brushed her thumbs across his cheek, blue eyes locked on blue. "Breath with me." Austin and Damon stood nearby just in case she would need any help.

"I.... Can't.... Breath...." Brad chocked out between battered breaths, his whole body shaking as he tries to calm down. Conner moved behind Brad rubbing his back as Erina kept her hands on his cheeks.

"Bryan, do something!" Damon said anxiously, running his hand through his hair. Erina looked up at him for a moment, silently telling him to calm down.

"Brad, take a deep breath for me." She took a deep breath Brad following her every breath. They breathe like that a few times until she could see that he was starting to calm down.

"Are you alright?" Brad nodded, leaning into her touch. He felt safe and loved at that moment. Erina's touch was soft and warm. Brad wanted to feel that all the time.

"How does the transplant work?" Conner asked as he stood behind Brad.
Erina dropped her hands from Brad's cheek. He already missed her touch. Erina got up to go to her desk. She pulled a few forms from her file, walking back to where Brad was sitting.

"Normally, we test the mother and father for a match first and then anyone that wants to donate. We also put her on the donor list." Brad snapped his head in Austin's direction, hearing that he could donate should he want to. He knew that technically, he wasn't allowed to donate. It was a stipulation his father had added when he took over the company.

"Austin.... if I am a match, I am donating." Brad gave him a stern look before turning back to Erina. "Won't it take too long if she's on the list?"

"No, she is critical and jumps to the top of the list. And as for you donating, we only need a small part of your liver."

"Then let's do this!" Erina nodded, handing Brad a form to fill out while she got the tubes ready to do some tests. Conner, Damon, and Austin also taking some forms telling her they want to get tested just in case.

After they filled out the forms, she started drawing the blood. Brad was the first one to have his blood drawn. He was lost in her eyes as she took some blood. She marked Brad's tube after she was done, putting it and his form in a plastic hospital bag and sealing it. Next was Damon, who winched as she pressed the needle in. She chuckled at the big baby sitting in front of her. Conner and Austin both having a turn as well.

Erina took the samples telling the nurse to take them to the lab for testing, Austin again following her. "Brad, you need to know that you might not be a match, either the mom or the dad is a match." Brad nodded, feeling this uneasy feeling in his stomach.

"Thank you. I am going to stay with Belle tonight if it's alright with you."

"Of course… Let me know if you need anything. I will be right outside." She walked to the door as Brad took a seat next to Belle's cot. Erina and the other guys walking out of the room, giving Brad time with Belle.

Belle had been in the hospital for only a few hours, and her color changed drastically. The yellowish tint could easily be seen. Erina knew they didn't have much time. With the amount of acetaminophen in her bloodstream, she should have been in a coma.

"Erina, do you have the test from the bottle?" Conner asked as they all stood outside the door.

"Yes…. It also had acetaminophen in it. It was a high dose. With Brad having the panic attack, I didn't want it to get worse by telling him the results of the milk test." Erina pulled out a copy of the test for Conner handing it over to him. He looked over the document, not sure what he was looking for.

"I hate that this is happening to Belle and Brad. But this is what Brad has been looking for proof that Amelia...."

"Is a murderous bitch?" Damon interrupted Conner raising his brow in question.

"Well, yes." Erina smiled, giving Damon a fist bump. Conner shook his head at the two.

"Guys.... I saw something in Nate's file a few days ago that has me concerned. I didn't want to tell Brad before I had the proof, but I have requested that test as well." Erina looked between Conner and Damon, who wanted to know what it is but knew she will tell them when she's ready. "If I show you, you need to promise me not to say anything. Brad is hurting as is." She gave them a stern look, both agreeing not to say anything.

She motioned for them to follow her, needing them to see it for themselves. They walked over to the nurse's station to use the computer there. She sat down behind the computer as she typed in her username and password. She went to Nate's file, clicking on a few icons. "Right there...." She pointed to a part in the file. Conner swallowed loudly, looking at Damon, who was just as shocked.

"I have an idea.... I need to talk to Austin, don't say anything about this to anyone." Erina nodded, closing the file. "I need to phone Mia. Brett died before he could give her the information he had about Amelia. I need to find out from her what they were looking into." Conner said as he pulled out his phone, already dialing Mia's number. "I will see you two tomorrow." He kissed the top of Erina's head before he walked down the hall and out of view.

"Shit Bryan this is big. You know what this means. If it is true, Brad will be free of Amelia for good." Damon smirked at her, giving her a wink. She knew what Damon meant by that, but the last thing she wanted was for Brad to lose his children just to be with him.

Damon and Erina talked for a while before he decided to go grab them all some dinner. Damon wanted to stay and be there for Brad, knowing this will be hard on him either way.

*****

Erina laid on the sofa in her office, Brad laying on the other one in front of Belle's cot, both of them finally falling asleep. Damon had taken the chair in the waiting room to sleep in.

The alarm of the monitors woke Erina up with a bang. She pressed the button calling a code blue as she rushed over to Belle's cot lowering the sides to get to her and start compressions.

"What's going on?" Brad asked with a sleepy voice, rubbing his hands over his eyes.

"Brad, I need you to step out!" He looked at her remembering the last time she told him to step out his son died. "I need you to go now!" She yelled while working on Belle. Within moments Christian and a nurse came running into the room assisting Erina. Damon rushed in with Austin, both of them leading Brad out of the room.

It felt as if everything was going in slow motion. All Brad saw was the doctors running around the room. Erina's mouth was moving, but Brad could not hear or understand a word she said. The last thing Brad saw before the doors closed was Christian's shocked face.

Chapter 10

Erina wiped her hands after washing them. She looked in the mirror at her reflection, her blue eyes shining with tears as she fought to save that little girl. "Do you want me to talk to Brad?" Christian stood behind her, seeing concern all over her face.

"No, I will do it." She turned, resting her hand on his arm. "This is not your fault." He nodded, feeling the guilt eat away at him.

"I should have done a blood test when I suspected that she was doing something. I just didn't want to put Belle through all the pain. She wasn't showing any signs of abuse or being drugged." His voice cracked as he spoke. He should have done more, then this little girl would be safe.

"Christian, she stayed with me more than once since the first time Damon brought her over, and I didn't pick it up. You were there only a few days, and the amount we picked up in her bottle when she came in was enough to kill her. Amelia was waiting for you to be out of the house to do this." She lifted his chin so he could look her in the eye. "I will not let my good friend and fellow doctor blame himself for this. All we can do is make sure Amelia gets caught." Christian nodded, giving Erina a hug. He was thankful to have a friend like her.

"You are the best, do you know that?" He brushed his hand over his face letting out a frustrated breath.

"Just telling you the truth." She patted his arm. "Let me go and inform Brad about Belle." Christian nodded as he walked back towards the PICU.

*****

Brad sat in a chair, his leg bouncing up and down, waiting for news on how Belle was doing. Damon and Austin were there with him. Both of them were too scared to say anything. They could see that Brad was on the edge of breaking down, and if he were to receive any more bad news, he might just tip over the deep end.

Brad took out his phone, checking the time. It had been two hours since they were woken by the beeping alarms of Belle's monitors. It had been two hours since he felt his heart being ripped out of his chest.

All three of the men snapped their heads towards the door as it opened, and they saw Erina enter the room. Brad felt his heart sink to the floor, not able to read her at all. She gave them all a nod before turning her attention towards Brad.

"Please don't say it." He looked down again, trying to swallow the lump in his throat. She took the seat next to him, reaching for his hand, giving it a soft squeeze.

"Brad…. Belle needs the transplant urgently. Christian is checking the records now to find out if they have any news. And I am going to the lab as soon as I am done here." Brad looked at her with his red-rimmed eyes as tears rolled down his cheek.

"She's alive….." He searched Erina's eyes for a moment. He was so sure that his little girl didn't make it. He was ready for the heartbreaking news.

"She is…." Erin straightened her jacket. "She's in PICU. We had to incubate her. She also had a collapsed lung." Brad gasped, shaking his head. She was still so small. His baby girl needed him now more than ever. "I inserted a chest tube for now to drain the fluid that had built up in her lung to help prevent that it will collapse again. We need to do a transplant before her organs start to fail." Erina could see Brad was struggling with the news. "Do you want to see her?"

"Could I?" Brad asked with insecurity in his voice. He wanted to see her but was afraid of what he was about to see.

"I can take you to her. You can see her, but not stay long." Erina got up, Brad getting up after her. "You need rest, and so does she." Brad nodded as they walk out of the room.

Erina guided Brad to the PICU. After putting on some scrubs and using the anti-bacterial scrub, she took him to where Belle was lying. He couldn't believe that it was his little girl, she had turned more yellow and had wires and tubes all around her, but she was still his perfect little baby.

"I'm going to give you a moment. I need to check on the results and if Christian were able to find a donor." Brad nodded, looking between Erina and Belle. He moved closer to Erina, pulling her into a hug, holding her for what felt like a few minutes, but in reality, it was a few seconds. He couldn't get enough of her.

"Thank you..." He whispered into her hair. He felt safe and loved in her arms. He felt as if she was his lifeline at that moment. All those feelings he had buried all those months ago coming to the surface again. He had new hoped that when he and Amelia are no longer married, that he could be with Erina at some point.

*****

Erina sat behind her desk, Damon and Christian standing behind her as they looked at the results she received from the testing. Austin took Brad home after Erina advised him to rest and make sure that Amelia came with him later the day. Brad had been at the hospital the whole night and needed some time to collect his thoughts.

"What are we looking for, Bryan?" Damon asked, looking at the papers in her hand. Christian pointed to a part on the document, and Erina shook her head in agreement, seeing what he saw.

"We were checking if any of you were a match. But none of you are, not even Brad." Erina looked up, meeting Damon's gaze. "That's not all. Do you see this?" She placed the one paper

108

down and then the other one, next to it, pointing to the two different pages.

"They aren't the same?" Damon pointed out.

"Exactly. Brad is ...." Before she could say anything more, there was an urgent knock on the door. She called for them to enter, seeing the Head of the hospital enter her office.

"Dr. Bryan, can I have a word with you, please?" Damon and Christian gave her a look. She nodded, telling them it will be fine. They walked out, closing the door behind them.

"Is something wrong?" Erina asked, motioning for him to sit down.

"I hate to inform you that your application for permanent employment has been declined by the board." He took out a document from his folder handing it over to her.

"What....." Erina grabbed the documents looking them over. "How could this be, my score is above the needed requirement, and my profession is of need in the hospital." She read the remarks *'Not qualified for the position. Her death rate is too high. - Denied'* And at the bottom of the page was Amelia's signature.

"I'm sorry, I wish there was something I could do." He rubbed the back of his neck. "I have to inform you that you have two weeks to leave the hospital." He got up walking to the door.

"I would just go if I were you." He turned, walking out the door, Christian and Damon rushing back in as soon as he was out.

"What happened?" Christian asked, concern dripping from his voice.

"I.... I have to leave the hospital within two weeks. I think I have just been fired." Erina slid the document over to Damon and Christian, both scanning over the papers. Damon smirked when he saw the signature.

"Bryan.... You are not going anywhere." She gave Damon a confused look. Christian catching what Damon was saying.

"I have no choice. My request was denied by Amelia herself...." She stopped talking with this look of realization on her face. "O, I get it now. I need to talk to Brad. But first, I need to get these results in. I then need to see Conner." She got up, grabbing the results.

"I'll drive you. We can go to Conner and then to Brad's house." Damon took his keys out of his pocket. Christian telling them he would work on getting a donor for the princess.

*****

Damon and Erina arrived at Conner's. She wanted to discuss the results with him wanting to find out if this would help Brad. They also wanted to inform him about Erina's request being denied by Amelia.

Walking into Conner's office, he greeted them. Erina got right to the point showing him the results.

"You never told me what this means," Damon said, staring at the paper. He didn't know what type of tests this was.

"You might want to take a seat because if I am correct, then someone has committed a crime. And I don't mean killing the babies." Erina raised her eyebrow, watching Damon take a seat. She leaned against Conner's table, keeping eye contact with Damon.

"When Nate died, I was waiting for a blood test to come back, so when they came back, I saw something that made me suspicious. Nate didn't share Brad or Madeline's blood group, though it is possible not to have the same, Brad is O Negative, and Amelia is A positive. Nate should have had one of those, and he didn't. He was AB positive. I then asked Austin, who gave me the approval to run a DNA test. You saw the results yesterday. I just wanted to make sure that it was true."

"I remember.... So what did you run a test on Belle as well?" Damon asked, looking between Conner and Erina.

"Yes...." Erina was interrupted when the door flew open, Mia walking in. She smirked at the three of them as she walked in with a man behind her.

"And let me guess it came back the same as Nate's." Mia chimed in while walking over to Conner's table, dropping a document on his table.

"How did you know, and who is he?" Erina asked, pointing to the doctor behind her.

"This is the fertility doctor that did the IVF on Amelia, and he has something to share with all of us. Conner, I believe you would like to get a recorder out for in case he decides to die." Mia pushed him forward and then pushing him down onto the chair. Conner took out the recorder from his drawer.

"Please state your name," Conner said with confidence, putting the recorder on the table.

"I am Dr. McDonald. I am here on my own free will to give a statement about what happened the day of the Mr. And Mrs. Davis's IVF." He sat there, rubbing his hands along his thigh nervously.

"Do you give consent for me to record your statement, to use if for any reason you are unable to do it yourself?"

"You do have my consent," Conner nodded, motioning for him to go on. "The day Mr. and Mrs. Davis came in, some of my staff was nervous. Everything went as planned. Mr. Davis had given his sperm to the nurse once he was done. The nurse was so nervous that she spilled the cup down the drain. Once she told me, I went to tell Mrs. Davis, who had asked Mr. Davis to give her some privacy. Mrs. Davis told me to just use someone else's sperm, that she didn't care who the father was just to make sure she walks out of there pregnant." He swallowed hard, looking down as he spoke the next words. "I... I used my own to get Mrs. Davis pregnant." He could hear the gasps around him, and he could feel the eyes on him.

"You mean to tell me that you are the father to the two babies Mrs. Davis was pregnant with," Conner asked with a harsh tone. All of this could have been avoided if the doctor had gone to Brad and not Amelia.

"Yes, they are my babies and not Mr. Davis's." He said loud and clear. Erina sank into the chair she was standing next to, her hand flying to her mouth at hearing his confession.

"You understand that we need to take this to Mr. Davis."

"Yes, and I want to help you." He turned to look at Mia. "There was a guard who came to see me a few months ago. He asked me questions about the IVF, and I told him everything, but he died that same day. I don't even know if he were able to tell anyone." Mia felt this pain in her heart, knowing that if Brett got to her in time, they could have stopped Amelia months ago.

"Unfortunately not…." Mia turned, looking out the window, not wanting to let anyone see how much losing Brett affected her.

Conner asked one of his guards to take Dr. McDonald to a room and keep him there until they were able to talk to Austin. Damon and Erina spoke to Conner and Mia about what they were going to do. Mia told them that Austin asked her to go see the doctor and get some information from him. Damon telling them that they need to talk to Brad about this. Brad needed to know that the babies weren't his.

"We should wait and hear what Austin says before we tell Brad. He is already lost with the fact that Belle is in the hospital. I think we need to approach this carefully." Erina swallowed to try and get her dry throat wet.

Mia considered it for a while. "I agree with Erina. We need to be smart about this. Amelia can fight us on the fact that we did a DNA test without her or Brad requesting it."
"I hate to say it, but what Mia says is true. We need to get Brad in on it." Conner said as he ran his hand through his hair. All of them know that it will break Brad's heart to know that the kids aren't his, and they all feel that this is why hurting them came so easy for Amelia.

"I need to see Brad about my employment. I will talk to Austin when I am there, and then we can talk to Brad."

Everyone agreed that Erina and Austin will handle giving Brad the news about the babies not being his.

*****

After a short nap and finally talking to Amelia about Belle and needing to go to the hospital, Brad headed to his home office. He had papers to go over before he headed back to the hospital. Amelia had told him she would meet him in an hour, and then they could go to the hospital together. He didn't want to go to the hospital with her, but he still had to play his part in upholding their marriage.

Brad met Austin at the bottom of the steps. "I need you to arrange two guards to be at the hospital. I have spoken to Amelia, and she will be going to the hospital with us. Meet me at my office in an hour." Austin nodded as Brad walked into his office. He walked over to the bar cart, pouring himself a drink, needing to numb the pain that he was feeling. He was sure that if Belle didn't get the transplant, she wasn't going to make it.

He walked over to his desk. He took a seat behind his desk. Before placing his glass down next to the documents, he had to go through. He looked at the first document while sipping on his scotch. He couldn't concentrate on what he was reading. His mind kept going back to what happened at the hospital and them having proof against Amelia.

Brad got up, pouring himself another scotch, feeling a little light-headed as he walked over to the bar cart catching himself against the wall. "I need more sleep if one drink does this to me." He chuckled to himself as he downed the second and then the third glass of scotch. He felt as if the room was spinning, trying to walk back to his desk where his phone was, his foot catching on the other one causing him to fall over, hitting his head against the side of his desk.

Brad doesn't know how long he was out. His eyes fluttered open, blinking a few times to try and see who was with him. He felt this pair of soft hands by his neck and on his chest.

He felt a gentle kiss on his lips, he still couldn't focus on what was around him. He had this aching in his brain that felt as if it was about to explode. Trying to lift his head, not able to get it off the floor. It felt heavy and as if he had no control over his body. His breath caught in his chest as he heard her voice.

*****

The drive over to Brad's place was tranquil. Both Damon and Erina were trying to wrap their minds around what was going to happen once the news was out about the truth around the twins' father. Not only what would happen to Amelia, but also what would happen to Brad. He fell in love with the twins the first time he saw them, and to know, after months of bonding with Belle to find out that she isn't truly his child was going to break him.

Damon pulled up near the front of Brad's house, parking his truck. Damon got out, walking around the truck to Erina's side to open the door for her. Getting out, she and Damon walked up to the front door.

"I have to grab something in my room. If you go down this corridor, turn right at the end, and the first door on your left is Brad's office. He should be in there." Erina nodded, watching as Damon walked down the other hall towards his room.

Erina turned, heading the way Damon told her to go. She hoped that Brad would be in his office. She has only been to his house a few times and never this far. She stopped in front of Brad's office, knocking on the door, waiting for him to call for her to enter.

"Brad...." She called out, hearing a noise coming from inside. She knocked again, not hearing him call for her to enter but hearing more of a moan. "Brad... I'm coming in." She slowly opened the door, walking inside.

"Brad....." She stopped looking at the sight in front of her.

Chapter 11

It only took Erina a moment to compose herself before she rushed over to Brad. She leaned down with her ear near his chest to make sure he was breathing. She kept her hand on his chest, moving her other hand to his neck, feeling for a pulse, letting out a breath she didn't know she was holding. She looked around the room, trying to figure out what had happened. All she saw was the empty scotch glass, but what was bothering her was the fact that there was still more than three-quarters of the bottle left.

"Brad.... I'm going to go get help." Brad moaned and murmured as he tried to wake up. "Shhh.... I won't leave you." Looking around the room, she saw his phone on the desk. She leaned down, giving him a quick kiss on the lips before she got up, taking his phone to phone Austin. She tried to calm her trembling hand, trying to unlock his phone. A tear slipped out of her eye, seeing his front page on his phone. It was a photo of her and him when they were at the beer garden before the twins were born.

She went to his contacts looking for Austin's name, dialing his number she heard it ring twice before he answered. "Sir, I'm on my way." She heard Austin's voice on the other side of the phone.

"Austin.... you need to hurry. Brad...." Her voice cracked as she spoke. Austin knew something was wrong.

"Damon, Brad needs us...." She heard Austin shout. "We are on our way. Just stay with him."

"I won't leave his side. Please hurry." Erina ended the call, putting the phone back on the table. She walked around to where Brad was lying, grabbing a cushion from one of the chairs. Lifting his head up slowly, she placed the cushion under his head, brushing a few strands of hair out of his face. "Brad.... please just hang on. Austin is on his way." Erina had a feeling she knew what was going on, but she wasn't going to speculate until she had the facts.

Moments later, the door burst open, Damon and Austin rushing in, their eyes landing on Brad lying on the floor.

"What happened?" Austin asked as he kneeled down next to Erina and Brad.

"He was like this when I got here... It looks like he had a scotch and fell, hitting his head." She motioned towards the glass, both Damon and Austin looking at each other with concern. "Damon, could you grab my medical bag out of the truck, please?"

"Sure... I will be right back." Damon turned, heading to the door. Austin turned, giving Erina a knowing look, both of them thinking the same thing.

"I have test kits in my bag. We will soon find out." Austin nodded, getting up to grab some ice and a cloth to put on Brad's head.

*****

Amelia walked from her room to Brad's office. She had only a long jacket on, knowing he would have taken a drink before starting his documents. She had given him 45 minutes, knowing that Austin wouldn't be around.

Coming down the stairs, Amelia stops instantly when she saw Damon running in with what looked like a medical bag in his hand. "Shit, what are they doing here?" She followed him, staying in the shadows, for Damon not to see her.

"I got the bag. How is he?" She heard Damon ask just before the door closed.

Amelia paced up and down, knowing that they will figure out that Brad had been drugged and she would be the

116

number one suspect. "I have to do something." She mumbled to herself.

"Why couldn't they just stay away. I'm pretty sure Dr. Perfect is in there playing the hero. I should have made sure she couldn't get near him." She berated herself for not paying attention and for not doing something about Erina a long time ago.

*****

Damon closed the door behind him, handing Erina her bag. "Thanks, Damon. I am going to hook him to an IV. It will help flush the alcohol and whatever is in his system out." Erina pulled an IV bag and some needles out of her bag. "Take this and get a few drops of the scotch Brad always drinks." She handed a dropper to Damon, he nodded, walking over to the bottle of scotch.

Austin helped Erina hold Brad's arm steady to put the IV in. She made quick work of inserting the IV line into Brad's forearm. "I am going to do a test on him as well." Austin nodded as she moved to the other side to get a drop of blood.

Austin sat with Brad while Erina took two test kits from her bag, one for blood drug testing and one for liquid drug testing. "This will only tell us if he has been drugged. I will have to take a sample of his blood and the scotch to the lab to be able to know what drug was used." Damon rubbed his hand over his face, turning to look at Brad. Erina dropped the liquid in both tests waiting for the results. "How do we know if it's positive?" Damon questioned as he leaned over her shoulder to see the test.

"Two lines means it's positive. Do you have to hang over my shoulder?" She quirked her brow at Damon.

"No, I just want to see what you are doing." Damon surged before squeezing Erina's shoulder.

Erina turned to Austin, holding the test in her hands. Austin looked up, seeing the look in her eyes. "It's positive. Brad was definitely drugged." Erina placed the test back in her bag, each in their separate plastic bag. "I am going to take a blood sample from Brad to have it tested to see what type of drug was used." Erina moved closer to Brad as he began to moan. He swung his one arm not connected to the IV around. "Brad…. You need to calm down." Erina took his hand, trying to stop him from hurting himself.

"Er…. Erin….." Brad tried to talk. Erina cupped his cheek, trying to hold his head still.

"Shhh…. Brad, we are here to help you. Do you think you can stand?" Erina whispered as she felt him relax at her touch. Brad reached up, placing his hand over hers, his eyes fluttering open.

"Belle?" He exclaimed in half a question. Erina looked up at Damon and Austin. Both nod, silently telling her they can't tell him anything while he is in this state.

"Brad, let's get you up to your room, then we can talk about Belle." Brad nodded, still not able to focus. Austin and Damon help him to stand, taking him on each side. Erina took the IV bag walking behind them as they took Brad up to his room. Austin and Damon held on to Brad, as he still didn't have control over himself, his legs still being wobbly.

Walking into his room, Erina stopped at the door. She has never been in his room before and felt like she was invading his privacy. "I will wait for you here." She held out the IV bag for Damon to take it as he had the arm with the IV line draped over his shoulder.

"You need to come with him to make sure he is alright." Damon gave her a pointed look before turning back towards the other side of the room where Brad's bed was. Erina huffed, following Damon. She knew that she wasn't going to win.

Damon and Austin laid Brad down on the bed, making sure he was comfortable. Brad had mumbled a few words on his way to the bed, none of them understanding him.

"I am just going to check his vitals. If they are stable, then a good night's sleep should do the trick. He would be as good as new tomorrow." Erina walked to his side, taking a seat next to him on the bed. She wanted to take his blood pressure and listen to his heart and breathing. As soon as she took his arm to place the blood pressure machine's cuff on him, he laid his hand on her thigh again, mumbling something she couldn't understand. When she was done with his vitals and saw nothing that concerned her, she tried to get up off the bed, but Brad held on to her wrist, looking at her with pleading eyes.

"Stay...." He whispered, pulling her closer to him.

"I can't.... Brad, your wife...." Brad tried to place his finger on her lips to stop her from talking but completely missed her lips. She bit down on her bottom lip to try and stop her from laughing.

"Please.... Stay.... Even if it's just.... for a little bit." Brad tried to catch his breath in between words. Erina looked from Brad to Damon and Austin, hoping they would have an answer for her. She didn't want to cause any problems with them building a case against Amelia.

"We will be right outside to make sure no one comes in," Austin said, hoping that Erina would stay with Brad. He knew that Brad needed someone to comfort him in his time of need, and he knew that Brad felt safe with Erina. He saw it in his office a few times. Her touch was able to calm Brad even before she had said anything.

"Fine.... I will stay. But only until you fall asleep." Brad smiled at her with this flirty look in his eyes. "No funny business, you need to sleep off the drugs." He nodded, holding his arm out for her to lay down with him. She lays next to him as he wrapped his arm around her, feeling calm just from her touch. Damon and Austin left the room, closing the door behind them.

*****

Austin and Damon were sitting in the sitting room just outside of Brad's room, unsure how long they had been sitting there. Both of them felt tired from the last few days. They haven't had much sleep. Knowing Brad would need them, they

119

didn't plan to sleep tonight. Austin had two guards right outside of Brad's room, and they were instructed not to let anyone in, not even Mrs. Davis.

"Austin…. I know Erina wanted to talk to you about the twins." Damon voiced, not sure if he should say anything. They had agreed that Erina would speak to Austin, and then they would speak to Brad.

"The twins aren't Brad's right. That is what she wants to tell me." Austin took a sip of his coffee, watching as Damon sat back against the sofa.

"Yes… How did you…. Did she tell you?" Damon was with her the whole time. He never heard them talk about it.

"No, I had a feeling. I have been doing my own digging, and I came up with some meaningful information regarding the twins, Amelia, and also the death of my guard Brett." Austin sets his cup down on the table, taking a deep breath before letting it out. "Let's just say that Amelia won't be getting out of this one." Austin sat back, thinking of the time just after Nate's death.

Brad and Austin were heading to the nursery to check on Belle. Brad was broken after losing his son, but he knew that his daughter needed him more than ever now. Walking into the nursery, they heard Belle crying none stop. Brad had asked the nanny what was wrong, to which she answered that she wasn't sure. Belle didn't want to take her bottle, she didn't want to be held, and she didn't want to sleep. Brad remembered Erina telling him that the twins shared a bond and that Belle might morn her brother even though she was still too young to understand what was happening.

Brad walked over to her picking her up and holding her close to his chest, just like Erina showed him. "There… There daddy's here." He softly said, rocking her from side to side. Belle finally calmed down, Brad still holding her against his chest. "Austin, I want you to do whatever you have to, to find out what is going on when I am not around." Austin nodded, telling him he will be back in a little while. Brad walked over to the rocker sitting down with Belle on his chest. The nanny gave him a blanket to cover Belle with while she was with him.

After a while, Austin entered the nursery with two other guards. Each of them with a photo frame in their hands. "These needs to be up on the walls," Austin explained. Brad quirked his eyebrow at them.

He watched as Austin placed the photo frames around the nursery. "Austin, why are you placing photo's in the nursery?" Brad asked, not sure what his head guard was up to.

"Sir, I will explain everything in a bit." Austin finished what he was doing. "Now, if you are done, I would like to see you in the security office."

Brad nodded, handing a sleeping Belle over to the nanny. "If Mrs. Davis asked about the photos, tell her I wanted something to remember Nate by." She nodded before walking over to the crib to lay Belle down. She took one of Nate's teddies laying it beside Belle.

Brad followed Austin back to his office, watching as Austin typed on his tablet as they walk into the office. He put the tablet down on the desk just as Brad takes a seat.

"I had nanny cams installed in the picture frames. These are all pictures that were approved by Amelia." Austin smirked as Brad shook his head. He shouldn't have doubted Austin.

"Now, let me explain to you how they will work," Austin explained to Brad what they will be looking for, and as soon as they get any proof of any kind, they will let him know, and then they can take it further. Brad felt more relaxed that they now had a plan in place.

Austin was brought out of his memory when Brad's bedroom door flung open. Erina came out, looking down at her phone. "Bryan, what's up?" Damon asked, seeing the concern on her face as she scrolls through her phone.

"It's Belle…. I missed Christian's calls." She braced herself against the wall as she put her shoe on. Damon jumped up, walking to the door.

"I'll take you to the hospital." He opened the door waiting for Erina to come. She turned towards Austin.

"I will let you know what happens, don't wake Brad until I have news. He needs to sleep."

"Are you sure? What if he is needed?" Austin walked closer to her trying to convince her to wake Brad up.

"Austin, I have a feeling that not even Brad will be able to do anything till the morning." She gave him an apologetic look, letting him know that Brad would not be able to do anything for Belle.

"Drive safe. I will make sure Brad is safe." Both Damon and Erina nodded as they head out the door. Austin walked over to Brad's bedroom, checking on him to make sure he was still sleeping. He could see that Erina had removed the IV and that Brad was more peaceful than when they first got to him.

*****

Erina ran into the PICU with Damon on her heel. She could see Christian standing by the nurse's station. He turned, seeing Erina running towards him. She slowed her pace, almost causing Damon to run into her as she saw the look on Christian's face.

"I'm so sorry.... I don't know how I missed the call." She explained as Christian pulled her to the side, motioning for Damon to wait by the nurse's station.

"Erina.... we need to get Brad down here." He ran his hand through his hair. "I did everything I could, her organs started failing, there was nothing I could do." Erina shook her head, looking down at her shoes. "We need to let Brad know." Christian placed his hand on her shoulder. He could see she was feeling guilty for not being there.

"Brad.... Uh um..... Brad was drugged, I was able to get an IV into him. He is sleeping it off at the moment." Christian raised his eyebrow at her. "I should have been here...." She sank down to the floor, her face in her hands as she felt the tears flowing down her face.

"Don't blame yourself. You weren't on call." He kneeled down next to her. "You needed to sort your own things out." Erina doesn't answer him as her body still shook from silent sobs. Not only was she going to tell Brad that the twins were not his, but she's also going to inform him that Belle died while she was with him.

After a while, Erina finally got up, wiping her eyes as she turned towards Christian. "I need to let Austin know to bring Brad over." Erina walked out of the room she was in with Christian. Damon took in her appearance, walking over to her. She shook her head at Damon, reaching for her phone on the chair Damon was sitting on.

"Bryan, what is going on?" Damon asked, following Erina to the room before Christian stopped him.

"Belle died about half an hour ago. She's about to let Brad know." Damon stopped and stared at Christian as if he was talking a foreign language. "You can't tell anyone. We are supposed to let the family know first." Damon could only nod as he tried to swallow the lump that was in his throat. He had grown to love little Belle. She was his goddaughter, after all. Erina stood in the empty room, waiting for Austin to answer his phone.

"Dr. Bryan, do you have any news?" Austin asked, half out of breath.

"You need to have Mr. and Mrs. Davis come to the hospital urgently." Austin could hear the hurt behind her voice.

"I will let them know. We will be there as soon as we can."

"See you then." Erina ended the call, turning to walk back to where Damon and Christian were waiting for her. Damon walked up to her pulling her into a hug. He had an idea of what was going through her mind.

"It's not your fault. This is all due to Amelia and her psychotic way of killing her children." Damon whispered to

Erina, making sure no one heard him. Erina gazed up at Damon, seeing the glistering in his eyes.

"Thanks, Damon…." She buried her face in his chest, feeling safe and knowing that whatever happens, Damon and Conner would have her back. Then she remembered that the hospital was letting her go in two weeks, and right now, she felt like she deserved it. She couldn't even help Belle.

*****

After hanging up the phone with Erina, Austin went to wake Brad up. He explained to him that they needed to get to the hospital. Brad still felt a bit groggy from the night before. All he could remember was that he was in his office and had some scotch. He doesn't remember that Erina was there or that she stayed with him for a while.

After a shower and getting ready, Brad followed Austin to the front door, where Amelia waited. Conner walked in just as Brad made it up to Amelia, Brad telling him to follow him to the hospital. Amelia hooked her arm through Brad's as they walked out to the car. Brad helped her into the SUV, closing the door behind her before he walked around to the other side.

"Austin, I want to know what happened last night. Why can't I remember anything?" Brad said in a hushed tone, not wanting Amelia to catch on to anything.

Austin looked at his watch before turning back to Brad. "We will tell you when you get back from the hospital." Brad nodded, opening the door before getting into the SUV.

The drive over to the hospital was quiet. Amelia didn't dare say anything, not sure how much Brad remembered from the night before. Brad was staring out the window. He had a feeling about what was going on at the hospital. He swallowed the lump in his throat, running his hand down his face to try and make himself feel better.

Austin parked the SUV at the back entrance to the hospital, wanting to give Brad and Amelia privacy for as long as possible. Ever since Nate died, they had press following them everywhere, waiting for the next juicy story from them. Brad got out, not waiting for Austin to open his door. He wanted to get inside and get it over with.

Amelia walked next to Brad as they entered the hospital. Amelia had no idea where Belle was as she hasn't been at the hospital since Belle was admitted.

As Brad came closer to the door of the PICU, his pace slowed down. He thought he was ready, but it turned out he was not. He couldn't hear them say those words. Amelia stopped glaring at Brad.

"What are you doing?" She asked through gritted teeth. Brad held up his hand as he stopped just outside the door. "Let's just get this over with." Amelia huffed as she pushed the door open. Austin came up next to Brad, patting him on the shoulder.

"Sir, we are all here for you." Brad gave him a thankful nod before following Amelia into the PICU.

Christian met Amelia and Brad at the entrance showing them to the waiting area where Erina was waiting. Damon had gone to get them all some coffee while waiting for Brad and Amelia to arrive.

Amelia walked into the room, seeing Erina standing by the window. "Dr. Bryan, you needed to see us." She turned, grabbing onto Brad's arm. He stood there, taking Erina in as she turned around, looking at them.

"Mr. And Mrs. Davis." Erina stood up straight. She locked eyes with Brad. Seeing Erina's bloodshot eyes, he couldn't control his emotions. "Please take a seat." She motioned to the chairs. Brad moved to the chair, watching as Amelia sized Erina up.

"Amelia… SIT DOWN." Brad's voice was harsh as he spoke to her. She turned to look at him before flopping down next to him. She grabbed hold of his hand, but he pulled it out of her grasp. "Please go on…" Brad nodded for Erina to continue.

"Belle went into total organ failure last night. Christian did everything he could, but he was unable to revive her. I'm

125

sorry she passed away at 01:20 this morning." Erina tried to keep her own emotions at bay. This was not her time to grieve the loss of a patient. She needed to be there for the parents.

Amelia stood up, walking towards Erina, her eyes narrowing the closer she gets to Erina. "YOU.... You killed my children...." She pushed Erina back until her back hit the wall.

"Where were you, while another doctor fought for my daughter?" She grabbed the front of Erina's shirt, slamming her back against the wall.

"AMELIA..." Brad yelled as he shot up, running towards Erina and Amelia. He pulled Amelia off Erina before turning to make sure she is alright.

"Brad, how can you defend her. If she was here, she would have been able to do something." Amelia shouted, seeing Brad caring for Erina.

"Ma'am..." Erina took a step past Brad. "It was my night off. I was a call away, and I came as soon as I could." Erina looked down at her hands, the guilt taking over her again.

"Dr. Bryan, you do not need to explain why you weren't there." Brad felt his heart rate pick up as he realized with Amelia going off like that, he didn't have a chance to process the news that his daughter died.

"I want her gone. She killed both my children." Amelia rushed over to Brad, grabbing onto his shirt. Brad took her shoulders, pushing her away from him, before storming out of the room, Amelia following him.

Erina took a moment to compose herself before walking out of the room, being met by Conner and Damon, both with wide eyes as they watch Brad and Amelia walk down the hall.

"That was intense..." Damon motioned to the two disappearing down the hall. "Are you alright, Bryan?"

"Yes, I will be fine. She blames me for killing the twins." Damon and Conner turned towards Erina.

"Don't ever blame yourself. This was her doing. I don't know why, but she didn't want these children." Conner pulled Erina into a hug, trying to comfort her.

126

Erina told them what happened, how Amelia pushed her against the wall. How she said, she wanted her gone. She told them about Amelia asking her where she was the night before and why she wasn't with Belle.

While they were talking, Conner received a text from Brad asking them to come to his office. "We need to go to Brad's house," Conner held up his phone, showing them the text.

*****

Brad sat at his desk, holding a picture of the twins. He felt his heart sink, knowing that he had failed the two most important people in his life. They were so small, and all they asked for was for their father to love and protect them, and he couldn't even do that.

Brad sat back in his chair, his head falling against the back of the chair as he tried to hold back the tears. He had been crying more in the last few months than he had ever cried in his entire life.

"Uh...Um, Brad...." Brad opened his eyes, seeing Mike standing in front of him with Mia. Brad wiped his face, turning away from them to not have them see his pain.
"Brad.... What can we do for you?" Mia said in a soft voice. She knew what happened. Conner phoned her to meet them at Brad's office.

"No one can do anything.... She died." Brad's breath hitched as he tried to talk.
Mike looked between Mia and Brad, just as the others enter the office. "I'm so sorry, Brad.... I know how much you loved her. You must be devastated to know you raised a child that isn't yours....." Everyone grabbed Mike as the words left his mouth, trying to cover his mouth, hoping Brad didn't hear it.

Brad froze hearing Mike, but not sure if he heard it correctly. He slowly turned around, standing up. He leaned forward, resting his hands on his desk as he took in the group in front of him.

127

"What did you just say?" He narrowed his eyes at Mike.

Chapter 12

Mike took a step back from Brad feeling his eyes burning through him. "Uh…um…. You know what, I am just going to go." Mike turned to head to the door.

"Do not move. What did you say about me not being Belle's father." Brad's voice ran through his office, making Mike and Erina jump. Mike swallowed, trying to find a way to explain it to Brad when he felt Erina squeeze his hand, taking a step forward with Austin right next to her.

Brad walked around his desk, stopping in front of Erina. She could see something other than anger and grief in his eyes as she stared up at him, something she couldn't explain. "Brad…. Please don't blame Mike." Erina felt her heartbeat out of her chest, taking a few deep breaths before she continued. "I was going to tell you last night but you…." Brad held up his hand to stop her from talking.

"I don't want to know all the detail now." He gently took her by the shoulders, his eyes never leaving hers. "Just tell me…. Were the twins my children?" Brad studied her as he waited for her to answer him.

"No, they were not…." She shook her head, saying the words Brad was waiting to hear. "The twins were not your children." Brad dropped his hands from her shoulders, walking towards the door without a word. Brad flung the door open with so much force that it bounced off the wall chipping the paint off the wall.

Damon, Mia, Conner, and Austin all waited for him to breakdown, but he didn't. He just walked out the door, not even glancing at them.

"Shit…. He is going to kill her." Damon ran after Brad, Austin on his heel. Mia smirked, knowing Amelia was going to get what was coming to her.

129

"Should we go help them?" Erina asked as Mia took a seat on the sofa by the window and Conner leaning against the desk. "Guys...."

"Nope, I am not going to get my hands dirty trying to save that....."

"Uh um...." Conner interrupted Mia before she could say more. "What Mia means is, Brad and the guards can handle Amelia. I am seeing the board members about his divorce in ten minutes. And Mia will be staying right here." Conner pushed himself up from the desk, grabbing his bag.

"That's not what I meant. I would kill Amelia with a smile, but I think Brad will do it better." Mia smirked, picking at her nails. Mike stood in the corner, watching them all. He knew he shouldn't have said anything to Brad. He just hated seeing his friend this upset.

"I am going to see if they need anything, like medical assistance." Erina followed Conner out the door.

"Wait for me...." Mike shouted as he hurried to catch up with Erina. She stopped to wait for him.

"Ugggg..... Fine, I will also come. Just to make sure I am there should you need a dagger, then I can give you one." Mia followed them. Erina smiled as they walk towards the stairs. Since she started working at the hospital, she has made a few friends that meant the world to her. Mia was one of her very good friends. Even if she was always in the background, she was there when Erina needed her.

The trio walked up the stairs heading to Amelia's room. As they walked closer to the door, they could hear Brad's voice booming from her room.

*****

Amelia sat in her room, going over her part of the statement she and Brad had to give regarding Belle's death. They weren't going to add anything, just that the twins had health issues, the reason being why they died at such a young age. Brad never gave more information on why Nate died, and going with health problems was the best for everyone at this stage.

"I need a plan. Without an heir, Brad will surely leave me." Amelia tapped her pen against the pad on her lap, talking to herself. She needed to find a way to stay married to Brad. She knew that Brad was looking for an out for a long time now, ever since he met Erina.

Amelia knew that if she got the kids sick, Brad would spend more time with her and the kids, and she hoped that he would eventually fall in love or just tolerate her more. She had hoped that getting through the heartache of losing one child would bring them closer as a family. She never meant to kill Belle. She just wanted her to get sick and have Brad with her. But then Brad got Christian to stay near Belle, and she had to up the dose Belle was receiving to get her to really get sick. Unfortunately, she had overdosed Belle and caused her death.

Amelia stood up, walking over to the window. She needed a change of scenery. She walked over to the fireplace to put it on when her door suddenly burst open.

"Of all the things you could do...." Brad stormed into her room, glaring at Amelia. His hands were in tight fists next to his body, his breathing was ragged as his nostrils flared.

"Darling, what's wrong?" Amelia batted her eyelashes at Brad, willing a tear to form in her eye.

"Don't.... Don't you dare darling me!" He paced in front of her, swinging his arms around in anger. "You...." He pointed at her as she took a step back. "You are done...." Brad took a deep breath watching Amelia to see her reaction.

"What are you talking about?" She squared her shoulders, glaring back at him. "Austin, Brad needs to cool down. Remove him from my room." She spat out, seeing Austin take a step closer to Brad.

"Don't you dare give my guard any orders." Brad took a step forward. "You lied to me. Those babies aren't even mine." He lets out a breath feeling the anger rush through him. He stalked over to her grabbing her wrist forcefully.

"Brad, I didn't know…." She tried to pull her wrist out of his grip, but he tightened his grip. "Brad, you are hurting me." She pulled her arms to no avail.

"STOP LYING…." He shouted, his anger hitting her like a ton of bricks, as he pushed her backward before turning around, walking back to Austin and Damon.

"Don't you dare yell at me! You had an affair, and you blame me." She picked up a vase throwing it at Brad. Austin pulled Brad out of the way just in the nick of time.

"YOU KNEW THE TWINS WEREN'T MINE." He shouted back. "Erina has nothing to do with this." He turned away from Amelia to try and compose himself. Damon patted him on his shoulder, giving him a reassuring nod.

"You killed my children….. You and that whore of yours. If she paid half the amount of attention to my children as she paid you, they might still be alive." Amelia picked up a knife, Damon seeing it just as she threw it at Brad.

"Brad, watch out…." Damon pushed Brad out of the way just as the knife cut through his upper arm, and Brad falling to the floor. "Fuck…." Damon yelled, grabbing his arm, seeing the blood trickling through his fingers. "I'm going to kill that Bitch."

"Get in line…" Brad pushed himself off the floor, pushing up his dress shirt sleeves, the anger evident on his face as he took a step forward. Austin placed a hand on his chest to stop him, giving him a knowing look.

"Actually, ma'am, I have proof that it was you that drugged Belle and also proof that you drugged Mr. Davis last night. This means you are the reason Belle died, and I am one hundred percent sure you are the one that caused Nate's death as well." Austin said confidently, while Brad looked at him with wide eyes.

"She did what?" Brad's breath was becoming faster, knowing what could have happened or what had happened.

"She drugged you, sir. I think Dr. Bryan messed up her plans when she found you and tended to you." Austin looked over to Damon, making sure he is alright. "Dr. Bryan was with you when the call came through about Belle." Brad stared at Austin, taking in what he just said. He looked past Austin, meeting Erina's eyes just when she walked into the room with Mike and Mia.

Amelia narrowed her eyes at the trio that just entered her room. "I don't remember inviting any of you here." She waved her hands around. Erina walked over to Damon, kneeling next to him to stop the bleeding, not caring about Amelia having a fit about them in her room.

Brad turned around calmly, clasping his hands behind his back. "Austin, I want you to arrest Amelia for the murder of her own children and for the attempted murder of her husband," Brad smirked, seeing the color drain from Amelia's face.

"You can't do this. I am your wife." She picked up another vase, looking from Brad to Erina, knowing he would try to protect her. She flung the vase at Erina. Damon and Brad both reached to pull her out of the way. The vase shattered against the floor where she was sitting a second ago, a few shards cutting Erina's arms and legs.

"YOU ARE FUCKING DEAD…." Brad lunged at Amelia. Austin and Mike pulled him back. Mike struggled to hold on to Brad as he fights to get lose. "Let me go." He pulled his arm out as two more guards held him back.

Amelia walked away from them, grabbing a pillow putting the one corner in the fire, lighting it. "You will not take me…" She yelled, dropping the pillow on the carpet.

Austin rushed forward, trying to catch her, but the carpet caught fire, instantly covering the room in smoke. "Get Brad out of the room." He ordered the guards as they pulled Brad to the door.

"No…. We need to help Erina and Damon." Brad pulled away from the guards going over to Erina, helping her up, before going over to Damon, helping him up. Mia rushed to Erina's side, giving Brad a nod, silently telling him she's got her.

"Get out of the room now…." Austin shouted as the fire became more intense, setting the sofa and curtains on fire. Brad

133

helped Damon as they walked towards the door. Mia and Erina right behind them. Mike ran into the room with a fire extinguisher in his hand, a few guards following behind him.

Austin came out of the room, coughing from all of the smoke in the room. "Sir, we need to get you medical attention." Austin stood next to Brad, seeing him stare into Amelia's room.

"Where is she?" He asked, his jaw clenching. He had a feeling that this was her plan, distract them while she escapes.

"We are checking now. With the smoke, we weren't able to see anything." Austin turned around, walking back into the room, he had to find Amelia, and he had to find her soon.

*****

A few days had passed since Amelia set her room on fire, and there was still no sign of her or how she could have gotten out of the house. Conner had been seeing the board members for the past few days trying to get Brad out of his marriage even without Amelia being present. He had the last meeting today, and he hoped that he would give Brad some good news after the meeting.

Brad had been in his office, waiting for Austin to come and get him. He was making a statement to announce Amelia's involvement with the death of the twins. He had decided to keep the fact that they were not his out of the statement. Since Nate died, the press has been haunting him for some answers, and now was the perfect time to give them the answers and hopefully flush Amelia out of her hiding place. The past few days since Amelia disappeared, Erina, Conner, and Austin had informed Brad of everything Amelia had been doing. They told him about her involvement in the twins' deaths, Austin showing him the video evidence he had. Erina told him about the doctor that did the IVF that came forward after Erina did the DNA tests. Erina and Conner also told him about the guy that attacked her a few months ago, telling her to stay away from Brad. Conner said to him that they decided that she move in with someone until they could tell him.

With everything they told him, Brad felt as if his whole world came crashing down. He wasn't able to protect the people he loved, not his kids, and not Erina. His heart sank hearing that Erina was attacked and didn't tell him. He now understood why she lived with Damon. He had all these feelings and emotions going through him and not knowing how to express them. Brad hasn't spoken to any of them since the day they told him everything. He needed to work through all the information and his feelings. He felt terrible that he was shutting everyone out, Damon had tried to talk to him or have a drink with him a few times, but he was just not in the mood.

Brad lifted his head, hearing a knock at the door, he called for them to enter, thinking it was Austin, but Erina walked in.

"Mr. Davis." She looked down at her hands. Brad shook his head, wondering when they became this formal. He didn't like it.

"Please, none of that. It's Brad." He got up, walking around his desk towards Erina. He leaned down, kissing her cheek.

"Sorry for just showing up." She looked up at Brad, seeing the tiredness in his eyes. He was pale and had black circles under his eyes. He had clearly not slept much over the last few days.

"No.... I uh um...." He rubbed the back of his neck in nervousness. "I should have reached out. You are welcome anytime." Brad smiled, motioning for her to take a seat.

"Thanks. How have you been?" Erina took a seat on one of the sofas, Brad sitting next to her, looking out the window letting out a deep sigh before turning back to her.

"I'm doing better. I think once Amelia has been found, things will be better." He sat back, watching Erina out of the corner of his eye. "Can I tell you something?" Erina gave him a sincere smile before nodding for him to tell her. "Don't tell anyone, but sometimes at night, I wake up all sweating and breathing fast from a nightmare. I keep thinking Amelia is going

135

to do something to me while I'm asleep." Brad looked down at his hands, not meeting Erina's eyes.

"Brad, that is normal. You have been through so much. You lost your children, and you found out your wife was behind everything." Erina patted his leg. He took her hand, giving it a soft squeeze.

"I'm sure you are not here to talk about my soon to be ex-wife." She shook her head back and forth.

"No…. the night you were drugged, I was on my way to come speak to you about my position at the hospital." She took out her documents handing them to Brad. "Amelia declined it, and I have about a week then I am done working for the hospital and would have to look at moving to another one."

Brad looks through the documents, rubbing his hand over his mouth, feeling the guilt of having Amelia go after Erina like that. If Brad had been more assertive and not shown his feeling towards Erina in front of Amelia, Erina would have been safe.

"Erina, this is no problem. I will approve your permanent employment. You can stay." Erina jumped forward, wrapping her arms around his neck, hugging him tightly, his hands going around her waist. Erina sat back, looking at Brad sheepishly.

"I'm sorry… I was just so excited." She looked away from Brad, feeling the blush creeping on her face.

Brad cupped her cheeks, turning her to look at him. "Don't be sorry." He brushed his thumb across her cheek, moving closer to her.

Brad's office door swung open, causing Brad and Erina to jump apart. Conner rushed in with a massive smile on his face.

"Brad, it's done…."

Chapter 13

"Brad, it's done...." Conner stopped feeling like he interrupted something. "Um... Sorry, should I come back?"

"No, please come in," Brad smirked, knowing Conner was feeling bad for just running into the office, but he had a good reason for that. "I believe you have some news for me." Conner walked into the office, taking a seat across from Erina and Brad.

Conner took out a document from his briefcase, handing it over to Brad. "You are a free man. The board members approved your divorce, even without Amelia. They say there is enough proof against Amelia. They feel that you are better suited to run the business without her. They also feel that she might have a mental disorder." Brad smiled, going through the document. "All you need to do is sign on the dotted line."

Brad jumped up, walking over to his desk, Conner and Erina sharing a look. They know how long Brad had been waiting for this. Brad grabbed his pen, leaning down to sign the documents. "Is that it?" Brad looked up when he was done.

"That's it.... You are officially unmarried." Conner walked over to Brad, clapping him on the shoulder, Erina following Conner. As soon as she was close to Brad, he pulled her into a hug. The hug feeling different than the ones before. This one was full of hope.

Conner explained to Brad and Erina what had happened in the last few days. How the board members went through everything, from the hospital reports to the attack on Erina. He told them that the board members had brought in an independent doctor from Chicago that also went over the hospital reports and information.

"Erina, you were right about Nate. He died due to shaken baby syndrome." Erina dropped her head feeling the tears form in her eyes, hearing that they finally had answers to Nate's death.

"The worse part is if you were able to admit Nate that first time Brad brought him in then, he could have been saved." Erina didn't lift her head, just shaking it. Brad took her hand, pulling her into his side. "Letting Amelia sign the against medical advise form helped our case even more." Conner could see how much this was bothering Brad and Erina. Erina felt like she should have fought harder to save Nate and Brad felt like he didn't protect his son.

Erina finally looked up, meeting Conner's gaze. "Thank... You...." Her breath hitched as she tried to calm herself. Brad handed her a box of tissues. As she took it, she gave him a grateful smile.

A knock at the door had them all turn to look at the door. Austin came in, telling them it's time for Brad to make the statement. Brad nodded, getting up walking over to his en-suite bathroom to ensure that he was presentable. Pulling his jacket on, Brad brushed his hands over his jacket and shirt. Before he walked out, following Austin.

Conner and Erina followed him, telling him they will see him outside. They met up with Mia and Damon standing next to the platform Brad was going to be standing on. Erina stood between Damon and Conner, all of them here to support Brad. Brad walked up to the press. He held up his hand to get the crowd to be quiet.

"Good afternoon. Thank you all for coming out today." Brad took a deep breath, knowing this is going to be hard for everyone to hear. "It pains me to give you the following news. Recently it was discovered that Mrs. Amelia Davis was behind the fatal injuries that both the twins had sustained. Due to this, my marriage to Amelia has been annulled." There were a few gasps and a few cheers from the crowd. Brad held his hand up again. "Unfortunately, Amelia escaped before she could be arrested. We are doing everything to find her. I ask that if anyone has any information about the wear bouts of Amelia, to let Austin or the police know." Brad looked down at the podium in front of him before looking over the crowd. "I want to thank you all for the good wishes during this difficult time. Unfortunately, this is all I have time for today. As soon as we have more, we will inform you. Thank you," Brad waved to the crowd as questions were being shouted at him. He didn't want to answer any question, not yet anyway.

Austin walked Brad back inside, where he was met by Conner, Damon Erina, and Mia. They all walked towards Brad's office, needing a drink after that press release.

"You told the truth, Brad, and with everyone knowing, we will be able to find Amelia sooner," Conner said as they all took a seat. Damon poured them each a drink, handing everyone's glass to them before taking his own seat.

Brad quirked his brow at them with this wicked smile on his face. "She better hope that I don't get to her first. I will not let her slip away again." Mia smirked at the tone Brad's voice had taken.

They all talked and laughed, letting the stress of the last few months wash away. Brad had apologized to Mia for how he acted. He explained to her that this was due to trying to protect her and Davis International's reputation. Brad, for this first time, told everyone what Amelia had done to him.

How she had told him she would turn his company against him, tell them that he was abusing her both physically and sexually. He told them how she told him to stay away from Conner and Damon that she would destroy all of them. This now made sense why Brad spent all his time with Amelia the last few months before the twins were born.

"Shit man, why didn't you tell us?" Damon slapped Brad on the back. He felt hurt that Brad didn't trust them all those months ago with this.

"I didn't want you and Conner to get hurt. Amelia knew you were hanging out with Erina, and she didn't want me near Erina." Brad looked at each of his friends, his heart swelling knowing no matter what, he would always have them by his side.

"We get it, but next time tell us from the start. We can help you." Mia said. All of them nod at Mia's words.

"Guys, there won't be a next time. I am a free man. I have done the whole arranged marriage thing. Now, if I ever do get married again, it will be for love, and my wife will be my equal." Brad beamed, meeting Erina's gaze. She blushed at the way Brad was looking at her. He knew that he needed to heal from his marriage to Amelia. He needed time to find himself. He only hoped that Erina would still be there when he was ready to move on. He didn't love Amelia, and he was more than happy with being rid of her, but she broke him emotionally. And he needed to heal from that. He needed to be able to trust again. He needed to be the person he was before he got married to Amelia.

*****

It had been eight months since Brad got a divorce, and they last saw Amelia. They didn't have any lead on where she was. It was as if she disappeared into thin air. Austin had guards watch her mother and father and their estates, and to date, there was no sign of her.

Brad had been feeling more relaxed about what happened. He had spoken to the doctor that was the twin's father. The doctor told him how sorry he was and wanted to come forward more than once, but Amelia had threatened him and his family if he ever came forward and told anyone. Brad took away his medical license. He felt that he did learn his lesson, but Brad didn't want anyone else to go through what he went through.

Brad had been thriving with the company. He showed them that he could run his company without having a wife, not that he wanted to be without someone to love his whole life. Now that he knew what love felt like, he knew that he wanted someone to love. For the first time since Amelia, Brad felt like he was ready to let someone in. Many businessmen wanted him to take their daughters on dates, but he just declined, not wanting to be set up again.

*****

Erina had finally moved back to her own place with the help of Brad, Damon, and Conner. She had gotten a new house near the beach after she received her permanent position at the hospital. She worked most of the time, but she loved to spend time on the beach or with her friends on her off days.

The last few months, Brad had been spending time with her, Damon, and Conner. They were never alone together, and she understood that he needed time to heal, time to get over the betrayal and the deception that Amelia had caused. Time to recover mentally and emotionally.

Brad would come to Damon's house and just spend time with her and Damon. They would just have dinner or watch a movie. Everything was casual, but Erina was feeling this pull towards Brad like she had felt when they first met. She knew she couldn't act on it, not with what Brad had gone through, and to tell the truth, she wasn't sure how long she would be able to wait for him.

*****

Brad walked from his room to the waiting SUV at the front of his house when he saw Damon heading his way. Damon was dressed in shorts and a plain blue T-shirt. Brad raised his brow, seeing Damon smirking.

"Brad, it's Friday. Why are you dressed like you are going on a date?" Brad was dressed in a black dress shirt and black suit pants. Damon knew that Brad wasn't meeting Erina as he was on his way to her. They were going to have a bonfire with Conner.

"Because I need to meet with an Australian ambassador. I wish I could rather be hanging out with you and Erina tonight." Brad ran his hand through his hair. When Erina invited him over early that week, all he wanted to do was go to her, but he had been swamped this week and had no free time. Now tonight again, he would not be able to join her and the guys for the bonfire, as he needed to meet with this Australian ambassador.

"I get it, duty calls." Damon looked at the front door before turning back to Brad. "Brad… I know you care about Erina, but are you ever going to ask her out on a date? You know she's a beautiful single doctor, who isn't going to wait around forever." Brad snapped his head over to Damon. He knew precisely that what Damon was saying is true. He just didn't want to hear it.

"I wanted to, more than once, but every time I think now is the time, something happens, and I don't get to see her." Brad lets out a heavy sigh stopping at the SUV looking back up at Damon. "I had planned on asking her to dinner tomorrow, but look at what I have to do now."

"You need time off. I tell you what, go to this meeting and in an hour I will call you, and then you come to join us." Damon smirked, feeling proud of the plan he just came up with.

"Let's see what happens. Call me in an hour, and I will let you know what's going on." Damon nodded before letting Brad get into the SUV. Watching him disappear from view, Damon turned around to go to his truck. He felt sorry for Brad. He hasn't had an off day in a few weeks.

*****

Brad sat at the table in a restaurant waiting for the ambassador to arrive, his mind going to Erina the whole time. He wanted to be there with them right now and not at this restaurant. Hearing the door open, he saw a middle-aged man and a well dressed young woman enter the restaurant. He had hoped that they weren't his meeting. He has spoken to the ambassador a few times before, but he has never met him, and there weren't any updated photos of him available.

The man locked eyes with Brad giving him a bright smile before heading towards him. Brad stood up, waiting for them to get to him.

"Mr. Davis" The man held out his hand for Brad to shake, and the lady gave him a flirty smile. "I'm Mr. Hamilton, and this is my daughter Gwen." He motioned to the lady next to him.

"It's nice to meet you both." Brad took his hand, shaking it before nodding towards Gwen.

They took their seats at the table, the waiter bringing out the drinks and appetizers that Brad arranged when he got there. Brad and Mr. Hamilton got right to the point, talking about what Mr. Hamilton and Davis International could do for each other. There was a trade deal that Brad wanted to have approved with Australia, but Mr. Hamilton wasn't convinced that it was the right deal for Australia.

Going back and forth over dinner, Brad decided that they would not come to a compromise. "Mr. Hamilton, why don't you come to my office on Monday and we could meet with some of the board members? Maybe we can find something that would work for both of us." Brad asked as he subtly glanced at his watch, wondering why Damon hasn't phoned him yet. It had been about two hours, and Damon was going to call after an hour.

"That is a marvelous idea, Mr. Davis." Mr. Hamilton said before looking over at his daughter. "I was wondering if you would mind showing my daughter around tonight. I am not into staying up late, and I know that she would want to go out." She gave Brad yet another flirtatious smile while her father waited for his answer.

"Uh…um, I am actually heading to friends of mine. We normally have a bonfire every Friday night. I do apologize for not being available." Brad took a sip of his scotch, meeting Austin's gaze across the room, silently telling him he wants out of this dinner.

Gwen leaned over, whispering into her father's ear before they both looked back at Brad. "Gwen would like to join you. She loves a good bonfire." Brad swallowed hard, knowing that he could not say no. He didn't want to lose this deal. But to be honest, he didn't want her to come with him, he wanted to see Erina.

"Sure, I'm sure my friends wouldn't mind." Gwen smiled excitedly at Brad. After the dessert, they all got up to leave. Mr. Hamilton saying good night to Brad before turning towards his daughter, telling her to enjoy herself. Gwen walked with Brad towards his waiting SUV.

*****

Erina stood on her porch, looking at her back yard. She was close to the beach; basically, there was a thick tree line between her and the beach. Erina wanted a walkway for her to get to the beach more comfortably. At the moment, she had to either walk through the tree line or around the tree line.

Damon had offered to build her a walkway down to the beach, all she needed to do was get some material, and he would do it for her. And right now, she was staring at all the wood and planks he had asked for.

"What happened?" Erina jumped, hearing Conner's voice right behind her. He chuckled, seeing her face as she turned around. "Sorry, didn't mean to scare you. Brad and Damon not here yet?" He asked as he put the drinks on the table.

"Only Damon is coming. Brad has a meeting." Erina turned her head back to the treeline, but not before Conner saw the sadness in her eyes. "As for all of that. It's for Damon. He is going to build a walkway down to the beach." She smiled as Conner came to stand next to her.

"I think we should start when he gets here. We can all help get you to the beach a little easier." Erina swatted Conner's arm, acting as if he hurt her feelings. Conner pulled Erina into a one-arm hug as they both laughed.

"This looks fun." Damon walked up to them, seeing them laugh. Erina greeted him, telling them she would take the drinks in and they could get started. "Ah, so that's why I was invited." Damon chuckled, walking to the treeline with Conner. They both stood there, checking all the wood and planks, Erina walking into her house to put the drinks in the freezer.

"What's Brad doing tonight?" Conner raised his brow at Damon. As they both bend down to take the first wooden beam.

"He had a meeting, but he was bumped that he couldn't be here." Conner shook his head in understanding. He knew that if Brad had a choice, he would have been there with them.

"Erina was also a bit upset that he couldn't be here." Conner helped Damon place the first wooden beam while they talk. Walking back to get the other side's wooden beams, they saw Erina walking up to them with a drink for each of them.

"Right boys, let's do this." Erina handed them the drinks as they cling them together. They started working on the first part of the walkway, talking and laughing as they went along. The sun began to set over the ocean once they got to the beach. The frame for the walkway was done. Damon added a few bolts and nuts to keep them together while Erina headed back up to get the snacks together.

"Shit...." Damon dropped his hammer, making Conner jump, giving Damon a confused look. "I forgot to phone Brad. I was going to be his out a bit more than an hour ago." Damon ran his hand down his face taking his phone out of his pocket, only to find out that it had died.   "Perfect, Brad is going to kill me." Conner laughed, taking out his phone, trying to phone Brad.

"His phone is just ringing...." Both Damon and Conner looked back at the tree line when they heard a noise.

"Did you hear that...." Damon felt his heart thundering in his chest, his first thought being that Amelia has not been found and Erina was alone.

"Gah...." Conner and Damon heard Erina's voice loud and clear. Both men running up towards the house.

Chapter 14

Erina headed up towards the house after helping Conner and Damon. She wanted to get the snacks ready and get the ingredients for the smors that Damon had promised her. Erina walked into the house, putting a cheese platter together. Taking the platter and a few beers to put them down on the table. She stood by the table with her back to the side of the house when she heard a noise.

"Hello...." She called out loud enough, hoping the guys would hear her. She waited but heard nothing. She took a step closer to the side of the house, knowing full well she shouldn't. Since the whole Amelia situation, she decided that she would not let anyone ever get to her again. Thanks to Austin and Damon, she had learned a few moves to defend herself and do some harm to the other person.

Erina heard the front gate slam shut, causing her to jump. She crept closer to the side to be able to see who came around the corner. As soon as she looked around the corner, she saw two figures walking towards the house. She stood with her back against the wall taking a few deep breaths. She could hear them get closer to her, she waited till they were by her when she turned to see who it was.

"GAH....." She yelled, tumbling backward. She felt a pair of strong hands grab hold of her waist to keep her from falling.

"Are you alright?" She looked up, seeing Brad's blue eyes staring back at her. He helped her back to her feet, never taking his hands from her waist.

"I'm fine.... I thought you wouldn't be able to make it." She smiled. Her hands still on his shoulders. Brad stood there, staring into her eyes as if he never wanted to see anything else. It felt like they were the only two people in the room.

Gwen stepped forward, "Uh...um." She cleared her throat. Erina looked over Brad's shoulder, seeing a beautiful redhead standing behind him. She swallowed as she dropped her hands from his shoulders, taking his hands from her waist, subtly nodding to the lady behind him. Brad's eyes grew wide, knowing that he forgot Gwen was with him.

"I apologize. Where are my manners." He stood next to Erina. "Erina, this is Gwen, the Australian ambassador's daughter. Gwen, this is Erina." He motioned between the two women. They all turn around, hearing Damon and Conner call out for Erina.

"They might think something was wrong." Erina turned to walk closer to the tree line. "Guys, I'm fine. It's just Brad and his date." Brad snapped his head towards Erina as he hears her call Gwen his date. Damon stopped in his tracks taking everyone in. Brad stood next to Erina, and just behind them was a tall redhead.

"You came." Conner walked up to Brad shaking his hand. Brad raised his brow at Damon, who just shook his head. Damon was annoyed that Brad showed up with some woman no one knew.

"Guys, this is Gwen, the Australian ambassador's daughter, Gwen these are my friends Damon and Conner." Brad motioned between them all. Everyone stood there with an uncomfortable silence between them.

Erina watched everyone just standing there and not moving. She knew she had to do something, even though all she wanted was to send everyone home and cry herself to sleep. "I have snacks and drinks. Let me just grab some for Brad and Gwen." Erina turned, walking towards the door.

"I'll help you..." Conner walked up to her. He could see the hurt in her eyes even though she was trying to play it off as nothing.

Damon went to stand next to Brad as Gwen stood off the side, picking at her nails. "What the hell are you doing?" Damon whispered just for Brad to hear. Brad shot him a look knowing how this might look.

"Why didn't you call me?" Brad glared at Damon. "As for her, I had no choice. Her father basically told me to take her with me." Damon nodded in understanding before he gave Brad an apologetic look.

"Sorry man, I was busy with this walkway and didn't notice the time, and when I finally wanted to phone you, my phone's battery died." Damon rubbed the back of his head, feeling guilty. "You want to see what we did for Bryan?" Brad nodded before he turned towards Gwen.

"Damon just wants to show me what he has done. I will be right back." Before she could say anything, Brad and Damon walked through the first set of the tree line. Damon explaining how Erina wanted it and what they have done.

Gwen stood there dumbfounded with Brad that just left her there with no one she knew or could talk to. She turned, seeing Erina walk out of the house with more drinks. She remembered Erina calling her Brad's date, smirking; she walks towards Erina.

Erina placed the drinks down on the table closest to the pit where Damon would make the fire. Erina smiled as Gwen comes to a stand next to her. "You are more than welcome to anything." Erina motioned to the snacks and drinks on the table.

"We already had dinner. Brad and I..." Gwen gave Erina a knowing look. Erina nodded before taking a sip of her beer. She felt her heart drop to her feet as she swallowed the sip she just took. She has waited for Brad to be free like he had asked, then she waited for him to find himself like he asked, and now he was going on dates with foreign dignitaries. Does he just want her to wait forever?

"We have dessert. Damon will be making his famous smors. It is to die for." She said without looking at Gwen.

Conner walked up to Erina placing his hand comfortingly on her shoulder, giving it a gentle squeeze.

"I don't eat sweets. I hope that if Brad is done with his friend, that we can go." Gwen blew on her nails, tapping her one foot against the floor.

Conner and Erina shared a look, knowing this girl is in for a feast. Brad was there to eat smors and drink beer. They heard Brad and Damon laughing even before they came into view.

Damon walked up to the fire pit to start the fire for the smors. Gwen patted the open seat next to her with a flirtatious smile, hoping Brad would take the seat. Brad ignored, taking a seat next to Erina.

"I told Damon I will help him to finish the walkway tomorrow." Brad leaned in to whisper to Erina.

"That would be great. If you have the time." She smiled subtly, nodding her head in Gwen's direction. Brad knew what Erina meant, he didn't understand why she thought Gwen and he was on a date, and he needed to fix it. He needed her to know that he wanted to be with her, and no one else.

"I have decided to take back my life, and that means making time for you and my friends." Brad could see the sparkle in Erina's eyes at his words.

Gwen got up, heading towards Brad as he stared into Erina's eyes. "Brad… Could you please walk with me?" Brad turned his head to look at Gwen, but Conner stood next to Gwen before he could say anything.

"I would love to show you around." Conner held out his arm towards Gwen. She took it as they walked away. He gave Brad and Erina a wink, making both of them blush.

Damon stood at the edge of the porch, Erina and Brad behind him. He wanted to give them a chance to talk, Brad needed to express to Erina how he felt, and he needed to do it now.

Brad and Erina sat there talking about their week, Brad telling her everything he had to do, from the board meetings to the trade agreement that still hasn't been agreed on. Erina told him about the hospital and the new interns that just started there. Brad smiled, watching her talk about her passion. Even though interns could be a hand full, she spoke of them as if they were her friends, and she was already proud of how well the interns were doing. He could see how proud she was of them.

"I have to go get some more drinks." Erina got up when she heard Gwen and Conner returning. She loved the time she could spend with Brad just now, but with Gwen back, Brad would have to spend his time with her. She was his date, after all.

Brad watched as Erina headed into the house. Damon gave him a look telling him to go after her. "I will be back. Keep Gwen here, or not." Brad smirked. Damon knew what he meant by that. Brad got up, following Erina into the house.

Brad walked in, seeing Erina stand by the fridge. She had her arms stretched out with her forehead against the refrigerator. She was mumbling something that he couldn't hear, but he hated seeing her like this. Ever since Brad met her, all he wanted was to be with her. If he wasn't trapped in that marriage with Amelia, he would have been with her by now. He didn't know why it took him another 8 months to see it.

He walked closer to her placing his hands on her waist. He could feel her body tense. "Erina, can we talk?" Brad whispered as he leaned against her. All Erina could do was nod. She was able to feel Bard against her, his hands on her waits. Brad's chest against her back. Brad turned her around to be able to look into her eyes. He wanted to see how she felt, what she thought.

Erina could feel the heat radiating from Brad, and she wanted more of it. She was trying to fight the urge to kiss him, knowing he was here with his date. He leaned down, stopping when their lips were only inches apart. She could feel his hot breath against her lips. "Brad…. what….." Before she could finish her sentence, Brad's lips crashed onto hers, his tongue swiping over her bottom lip, asking for entrance. She parted her lips for his tongue to find hers. The kiss started out soft, becoming heated very fast. Brad walked her backward until her back hit the fridge. His arms wrapped around her waist as hers were wrapped around his neck.

Reluctantly they pulled apart breathless. Brad resting his forehead against hers. "Gwen is not my date. Her dad had a meeting with me, and she came with me. She basically invited herself to join me." Brad kept his gaze on Erina, his arms still around her waist. Her fingers were playing with the hairs at the back of his neck. "I came here because I wanted to see you at...." He lets go of her for a few seconds only to hook a stray strand of hair behind her ear. "I want to be with you. I think we have wasted enough time" He smiled, leaning down, giving her a lingering kiss.

"What are you saying?" She had this hopeful look in her eyes. She cared about Brad and knew that he felt something for her. She just wasn't sure how much he cared for her.

"I want to take you on a real date. I want to be seen with you out in the open. I want to spend the night with you here at your house or at my house. I want you on my arm when I have a function or a dinner meeting to attend. I want everyone to know that the CEO of Davis Intentional is taken." Brad chattered, causing Erina to chuckle.

"Take a breath, Brad." She cupped his cheek in her hand before she leaned forward, kissing him again. "I want that too." Brad picked her up, twirling her around as she lets out a hearty laugh.

Gwen sat outside by the fire, looking at her watch before seeing Damon and Conner deep in conversation. She got up, turning to walk towards the house. "Gwen.... I wouldn't if I were you...." Damon stated as he saw her walking to the door. She just waved him off and kept on walking.

Gwen walked into the kitchen, seeing Brad locked in a heated kiss with Erina. His hand was under her shirt, while hers were in his hair. Brad had Erina pinned against the kitchen wall away from all the windows, but Gwen could see them from the door. Gwen could see how Erina arched into Brad, her head falling back as he trailed kisses down her neck, his hand moving up her shirt even more.

"Oh…. Brad…." Erina moaned as Brad found that spot just behind her ear before capturing her lips again. Gwen could feel the anger and disappointment coursing through her. She turned on her heel, stomping back to where Conner and Damon were standing.

"Who does he think he is." She spat out, Damon and Conner's eyes going wide, wondering what she was talking about.

Conner pushed Damon forward, silently having a debate about who was going to talk to her. Damon shook his head at Conner, pointing for him to speak to her. Conner gave Damon a sly smile before pushing him all the way to Gwen. She looked up at Damon, glaring at him.

"What happened?" Damon asked with what he hoped was a sincere smile. Gwen eyed him before answering.

"I am here because my father wants me to be with Brad. He had heard that Brad is single and not seeing someone, but it all makes sense now. The way Brad kept sitting next to her, how he kept looking at her. Brad is in love with Erina." She paced in front of Damon, rambling.

"I'm sorry…." Gwen held her hand up, stopping Damon from talking.

"Don't…. Just take me back to the hotel." Gwen walked towards the gate, Damon following her. He was about to let her know that Erina and Brad have a history and that Brad would have told her if she asked Brad.

"Good luck. I will tell Brad that you took her back. I don't think he will be going back to his place tonight." Damon clapped Conner on the back knowingly as he walked after Gwen.

Conner walked towards the kitchen, clearing his throat before he walked in, but Brad and Erina were no longer in the kitchen. He wrote a note for them and left it on the fridge before closing the door, locking it with his spare key. He knew that Brad and Erina needed time together, and they were all happy to let them have it.

*****

It has been a few months since Brad and Erina decided to express that they wanted to be together and give it a try. They were always together. Everyone could see how close they were getting.

Erina was still working at the hospital, even though everyone knew that she was Brad's girlfriend. It didn't bother her one bit for everyone to know. She wanted nothing more than to spend her days with Brad.

Brad had assigned two guards for Erina. With everyone knowing they were together, he wanted her to be safe. They still had no leads on where Amelia could be. It was as if she had vanished into thin air. It had been nearly a year since the whole ordeal with Amelia, and Brad still didn't want to let loose and just forget that she is still out there.

Brad and Erina had gone to a few social events in the past few months, and most of the people she met found her intriguing and could understand why Brad was fascinated with her. Hearing that she was the chief of pediatrics made them respect her even more.

Mia, Damon, Conner, and Austin could see the old Brad returning more and more each day. This was the Brad they grew up with, the one that had hopes and dreams. The one that wanted the best for Davis International and for the monarch. This was the Brad that believed in love, and they could see the love Brad and Erina had for each other.

*****

Brad sat in his office listening to Neville go on about his proposal for another golf estate in some small town. Brad wasn't

153

interested. He felt the money could be better spent on something someone needed. Neville always came to Brad with some kind of proposal that would only benefit Neville.

"You can see on page three just how much economic the new course will bring in. That would be beneficial to the town." Neville pointed to the graph on page three as Brad only nodded. He was relieved when there was a knock at his door. He called for them to enter, giving Neville an apologetic look.

Austin walked in with a smirk on his face. "Sir, it's time." Austin gave him a knowing look as Brad stood up from his chair, grabbing his jacket, putting it on.

"I'm sorry to cut this short, I have another appointment. We can retake this next week. Please make an appointment with my assistant." Brad walked out without giving Neville any time to respond. He wanted to get to where he was needed as soon as he could.

"Are you ready?" Damon asked, joining them as they walked towards the waiting SUV.

"Yes…. Do you have everything you need?" Brad inquired as they slid into the backseat. Austin getting into the driver seat, looking in the rearview mirror. He couldn't help but smile at the excitement in Brad's eyes.

"Everything is taken care of." Damon shoved Brad's arm. "Do you have it?" Brad nods as he pats his hand on his breast pocket.

*****

Erina stood at the nurse's station in the pediatric ward talking to Christian and going over some of the charts. It was her weekend off, and she was going to Chicago with Brad. She couldn't wait for it, as she loved the snow.

"Dr. Bryan…." A little boy pulled on her white coat. As she turned around, she saw the white rose he was holding in his hand.

"What can I do for you?" She asked, smiling warmly at her patient. He held out the rose for her. "Is this for me?" He only nodded before running back to his room. Erina smiled, looking at the rose as the little boy disappeared into his room.

A few more kids came to give her a rose for an hour. They would either have a white or red rose to give her. Christian chuckled, knowing exactly what was happening.

Erina stood with her back against the wall outside the NICU, going over a chart when a young lady tapped her shoulder. She looked up, seeing the little one in her arms. She was no more than 1 year old. Erina couldn't help but think of the twins. They would have been about the same age as this little girl.

"Is everything alright?" Erina asked, putting down the chart she was working on, moving closer to the lady.

"Yes, we were asked to give you this." She handed the baby the rose with a letter on. "Give this to the doctor." She took the baby's hand, holding it out to Erina.

Erina took the rose, leaning over kissing the top of the little girl's head. "Thank you so much. I wonder who has been so sweet to give me all these roses." She pointed to the table with all the other roses. The lady smiled before turning to head back to the room where her baby's bed was.

Erina took the note from the rose before putting it in the vase with all the others. She opened the note to read it.
Please meet me in the attending's lounge.
Love Brad.
Erina smiled as she read the letter repeatedly. Before she walked over to the nurse on duty, telling her she would be right back, the nurse nodded, watching as she walked out of the ward. The nurse took out her phone, sending a quick text letting them know Erina was on her way.

Walking down the hall towards the attending's lounge, Erina couldn't help but notice the giggles and stares she got from the other doctors and nurses. She stopped in front of the door, taking a deep breath, but before she could enter, Conner stopped her taking her doctor's coat from her, motioning for her to go ahead.

Erina entered the room, seeing it filled with red and white roses, and right in the center was Brad down on one knee. Her hands flew to her mouth as she realized what was happening.

"Hello, love...." Brad smiled as she walked closer to him. He took her hands into his. "I have waited for so long to do this." He rubbed soothing circles on her knuckles with his thumbs.   "You have been my rock and my guiding light through so much. You have seen me on my worse days, and you have seen me on my best days. I love you so much it hurts." Erina lets out a giggle as the tears rolled down her cheeks. "Erina Bryan, will you please do me the honor of becoming my wife, my other half?" Erina gasped as Brad opened the red velvet box in his hands, revealing a beautiful princess cut diamond ring. "Will you marry me?"

"Yes... Brad, thousand times, yes!" Brad got up, pulling Erina into a passionate kiss, holding her close to him. Breaking apart, he slipped the ring onto her finger. "It's beautiful." She kissed him again just when everyone else walked in, clapping their hands for the happy couple.

Conner and Damon hugged Erina before congratulating Brad as well. They all had some cake and ciders. Erina couldn't help but admire the ring on her finger. Brad never once left her side. He wanted this to be perfect and knew that she had limited time with the patients and the interns needing her attention.

"Brad, this was amazing." Erina turned, wrapping her arms around his neck, his going around her waist. "I love you!" She gave him a sweet kiss.

"I love you too.... Now, are you ready for the snow?" Erina nodded, turning away from Brad as they both say goodbye to everyone. Brad took her hand after saying goodbye, Damon and Conner following them.

As they walked out, a man watched them leave. He took out his phone, dialing a number. "He's getting married to her."

Chapter 15

Erina looked at herself in the floor-length mirror, brushing her hands down the front of her dress. It had been six months since Brad asked her to get married, and here she was in her wedding dress waiting to get married to the love of her life. When she met Brad, she never thought that this would ever happen with Brad being married to Amelia. To say that today was a dream come true was an understatement.

After Brad asked her to marry him, they went to Chicago for a weekend away from everything. Brad took her to a cabin just outside of Chicago. They were surrounded by trees and snow. They enjoyed the time getting lost in each other and just relaxing without any distractions.

Over dinner one night, Brad told her what he wanted their wedding to be like. He had already had a big wedding, and Brad wanted an intimate ceremony with just his bride and close friends. Erina was more than happy with a small wedding. She wasn't one for extravagant things. She wanted it to be on the cliffs overlooking the ocean.

And now, six months later, it was finally time for her dream wedding. Standing in the room with Mia as her bride's maid. They were waiting for Damon to come and tell them it's time.

"Are you nervous?" Mia asked as she helped Erina put her veil on.

"No, I just want to see him. We have waited so long for this." Erina walked over to take her bouquet of roses from the table, smiling back at Mia.

Both of them turned, hearing the knock at the door, following Damon's voice. "Ladies, it's time." Mia opened the door seeing Damon and Conner standing on the other side of the door.

"Gentlemen, we are ready," Mia smirked as she walked down the hall with Damon. Conner walked into the room, seeing Erina standing by the window.

"You look beautiful. Let's get you married." She turned, smiling at him as she lifted her dress with her one hand. He took her flowers before holding his arm out to her. Erina had asked Conner to walk her down the aisle, he was the closest she had to family, and she couldn't imagine anyone else walking her down the aisle than Conner.

"I am ready. Let's do this." They walked down to the front of the house, where the SUV was waiting for them. Conner helped Erina into the back of the car before getting in next to her. One of the senior guards driving them to the cliff where the wedding was being held.

The drive over to the cliffs was quiet, Erina staring out the window, grateful to be getting married to Brad today. Things could have been so much different if Amelia was never caught doing what she did. Brad was still on edge with Amelia on the loose and not knowing where she is. It had been more than a year since she was last seen, and they still had no lead on her where abouts.

Brad had made sure that the wedding location was kept a secret. The guest were all picked up at the hotel and taken to the wedding location. Only Brad, Erina, Damon, Conner, Mia, and Austin knew where it was held. And only today, they had shared the location with two senior guards that had to drive the guests and Erina to the location.

*****

Brad stood at the front of the aisle with Thomas and Austin. Brad was thankful that Thomas could join them and even more grateful that Thomas had agreed to be the officiant for the wedding. When Brad got married to Amelia, he had lost touch with his brother, and he hoped that he would be able to build a relationship with his brother again.

Brad couldn't believe that day had finally arrived. The day he got married to Amelia, he didn't nearly feel like he was feeling today.

At his wedding to Amelia, Brad was just standing there nodding at all the right times. And after the wedding, he sat at the bar with his friends. Brad didn't even spend his wedding night with her. He dreaded every day he was with her. Even more so when he met a beautiful pediatric doctor at the hospital.

Today was a dream come true for Brad. He was finally happy and was getting married to the only woman he will ever love. They have been through so much that even though he was married and had babies, she was still there for him whenever he needed to talk. Brad knew without a doubt that Erina was his soulmate, the woman he was supposed to spend the rest of his life with, his queen and soon to be wife.

Thomas tapped Brad on the shoulder, subtly nodding towards the end of the aisle where the SUV's with Erina and Mia just pulled up. Brad's smile grew wider, knowing that Erina was in the SUV at the back.

Damon got out of the first SUV, walking around to open Mia's door to help her get out. He smiled as he held out his arm to her, taking it. She nodded as they make their way down the aisle. Mia gave Brad a sly smile as she walked past him taking her place.

Conner got out of the next one smirking at Brad as he slowly walked around the SUV to open the door for Erina. Conner stood in front of the door, making sure Brad couldn't see Erina as he helped her out of the SUV.

Brad gasped as soon as Conner stepped aside and Erina came into view. She looked radiant in her dress. Erina wore a mermaid style dress with beading at the neckline. Her hair was hanging over her shoulders in loose curls. Brad felt as if he couldn't breathe, that if he blinked, she would disappear.

Conner walked down the aisle with Erina on his arm. She couldn't take her eyes off Brad, not even seeing anyone else except Brad standing in the front waiting for her. Stopping in front of Brad. Conner lifted her veil, kissing her cheek, before turning to Brad shaking his hand. He stepped away, letting Brad take Erina's hand, pulling her closer to him before Conner took his place on the other side of Damon.

"You look beautiful, Love." Brad leaned down, kissing her cheek.

"You look dashing yourself." Erina smiled as they both turn towards Thomas.

The ceremony was beautiful, not a dry eye among the guests. Brad's vows had everyone wanting that kind of love, and Erina's had everyone in tears. Thomas stood there looking between the two, happy that his brother had finally found love.

"It is with pleasure to present to you, Mr. And Mrs. Davis." Thomas smiled proudly as Brad and Erina turned towards the guests, Brad's arm around Erina's waist as she beamed at him.

*****

3 months later

Erina walked down the stairs on her way to Brad's office. They had a meeting at one of the new hotels they needed to get to. Erina was running late after she spilled her coffee all over her outfit.

Since they had gotten married. Erina had adjusted to helping Brad with the company. Even though he didn't expect her to take on a role in the office. She had decided to give

Christian the pediatrics department at the hospital, knowing that she would not be able to work there anymore. She wanted to focus on Brad and spending time with him. Christian had fallen in love with pediatrics when he was helping Erina. She still helped out sometimes, especially with the NICU where her heart was, and Brad supported her with it entirely.

Erina knocked on Brad's door, waiting for him to call for her to come in. Hearing him call for her, she entered the office, giving him a small wave. "There you are." He got up, walking around his desk, stopping in front of her. "Are you feeling better now?" He raised his brow at her as she nodded.

"I am fine. I just spilled my coffee." She leaned up on her tiptoes, kissing his lips sweetly. "Are you ready?" She asked as he took her hand.

"Yes, let's get this meeting over with." Brad and Erina walked out of his office, heading for the waiting car.

"Mrs. Jones told me she had to hire a few more ladies. Do you know what that's about?" Erina asked as she got in the backseat. Brad met Austin's eye across the SUV's roof, silently asking him what was going on.

"I did not approve it. I will have to have a word with Mrs. Jones and Austin." Brad took Erina's hand in his, concerned that he didn't know about the new ladies hired and now had access to the house.

"Brad, is everything alright." Erina could see the wheels turning in Brad's mind. He looked at her kissing her softly.

"Yes, my love. Everything is fine." Brad again met Austin's eyes. He hoped that there was an explanation for what was going on.

After the meeting, Brad and Erina went for lunch and talked about their upcoming events. Brad had decided to have a charity ball for the orphanage. They needed funds to repair the orphanage, and a few of his business associates felt that it was perfect. They could all help raise funds for the orphanage.

Erina watched as a man and woman entered the restaurant. The woman had her hand protectively on her baby bump. Erina smiled as she saw them before her eyes grew wide.

"Shit...." Brad snapped his head over to Erina as she grabbed her bag to look for her phone.

"Honey, what is it." Brad moved closer to her, concern lacing his voice as he took her hands in his before she could get her phone. "Talk to me."

"Brad, what's the date?"

"It's the 27th. Why?" Brad brushed a tear away that slipped out of her eye. She took a deep breath before she smiled.

"I'm late.... By almost two weeks. I have been so busy I didn't notice it." Brad looked at her confused, not entirely sure what she was talking about. Erina didn't know how to feel about the way he was looking at her. She knew that Brad always wanted a family. She just wasn't sure if he wanted it this soon. Not with what happened with Amelia and the twins. They never talked about having children.

Brad's face lit up with the realization of what Erina was trying to tell him. "You mean....." He took a breath. "You mean.... You might be.... You know...." Erina nodded knowingly at Brad. He stood, pulling her up from her chair before crashing his lips onto hers. He smiled into the kiss, feeling like the luckiest man alive.

"We will have to go to the hospital to have it confirmed, but I am almost certain that I am." She looked up at him as he held her close.

Brad took her hand as he told Austin to take them to the hospital. Erina phoned Christian asking him if he would do her the favor of doing the test. He was over the moon, telling her nothing will make him happier than to do this for them.
After arriving at the hospital, they were taken to a private room where Christian was waiting for them. He greeted them, telling Erina to get onto the bed. She did as she was told.

"Now, I am going to draw blood to have your levels checked. I will be doing an ultrasound, as well. Not sure if we will see something..." Erina swallowed, looking at Christian nervously. She was sure what he was about to say. "I'm not doing that one, even if we don't see anything like this. You will have to see Dr. Barry for that. You're my best friend and that...." He motioned to her lower half. "Is something I don't want to see."

Erina laughed as Brad placed his hand on her thigh, raising his brow at Christian. "I don't think I want you to see that." He smirked at Christian's face.

"Enough, you two. My bladder is full. You should be able to see something." She pointed at the two men, both of them smiling back at her as if they weren't just talking about her or her lower half.

Christian made quick work of drawing the blood and setting up the ultrasound. He smiled as he moved the wand over Erina's tummy before turning the screen for them to see. "I believe congratulations are in order." Brad and Erina looked at each other before looking back at the screen, both of them with bright smiles.

Christian showed them the baby, telling them that Erina was 6 weeks, 5 days. After he was done and cleaned Erina, he left the room to give them some time alone.

Brad pulled Erina into a passionate kiss. He could not believe that they were having a baby. Right at this moment, Erina had made all of Brad's dreams come true. He was married to the most perfect woman, and they were starting a family.

"I take that as you are happy," Erina said, half unsure. Looking at Brad with a hopeful look.

He took her hands into his own. "I am beyond happy. I am having a baby with the love of my life. You make me fall in love with you more and more every day." She wrapped her arms around his neck as he pulled her closer to him.

*****

The next few months went by quickly for Brad and Erina. They had the charity ball for the orphanage, making more than enough funds for the upgrades and the renovations. Again

163

Damon offered to help with the construction part of the upgrades. He loved being able to help with all the things Brad was doing.

At 16 weeks, it was leaked to the press that Erina was pregnant, not that Brad or Erina cared that they knew. They just would have like to be the ones to tell the press, but what's done was done. Not that Erina could hide her growing belly.

Erina and Brad had gone back to the cabin in Chicago for Christmas. Erina was almost 20 weeks pregnant, having more energy than what she had a few weeks before. They were spending Christmas with their friends and family. Mia had offered to make them Christmas dinner, which was a feast, as Mia rarely cooked. On a few occasions, the press had asked if they knew what they were having, to which the answer was always no. They didn't know what they were having, and they didn't want to know. They wanted it to be a surprise. Brad didn't care what they were having. All he knew was that this baby was made with the love that he and Erina shared.

Erina walked down to the ballroom after trying to get a dress to fit for the third time that day. She was now 30 weeks pregnant and had a noticeable baby bump. She rubbed her hand over her stomach as she walked towards the ballroom, it was her and Brad's baby shower today, and she couldn't wait to see all her friends again. All the business associates were invited, and Erina was a bit nervous about seeing Amelia's parents for the first time.

Since Erina and Brad had gotten together, Godfrey and Adelaide didn't show up to any of the functions or board meetings, always sending their regrets for not being able to make it. Brad had thought that it was strange that Adelaide didn't show up to any of the events, knowing how much she enjoyed it.

The baby shower went off without any drama, everyone enjoying themselves. Godfrey and Adelaide had expressed how sorry they were for what Amelia had done and that they would help Brad in any way to find her. Adelaide told Brad that she told Amelia to get pregnant for them to have an heir. She also knew that Amelia had fallen in love with Brad since the engagement. Amelia wanted more out of their marriage than what Brad was willing to give her. Adelaide knew that Brad never loved Amelia and felt that Brad might have fallen for her if her daughter acted differently. But seeing Brad with Erina and how in love they were made her realize that Amelia was never the one for Brad.

*****

Damon walked down the corridor on his way to Brad and Erina's room. Brad had phoned him asking him to check on Erina. Brad was in Brooklyn at a meeting that he couldn't reschedule. He didn't want to leave Erina as she was 38 weeks pregnant and could go into labor at any moment.

Brad had received a text from her telling him she wasn't feeling well and that she would be heading to the doctor, but when he tried to contact her, he couldn't get a hold of her. That's the reason he phoned Damon asking him to check on her and that he would be there in about an hour or two.

Damon walked up to the door, not seeing the guard that was supposed to be there. He swallowed nervously, not knowing what he would find. He opened the door calling Erina's name but not hearing anything.

"Bryan.... Come on.... Brad is worried...." He called out, walking into the room; nothing was out of place. Brad's room was almost the size of a small apartment, with a living area, small kitchen, and a bedroom to the side. He walked to the living area, not seeing anything out of place there. As he walked back, the room's door opened even more. "Fuck...." Damon jumped when the guard stepped in.

"Sorry, sir..." The guard held up his hands in defense.

"Where were you?" Damon eyed him as he walked past him.

"I had to help one of the maids carry something. Mrs. Davis's orders." The guard followed Damon feeling this nervous feeling the closer they got to the bedroom.

Damon knocked on the door, waiting for her to call for him to enter. Not hearing anything the first time, he knocked again. "Bryan…. Brad asked me to check on you." Damon explained, reaching out for the doorknob. Damon and the guard shared a look, both knowing what to do.

Damon slowly opened the door, his eyes landing on Erina on the bed in a pool of blood. His heart stopped as he ran towards her. "Get help…."

Chapter 16

Earlier that day

Brad walked out to the bathroom to get his jacket from the bed, watching Erina pull one of his t-shirts over her head. She was 38 weeks pregnant and uncomfortable. She was waddling around the room and house, which Brad thought was kinda cute.

"How are you feeling love," Brad asked as he wrapped his arms around her from behind, kissing the side of her neck.

"Uncomfortable, but hanging in there. I am so ready to meet this little one." She leaned into him, her back flush against his chest, his hands resting on her tummy. "Do you really have to go today?" She asked with her eyes closed as she took in the feeling of him against her.

"I have to…. This meeting can't be moved. I will be in Brooklyn for most of the day, but I am only a call away." He kissed her temple before stepping away to grab his watch. "Damon will also be here the whole day if you need anything. I should be back no later than two in the afternoon." Erina nodded as she watched him get ready. She didn't know why, but she wanted him to stay with her today. She felt needy and clingy, but she didn't care. She wanted her husband with her.

"If you must…. I know Christian is coming a bit later to discuss a few procedures he needs to perform next week." Brad turned to her pulling her closer to him, at least as close as she could get.

"I will phone you when I get there and before the meeting. I love you with all my heart." He kissed her deeply before kneeling in front of her. "I love you too…" He kissed her baby bump while she ran her hands through his hair. Brad stood back up, brushing his hands over his knees. "I will see you later." He kissed her before walking towards the door. He stopped at the door and turned back towards Erina, looking at her with this uncertainty in his eyes. For some reason, he felt like not leaving her, like he wanted to stay and make sure she was alright.

"Go, I will be fine. We love you." She blew him a kiss as he walked out of the room, following Austin.

Erina went to take a shower. After she was done, she went to put on some shorts and Brad's T-shirt again. She wanted to be comfortable if she would be cooped up in their room for the rest of the day.

She walked out, grabbing herself a bowl of fruit salad and a glass of apple juice. "I am sure this is what you want, baby." She rubbed her hand over her tummy, feeling the baby move. Space was cramped, and that made her feel every move the baby made.

Erina was startled when the door to her room opened. One of her maids came walking in, or so she assumed. "Mrs. Davis, I am sorry. I wasn't aware that anyone was here." She lowered her head.

"It's no problem." Erina waved her off as she settled back against the sofa, flipping through the channels on the television.

"Could I get you some tea, ma'am?" The young girl asked as she looked at Erina nervously.

"That would be great, thank you." Erina smiled at her before turning her head towards her ringing phone. She picked it up as soon as she sees it's Brad calling her.

Erina spoke to Brad for a while as he wanted to make sure that she was feeling alright. She told him that she would just lay on the sofa and watch Vampire Diaries until she fell asleep and would see him when he gets back home and that should anything happen, she would let him know.

The maid brought the tea she had made for Erina, setting it in front of her while trying to listen to Erina's conversation with Brad. Erina took a few sips of the tea while talking to Brad. After ending the call, she stood up, her head spinning as she tried to catch herself on the armrest of the sofa.

"I need to eat something. My blood pressure must be low." She noted to herself as she stood there, waiting for her head to stop spinning. She took a few steps forward, feeling as if her legs were heavy. She took out her phone, sending a text to Brad, telling him that she was not feeling well and was going to the hospital.

"Ma'am, are you alright?" The lady came next to Erina, taking her by the arm, leading her to the bed.

"No.... I need you to get my guard...." She whispered as the lady lead her to the bedroom. "Stop...." Erina tried to pull her arm from the lady's grip. "I need.... I need a.... doctor." She pleaded with the lady next to her, clutching her tummy. Her breathing became uneven, and she could feel her heart beating out of her chest. Erina knew she needed to get to a doctor and soon.

"Don't worry, ma'am, I will get someone for you." The lady smirked as she helped Erina on to the bed. She helped her lay back against the pillows covering her with a blanket. "I am just going to give you something to sleep. And when you wake up, everything will be over." The lady took a syringe out of her front pocket.

"Please no, please the baby...." Erina shook her head back and forth, the sweat dripping from her forehead. She was trying to fight, but she couldn't. It was as if she had no control over her body. In her mind, she was hitting back and yelling for help, but in reality, she was just laying there, watching as the lady pushed the needle into her arm. She felt her eyelids drooping before everything turned black.

*****

Christian walked around the living room of his house. When Erina got married, he brought her house as she wasn't going to need it anymore. With his wife also pregnant, they needed a bigger place, and he was happy to have this one.

"I'm heading out to meet Erina…." He shouted from the front door, waiting to hear if his wife would say anything. He smiled as he was met with silence, knowing that she probably went right back to sleep. Walking out, he locked the door before he got into his car.

He tried to start the car, but there was nothing, no sound, no power. "Shit…." He got out, popping the hood of the car to see what was wrong. "What the…." Christian looked at his vehicle with confusion. His battery had been removed entirely as if to stop him from going anywhere. He took out his phone, dialing Conner's number, having this uneasy feeling inside of him.

"Christian, is everything alright?" Conner asked as he answered the phone. He knew that Christian was on his way to see Erina, and his first thought was that something happened to her. He also knew that Brad was in Brooklyn in a meeting.

"I'm not sure…." Christian hesitated for a moment before he spoke again. "My car's battery has been removed, and some wires were cut. I can't go anywhere." He paused for a moment walking back towards the house. "Conner, something's wrong!" Christian said as he walked into the house.

"I'm on my way. Don't touch anything…." Conner said. He stopped talking as he heard the next words.

"I smell gas…." Christian ran to his bedroom. His wife was sleeping as he picked her up, his phone still in his hand. "Baby, we need to get out of here." He ran with her in his arms out the sliding door leading to the walkway to the beach. They needed to get as far away from the house as possible. Just as he made it to the walkway, the house exploded. Christian flew forward from the blast, with his wife still in his arm as they both hit the ground with a thud.

"Christian, what was that?" Conner yelled, waiting to hear something when the phone started making a connection lost noise, and then it went dead.

*****

Conner ran from his study towards his car, needing to get to Christian's house as soon as possible. He had already phoned the police and the hospital, letting them know they needed help at Christian's address.

He jumped in his car, calling Austin from the hands-free kit. Not getting an answer from Austin, he left a message knowing Austin would phone him back as soon as he gets the message.

Conner tried to get to Christian's house as fast as possible, but he was an hour and a half's drive from there. As he pulled into the driveway, he gasped, seeing the sight in front of him. There were firemen, paramedics, and police officers everywhere. The house was on fire, and that's when Conner saw the two gurney's, one with a body bag and one with a patient on it. From where Conner was sitting, he couldn't see who the survivor was. All Conner knew was that losing Christian would break Erina. He was her best friend.

"I'm sorry, sir, this is an active crime scene." One of the officers that stood next to Conner's car stated.

"My…. My friend lives here…. I need to…." Conner brushed his trembling hand over his mouth. He needed to know what happened. "I need to see them." He spat out, trying to stay calm.

"I'm sorry you will have to follow them to the hospital for that. I am not allowed to share anything with you. All I can say is prepare to say your goodbyes." The officer patted Conner on the shoulder as he motioned for him to make way for the ambulance to come through. One had Christian in, and the other had his wife, Conner still not knowing which one was alive and which one had died.

*****

Brad sat in the meeting, his mind going to Erina and how much she wanted him to stay. He took his phone, looking at it when he realized that he had no signal inside the room.

"Excuse me…. I just need Austin to take my phone to see if he can get a better signal. As you all know, my wife is nearing her due date, and the baby can be born at any moment." Everyone nodded, understanding that Brad needed to have an open line, incase his wife might need him. "See if you can find a signal and make sure Erina is alright. I have this uneasy feeling about all of this." Brad held out his phone to Austin, giving him this pleading look.

"I will get right on it, sir." Austin took the phone, heading out of the room. He didn't even notice that there wasn't any signal there because it was in the middle of Brooklyn, and he needed to find out why the signal was lost.

Brad sat back down, continuing with the meeting as he watched Austin walk out of the room.

Austin walked around the building, not finding any signal. He told two of the guards to stay with Brad while he was going to see if he could find a better signal. Austin walked out of the building towards a park on the other side of the street. As he walked towards the fountain in the middle of the park, his phone and Brad's phone started to light up with messages and missed calls.

Opening Brad's phone, he saw a message from Erina, he tried phoning her, but there was no answer. Austin checked his phone, seeing the call and messages from Conner. Austin looked up at the building in front of him before running towards the building he needed to get Brad.

Brad watched as Mia pointed out a few things on the board, things they needed to change to ensure that the hotel they were planning on building in Brooklyn met everyone's expectations. Mia jumped along with all the others in attendance when Austin ran into the room out of breath.

"Sir, I need you and everyone else to evacuate the building." Austin walked towards Brad, ushering him up as Austin and some guards covered him. They walked out of the building towards the park, making sure Brad was secure and safe before Austin showed him the message.

There is a bomb in the Brooklyn building. Get Mr. Davis out.

Brad was just done reading the text when the bomb went off. He sank to the ground watching in horror as the building he was in only a few minutes ago went up in smoke. Brad stood up, his legs feeling like jelly. What could have happened if Austin didn't get them out?

Austin showed him the message from Erina, Brad trying to phone her, and again there was no answer. Austin also told him about what happened to Christian, and now with what happened to the building, he was almost sure someone was trying to keep him from Erina.

Brad took his phone, dialing Damon's number. It took him a while to answer.

"Brad…. I am kind of busy right now." Damon hissed as he tried to talk and work.

"Damon, I need you to check on Erina. She was not feeling well, and now she is not answering," Brad pleaded with Damon to do this for him.

"Brad…. I…. the horses are dying…. I don't know what to do." Damon explained, he knew that Erina was top priority, but he couldn't just leave the horses.

"Damon, she's my wife, please…. I am too far to get to her. You are right there with her... Please, Damon….." Damon rubbed his hands over his mouth, giving the stable hands a few instructions as he headed towards the house.

"I'm going. Don't worry, she will be alright."

Brad ended the call giving Austin a knowing look. "I already phone the hospital. Erina did not arrive there. I have asked them to send an ambulance to your house. Conner is going with the ambulance. They are closer than what we are sir." Austin tried to calm Brad. He couldn't move Brad until they knew the SUV's were clear. Right now, Brad was safe with guards around him and with the protection of the trees.

*****

Erina started to stir, moving her head from side to side. She opened her eyes, blinking a few times to adjust to her surroundings. She felt as if her head was going to explode. Trying to move her arm, she felt that it was tied to the bedpost the same with her legs.

"Brad...." She called out, trying to lift her head, but she wasn't able to.

"Well, well, well, you finally woke up." Erina's eyes shot open, hearing the voice of the one person she thought she would never see again. She pulled on her restraints to no avail.

"Amelia.... the house is full of guards. Someone will hear me." Erina pulled on her arms again, her mind going to her baby and to keep the little one safe.

"No, they won't. I have people that took care of that." Amelia sat next to Erina brushing her hand over Erina's baby bump. "And no, your precious doctor also won't be showing up. He and his wife is a bit...." Amelia tapped her finger against her lip as if wondering what the right word would be. "Dead..."

"No.... Please no....." Erina gasped, trying to get herself loose from her restraints, but the more she pulled, the tighter it went.

"Just shut up.... You don't get a say in any of this." Amelia smirked, making sure Erina cannot get lost from her bindings. "You thought you could take my life from me...." She ran a manicured finger along Erina's face. The tears flowing down Erina's face as she tried to think of a way out of this. "You

174

brainwashed Brad against me, and now I will take from him what he most desires…."

"Amelia…. Please, you can do to me what you want. Just leave Brad and our baby out of it….. They did nothing…." Amelia pulled her hand back, slapping Erina across her face. Erina lets out a whimper as she felt the sting on her cheek.

"You will not tell me what to do…. I have taken care of Brad already. Now it's you and this baby's turn." Amelia chuckled as she got up from the bed. Erina tried to calm her breathing, not knowing what Amelia was thinking. The tears rolled down her cheeks, not knowing if Brad was safe.

"What have you done…." Erina's lips quivered, her voice breaking as she looked at Amelia walking closer to her.

Amelia walked over to her, taking duck tape to cover Erina's mouth. "I need silence for what I am about to do…. I am going to make you wish that you never set foot near Brad or me…." Amelia glared at Erina.

Chapter 17

Erina watched Amelia walked towards her closet, not sure what she would be doing in there. She could hear her shuffling in there, and when she came out of the closet, her eyes grew wide. Erina shook her head from side to side, trying to get Amelia to stop, but with her mouth covered by the tape, she couldn't get a word out.

Amelia emerged with a medical bag from the closet, seeing Erina thrashing on the bed. "I knew you would have a bag here somewhere." She smirked, putting the bag down, on the ground next to the bed. She headed over to the vanity where her tablet was lying. Picking it up, she walked over to Erina, not looking up from her tablet.

"Right, I need warm water, towels, and a blanket." She looked up, meeting Erina's tear-filled eyes. "Don't worry, I give you ten minutes max after I started before you will pass out." Erina shook her head, praying that anyone would find her before Amelia did something to her or the baby.

Amelia set her tablet down and in a position that she would see on the tablet if she was sitting between Erina's legs. She needed it to not make a mistake. After she is done with that, she turned around and called for the maid. "I need you to get me four towels and some warm water." The maid nodded, walking out of the room.

Erina could see everything that was happening remembering the new ladies that were hired a few months ago. Neither she nor Brad ever met them, even though Brad had asked a few time to have a meeting with the staff, the new ladies just wasn't there once. This is what Amelia had planned all along, maybe not this exactly, but she wanted to get inside the house undetected.

The maid came in with the items that Amelia had asked for. Amelia told her to put them down next to Erina. The maid walked up to Erina tied to the bed, looking at the heading on the tablet. Her eyes grew wide before turning back towards Amelia. "She will die if you do that." She pointed to the screen of the tablet.

Amelia turned around, watching the maid intently. "That's the plan. She dies, Brad is heartbroken, I come to comfort him, and he takes me back. That's if he survived the bomb at the Brooklyn building." Amelia pulled a pair of surgical gloves over her hands, walking back towards the bed. "Now get rid of the guard, tell him Mrs. Davis wants him to do something for her. That she's in the bath, and that is why she's not asking him herself." She gave Amelia a nod before walking towards the door, this feeling of guilt eating her up inside.

Amelia sat down next to Erina, opening up her medical bag. "You have everything I need." Amelia took out a scalpel, clamps, and a few other equipment she might need. She placed everything down on the bed, taking a towel and lifting Erina to put it under her.

"I will share this with you." Amelia brushed the hair out of Erina's face. "This is going to hurt like hell. I am going to cut you open and take what was supposed to be mine. This baby is Brad's baby, the one he should have given me." Amelia took her place between Erina's legs picking up the scalpel.

Shit.... Please, Brad.....I need you. Erina closed her eyes, knowing that no one will hear her scream and no one will be here for hours. Christian was her only hope, and Amelia did something to him. *Damn, that hurts.* Erina tried to take a breath as she felt her skin being cut into. She could feel that this was the first incision to a c section being done. *No, please no..... My baby.....* Erina's body began to shake as the shock from the pain took over. She tried to stay awake but knew that with her blood pressure lowering, the pain, and the blood loss, she would pass out no matter how hard she tried to stay awake.

Erina's eyes shot open, feeling Amelia cut into her more. She felt the pain shoot through her lower half. It felt like her whole body was on fire and being ripped apart. *You don't know what you are doing..... I will die.... my baby might die as well.....* Erina's body shivered from the shock. She felt the sweat forming on her body, knowing that soon she will lose consciousness. *Amelia.... think about what you are doing....* this was the last thought that went through Erina's mind before everything went black.

*****

Amelia took a towel, wiping some of the blood away as she made the next incision. She had already cut through the skin and muscles. She watched on the tablet for the next thing to do. She had prepared for this the last few months, wanting Brad's baby no matter what.

Amelia performed the next few steps just as they were telling her on the video she was watching. She pulled a clean towel closer, as she was able to see the amniotic bag with the baby inside. She made the last incision pulling the baby out. "Welcome little princess." Amelia clamped the umbilical cord before cutting it. Taking the clean towel, she cleaned her up, making sure she was breathing and everything was as it should be. After Amelia cleaned her mouth and nose, she lets out a faint cry.

"There, there little one.... Mommy is right here." Amelia said as the baby fussed in her arms. She wrapped the baby girl in a blanket before walking towards a secret passage. She opened it, going through it. Knowing this was her way to escape the house once again.

*****

"GET HELP…." Damon shouted at the guard as he ran to Erina's side. The guard stood frozen, seeing Erina's motionless body lying on the bed in front of him. "You need to call for help…." Damon shouted again. The guard nodded, running out of the room to get help.

Damon stopped next to the bed taking in the scene. He ran his hand down his face seeing Erina laying on the bed in a pool of her own blood. "Shit, the baby…." Damon grabbed a few towels lying on the floor, pressing them to the open wound on Erina's stomach. He could see that the baby had been removed from her. He shook his head, trying to get the thoughts out of his mind.

"Bryan…. You have to hold on…. You can not give up. Brad and the baby need you." Damon swallowed the lump forming in his throat, taking in the way Erina looked. She was pale, her skin damps from the sweat. "You can't leave us…. Brad just found his happiness." Damon pleaded as the first tear slipped out of his eyes. He knew she was in a lot of pain, and she didn't have much time left. Keeping his one hand on the wound, Damon reached up to feel her pulse. He closed his eyes when he felt a faint pulse. He turned his face towards the door as he heard footsteps. "Get someone here now," Damon shouted urgently, just as two senior guards came running through the door.

"What happened?" The older man asked as he started to untie Erina's wrist, the other guard doing the same. Damon looked up, not ashamed that he didn't even notice that her hands were tied. He reached up again, this time to take the duck tape from her mouth.

"I have no idea. All I know is someone stole the baby from Mrs. Davis's womb." Damon's voice cracked as he tried to keep himself from breaking down. "Her pulse is weak, and she has lost a lot of blood. We need to get her medical attention. And the place needs to be locked down. No one in or out, except the medical team." The guards nodded. The older gentleman started calling orders to the rest of the guards around the house.

Damon stood up from the bed as one of the guards took over from him. He needed to get her to the hospital. As he walked out the door, he saw Conner and paramedics run through Brad's room's front door. "She's in the bedroom, she has lost a lot of blood, and her pulse is weak," Damon said in a hushed tone to the one paramedic ushering him towards the bedroom. Damon turned towards Conner, who had not heard what Damon said. Conner took a step forward to follow the paramedic into the room, but Damon stepped up in front of him.

"Damon???" Conner gave him a look as he tried to step past Damon.

"You can't go in there…." Damon shook his head, putting his blood-covered hands on Conner's shoulders. For the first time, Conner took Damon in, seeing his red-rimmed eyes, the blood on his clothes and hands. Conner took a deep breath feeling the knot in his stomach.

"I need to see her…." Conner tried to push past Damon, but his hold was firm. Damon held him back, trying to get him to calm down. "She…. She might need me…." Conner's voice cracked as he tried to push past Damon again. This time Damon pushed Conner against the wall.

"She…. She won't need you…." Damon looked down at the ground gathering his thoughts. "We need to let Brad know." Conner shook his head, putting his hands on Damon's arms.

"No…. Please no…. She's my best friend…." Conner sank to the floor, pulling his knees up to his chest as he sobbed. Since meeting Erina, she had been his friend. Not once did he see her as anything more. She was like a sister to him, and he wanted to keep her safe. He had failed her and her baby. "Brad can't lose her…. I can't lose her…." Damon crouched down next to him, resting his hand on Conner's shoulder.

Just as he was about to say more. The paramedics came rushing out of the room with Erina on a gurney. She was covered with a silver emergency blanket. Conner stood there, shocked as they wheeled her past him. Her complexion had changed. She was now a pale greyish color. She had an oxygen mask on and wires and tubes coming from her body.

"We need to get Mrs. Davis to the hospital. We are airlifting her." The one paramedic said in a rushed tone as they passed Conner and Damon. "We need one of you to come with us." He looked between Damon and Conner.

Conner was unable to move, watching his friend's lifeless body being pushed past him. He felt his mouth go dry as he tries to swallow the lump in his throat, his hands were trembling, and he was unable to speak. Damon watched as Conner stood there frozen, knowing what seeing Erina did to him.

"I will come with you. Let me just arrange someone to take Conner to the hospital." The paramedic nodded, telling Damon to hurry. Damon walked to one of the guards telling him to bring Conner to the hospital.

"Sir…. Sorry to interrupt. We have located the maid that told the guard to help her." Damon turned to look at the guard as the sadness had turned into anger as he heard they found one of the people involved.

"Take her to the police station. I will let them know what happened. See if you can find out who did this and where the baby could be." The guard nodded as he walked away to do as Damon has told him.

Damon followed the paramedic as they wheeled Erina out to the waiting helicopter. He had made sure that Conner had left before they were to leave, knowing that Conner was much closer to Erina than Damon was.

*****

Brad sat against the tree, Mia sitting next to him as they waited for news that it was safe for them to go. Austin stood there, talking to one of the officers about everything that had happened that day.

"From my point of view, it looks like someone planned this. First, the doctor that's good friends with Erina, then you and you say that something was going on at the stables. It was as if someone wanted to keep you all busy." The officer gave Austin a knowing look telling him they need to find this person.

Austin stood frozen, thinking of everything that had happened, the new staff that was hired without his, Brad, or Erina knowing. And every time they tried to meet with the new staff, something would happen, and they wouldn't be able to see them. "Mrs. Davis....." Austin turned around, rushing back to Brad, as the realization hit him. This was all done to make sure no one could get to Erina.

Brad looked up just as Austin stopped in front of him. "Sir...." Austin is interrupted by Brad's phone going off. Brad saw Damon's name flashing on the screen. He held his hand up to Austin as he pressed the answer button.

"Damon...." Brad answered. Hearing the background noise, he moved his phone from his ear to switch it to speakerphone.

"Brad.... I need you to get to the hospital." Brad could hear the faintest concern in Damon's voice, even though he tried to hide it.

"Damon.... my.... my wife?" Brad's said in a hushed tone. Austin and Mia moved closer to be able to hear them better.

"Just get to the hospital." Damon's voice was soft as he repeated himself. Brad got up, walking towards the SUV.

"Stay with her. I am on my way." Brad ended the call when Austin grabbed his arm, stopping him. Brad glared at him, his eyes moving from Austin's to his hand on his arm.

"Forgive me, Sir. The SUV hasn't been cleared. I can not let you get into that vehicle." Brad shook his head. He didn't care about himself at this moment. He just wanted to get back to his wife. He wanted to make sure that she was safe.

"I.. Don't... Care.." Brad said with each breath he took. "My wife needs me." Brad took a step closer to Austin, glaring at him. "Get me a car." Austin nodded as his eyes locked onto the officers that spoke to him a few minutes ago.

"Sir, let's get you to the hospital." Austin walked past Brad straight towards the officer. "Could you please escort us to the hospital? Mr. Davis needs to get to his wife." She nodded at Austin, ushering them all to her squad car. Brad, Mia, and Austin all got into the back of the vehicle, the officer getting behind the wheel. She switched her lights on as she drove off towards the hospital.

*****

Once the helicopter arrived at the hospital, Erina was rushed into the OR. They were met by a few doctors, that had everything ready to save her.

Damon followed them when one of the doctors stopped him. "I'm sorry, this is where you need to stop." The doctor pointed to the red line on the floor. "We will take good care of her." Damon nodded as he watched them disappear through the doors, hoping that this was not the last time he sees her.

A nurse came to take Damon to the waiting room, telling him someone will be out as soon as they have any news. Damon paced up and down, the image of Erina on the bed flooding his mind. He knew that whoever did this had this planned down to every detail, and he was almost sure that he just missed the person, which would mean the baby could still be in the house. Brad ran into the hospital once they arrived, the nurse seeing him, pointed down the hall. From the look on his face, she could see that he was worried and knew that he was there for his wife. Brad ran down the hall, his face flushed as he tried to control his breathing.

He stopped in front of the waiting room, taking a deep breath. He wasn't sure what to expect. Damon being vague over the phone, just telling him to get to the hospital. He opened the door walking into the waiting room. Brad saw Damon covered in blood, and he instantly knew that something horrific happened to Erina. Damon snapped his head towards the door seeing Brad enter.

"Damon...." Brad's voice sounded hoarse as if he had been shouting the whole day long. Damon walked up to Brad, pulling him into a hug, silently telling him he was there for him.

"Where is she?" Brad asked as they pulled apart. Damon turned around, motioning for him to sit down.

"Brad.... She's in the OR.... It's not good...." Damon stopped talking when Austin and Mia enter the room. They both nod at Damon as they take a seat near Brad. "When I found her, she had already lost a lot of blood...." Brad hung his head hearing the words. He wasn't there to protect his wife. He should have stayed with her.

"The.... The Baby?" Brad asked softly as he covered his face with his hands. He wanted his wife to be safe, and he wanted his baby to be safe, but if he had to choose, which he hoped he never had to, he would choose her. Brad would never be able to live without Erina. She was his life, the air that he breathed, the blood that pumped through his veins.

Damon looked from Brad to Austin, rubbing the back of his neck. "There is something you should know... The baby.... uh um.... how can I put this."

"JUST SPIT IT OUT...." Brad shouted before he stood up, tears falling down his face.

"The baby was stolen." Everyone gasped at Damon's words. Brad stared at Damon feeling like the air was pulled out of him. Brad clawed at his chest, feeling as if his heart was being crushed. "You.... You need to breathe..."

"How?" Brad spat out before turning towards Austin.

"They stole the baby out of Erina's womb." Brad looked at Damon, even more, shocked. Someone violated his wife's body to steal their baby. Brad felt the sadness and anger building up inside him, all these questions running through his mind. How did they get into their house? Where were the guards?

Brad pushed Austin against the wall. Pulling back his fist, he slammed it into the wall next to Austin's head. "What type of head guard are you...." Brad shouted. Damon and Mia tried to pull Brad away from Austin, but he shook them off. "You failed my wife.... I told you to make sure she was safe...." Brad slammed his fist into the wall again, this time closer to Austin's head. "My child was stolen from my wife..." Brad shouted while Austin held up his hands in defense.

"Sir, Please.... I will find out what happened." Austin swallowed hard as he saw the anger in Brad's eyes. Damon pushed himself in between Brad and Austin, giving Austin a chance to move away from Brad.

"Go to my house and find my baby. So help me God, if I get there and you don't have something for me." Brad spoke through gritted teeth, his back was towards Austin, but Austin could see his shoulders shaking as he tried to regain his composure.

"I will find the baby, sir." Austin walked to the door. Mia grabbed his arm, telling him to wait.

"I will go with him." She walked over to Brad putting her hand on his shoulder. "Brad, do you know what you were having." She asked in a soft tone. He shook his head, unable to say anything, he hung his head pinching the bridge of his nose.

"I don't know. We wanted it to be a surprise." Brad said in a calm tone, not meeting anyone's gaze.

"Uh um.... Guys, they have one of the maids at the police station. She was the one that made sure no one got near your room." Damon felt guilty for not telling them sooner.

"I will lock down the city if I have to, and we will search every inch of the city until we find the baby. I will also talk to the maid and see what she knows." Austin spoke with confidence, knowing exactly what they needed to do. First, he needed to find Dr. Barry and determine if she knew what the baby was a boy or girl.

Damon nodded to Austin and Mia, telling them he will stay with Brad until the doctor came to see them. As Austin and

Mia walked out, Damon turned towards Brad, seeing him staring at a spot on the wall deep in thought.

"Brad…. We will find them." Brad didn't move. He just stood there. Just as Damon thought Brad was not going to say anything, he turned towards Damon.

"I am going to kill the one that did this. Even if I have to do it with my bare hands." Brad had this fire in his eyes that Damon had never seen before, and he was sure that if he were to stare into Brad's eyes, he would be set on fire.

The two of them were sitting in the waiting room, hoping that the doctor would come and tell them that Erina was alright and that they could see her. She was the only one that knew who they were looking for. Brad knew that she wouldn't know what they had, being sure that she would have passed out from the pain and shock to her body.

*****

Conner climbed out of the SUV heading towards the hospital. He slowed his pace, not knowing what to expect when he got there. He knew that Brad was already there. He just didn't know if they had any update on Erina's condition.

As he entered the hospital, a nurse told him where to go and that Brad was already there. He thanked her before walking to meet Brad and Damon. He was going to see how they were doing before he would check on Christian.

Conner came around the corner on his way to the waiting room when he saw Brad talking to the doctor. He couldn't hear what they were saying, he only saw Brad shake his head back and forth, and in a blink of an eyelid, Brad collapsed. Damon just being able to catch him before he hit the ground.

Chapter 18

Brad stood up, walking out the waiting room door. He wanted some answers as to how his wife was doing. He was done waiting. He wanted answers right now.

He walked out with Damon right on his heel. Just as they made it to the nurse's station, the doctor came walking towards them. Brad froze as he saw the look on the doctor's face. Erina was loved among the doctors at the hospital. For them to have to work on a colleague, a friend must have been hard on them.

"Mr. Davis" The doctor raised his eyebrow at Brad. "I'm Dr. Sloan. I have been working on your wife." Brad felt his heart drop just hearing that this is the doctor that was assigned to his wife. "Mrs. Davis came in with an open abdominal wound. She had lost a lot of blood. We were able to stop the bleeding...." Dr. Sloan placed his hands into his pockets, looking down. "Sir, Mrs. Davis is critical.... the next 24 hours will be touch and go." Brad felt the air leave his body as the words hit him like a ton of bricks, his wife. His everything might die, and he will be left with nothing. His breathing became shallow as he felt like screaming to wake up from this nightmare. All he could do was stare at the doctor as his voice did not want to come out. "We were lucky. We almost lost her a few times. If she was brought into the hospital a few minutes later, this would have been a whole different conversation." Brad tried swallowing the lump in his throat, not even comprehending what was happening. All he thought about was the fact that his wife might die and that he won't be able to go on without her.

"I… I… Can't breath…." Brad scratched at his chest, trying to get the words out. Dr. Sloan moved closer to him, but before he could even touch Brad, everything around Brad went black as he fell to the floor.

Damon rushed up to Brad just in time to catch him before he hit the floor. "Shit…. Come on, wake up." Damon lightly slapped Brad's face trying to wake him up before looking at the doctor for help.

"Mr. Davis had a mild panic attack. He just needs to rest." Dr. Sloan motioned for a nurse to help them get Brad into a room and get an IV into him. He was sure that the day's events had been too tiring for Brad and that he might be dehydrated as well.

*****

Conner stood frozen, watching Brad fall to the ground. He felt his heartbeat out of his chest. He stood against the wall, trying to get his breathing under control, the tears hot against his cheeks. He could see by the way Brad reacted that it wasn't good news, and the fact that Damon went with Brad meant that they aren't able to see Erina.

After a while, Damon came out of the room Brad was in, seeing Conner standing against the wall, his head thrown back and his eyes closed. He walked over to Conner, wanting to tell him the news about Erina.

"Conner, you made it!" Damon stood next to him against the wall, giving him a side glance. "How you holding up?" Conner opened his eyes, turning to look at Damon.

"How…. How is she…." Damon turned, looking down the hall before turning back to Conner, motioning for him to follow him. Conner closed the door as soon as they were in the room Brad was in.

"The next 24hrs are critical. We almost lost her." Damon rubbed his hand over his face for the first time, feeling how exhausted he was. Conner sat forward, hanging his head in his hands. "We should let Christian know." Conner snapped his head over towards Damon. He never had a chance to tell them what happened to Christian.

"There is something you need to know...." Conner got up, walking towards the window, taking a deep breath. "There was an accident at Christian's house. A gas leak is what the fire chief said." He turned around, the tears prickling in his eyes. "Christian is in ICU. He took a bad hit to the head and has some swelling on the brain. They don't know when he will wake up. His wife and daughter didn't make it. They said that she fell on her stomach and a wooden pole stabbed her in the neck." It was Damon's turn to hang his head in his hands. "I think everything that happened today was to make sure we wouldn't get to Erina in time." Damon nodded as he thought about everything that happened, the horses getting sick would have kept him busy most of the day, Brad having the bomb threat and then the explosion. They wanted Brad out of the building, then Christian's house blowing up, nearly killing him.

"Conner, you are the only one nothing happened to today," Damon explained as Conner looked at him with horror in his eyes.

"Damon, I wasn't supposed to be in the country today. I was supposed to be in Italy for a summit there." Both Damon and Conner grabbed their phones, trying to see if anything happened at the summit. Conner sank back into his chair, reading the headline. *SUMMIT CANCEL DUE TO FOOD POISONING*. "This would have made sure that I end up in the hospital like all the other dignitaries."

"This has Amelia written all over it. We need to find the baby." Damon felt as if the world was crashing in around them.

How could she do something like this? How could she get everything planned to perfection without being seen by anyone?

*****

Amelia walked to the back of the hospital, ready to meet her accomplice. She needed to have the baby checked out. She stood in the shadows waiting for the person to arrive. Amelia was unaware that Erina had survived and that the hospital was full of guards.

When the door opened, Amelia made sure that it was the doctor she was waiting for before she came out of hiding with the baby.

"You took your time." Amelia scoffed as she followed the doctor into a secluded room on the side of the hospital. "Did you bring it?" Amelia closed the door behind her.

"Yes, let me see how she's doing, and then I will explain to you how this works." The doctor held her arms out to take the baby. "We might have a problem." Amelia raised her brow, watching the doctor work on the baby.

"What might that be?" Amelia took a seat at the table, waiting for the doctor to continue.

"Damon found Erina, and they were able to stabilize her. The plus point is that I was able to get you some breast milk for a few feeds without anyone noticing." The doctor turned towards Amelia with the baby in her arms, handing her back to Amelia. "The baby is healthy and won't need anything. How has she been since birth?" The doctor turned to take out the bottle with the breast milk.

"Will that milk be safe for her?" Amelia asked with concern, knowing that if Erina made it, they would have pumped her full medication, and she doesn't want the baby to get anything in that she shouldn't.

"Yes, I got this before they started with Erina. It's not much, but this is all I could get." The doctor placed the bottle down on the table before taking some pills out of her bag. "Now drink two now and then one every four hours until you have

190

enough milk to feed the baby." Amelia nodded, taking the pills from the doctor.

"Finally, I have the baby I always wanted. And if Brad sees how good I have been to her, he will have to take me back." Amelia swayed the baby in her arm, talking with the doctor for a few more minutes, telling them to do whatever they could to make sure Erina doesn't make it out of the hospital.

*****

It has been two days since Erina was rushed to the hospital, two days since her and Brad's baby had gone missing, two days since Brad's whole world came crashing down. He was torn between trying to find his baby and getting his wife to fight for her life. The first 24 hours was a nightmare, with her barely hanging on, and now two days later, she wasn't awake.

In the past two days, Austin had been following up on each and every lead he got. The longer it took to find his baby, the less likely it became to find the baby. The maid finally did tell them that Amelia was behind everything. Also that she had been hiding in the mansion for the past few months. She changed her whole look and even was around Erina a few times without Erina noticing it.

She had vowed to help them with any and all information if Mr. Davis would show her some mercy when it came to her charges. Austin told her that he would take it up with Mr. Davis, depending on what she would give them.

She told them about the plans Amelia had and that she had three men working with her. One made sure that Christian wouldn't get near Brad's house. He also was the one that planted the bomb in the building Brad was in. She gave them a description of each of the men. She also told them that the other one poisoned the horses, knowing that Damon wouldn't leave the horses to die, but she never thought that if Brad told him to check on Erina, then Damon would do it. And then the last guy was to make sure that the summit got food poisoning. She told them that Amelia didn't want anyone to be hurt badly except for Erina. Amelia wanted her dead.

She had also told them about the c section that Amelia performed. Unfortunately, she was sent out of the room before Amelia started, and that she didn't see whether the baby was a boy or a girl. All she knew was that Amelia wanted the baby because it was Brad's blood, and she wants Brad.

After Austin got all the information, he had told Brad all that he had found out and that he was going to start with trying to find the three men who worked with her. He also told Brad that he was sure a doctor in the hospital was working with them. The fact that Amelia knew every detail about everyone had him wondering who else was working with them. That they couldn't trust anyone, not even the employees at the mansion.

Austin and Thomas were on the way to see Dr. Barry after not being able to see her for the past two days. She had been in and out of Erina's room, never being able to talk and never staying too long when someone was there, and Brad was there all the time, not wanting to leave his wife.

After Conner had phoned him informing him of what happened, Thomas had arrived the day after everything had happened. He didn't even hesitate to get on a plane and come help with finding his niece or nephew. He had some things he wanted to say to Amelia that you couldn't say over the phone.

*****

Brad sat next to Erina's hospital bed, her hand in his. He hated seeing his wife like this. He wanted to be able to hold her and see her beautiful blue eyes. He wanted to hear her voice, telling him that everything was going to be alright.

"Love…. I need you to wake up…." Brad whispered as he brushed his hand along her cheek. "I can't do this without you…. You have been my everything…." Brad got up, brushing his lips against her forehead. A tear dropped down his cheek. "Please just give me a sign that you can hear me." He leaned over the bed, his face buried in her neck as he tried to calm himself. "I love.... you so... so much," He cried into her neck.

Brad.... I'm trying.... Erina could feel the weight of her husband against her chest. While he wanted to hold her close to him without hurting her. She could feel his tears damping her neck as he cried, and there was nothing she could do to let him know she was there. *I want to hold you.... damn, I'm in so much pain.... why can't I lift my arm.... Brad....* Erina's breath became uneven as Brad took a step back from her bed when the monitors started going wild as her heart rate picked up. The nurse came running in, telling Brad to wait outside. *No.... nooooo..... don't let him leave..... he's my strength..... if he leaves, I have nothing to hold onto..... please don't let him leave.....*

"Sir.... You need to step out." Brad was frozen, seeing Erina's body shaking. He wanted to run up to her and hold her close and never let her go. Damon came into the room with all the commotion going on. He could see they needed to work on Erina. He took Brad by the arms pulling him towards the door.

"I need to stay with her." Brad sobbed as Damon pulled him to the door. *Yes..... Brad stay..... I want to wake up....*

Damon and Brad both stopped when they heard a faint voice. The whole room fell silent. *"It's a girl...."* that was all they heard before the alarms went off again, and the doctors and nurses started screaming orders again.

*****

Austin and Thomas knocked on Dr. Barry's door, waiting for her to let them in. Once they were inside, they took a seat on the other side of her desk.

"Thank you for seeing us." Thomas placed his hands on his lap, taking the doctor in, she seemed nervous, and he wanted to know why.

"I will help. However, I can." She smiled at the two of them, never meeting their eyes. She knew that once she did, Thomas would see right through her.

"Could you tell us what Mr. and Mrs. Davis were having? We need to know if we are looking for a boy or a girl. It will make it so much easier." Austin came right out with what they needed to know. He didn't have time for sweet talk. She nodded, taking the file with all Erina's information in. Thomas observed her as she went through the documents, his eye-catching something that she didn't want them to see.

"It seems like it was a little boy. I did ask them if they wanted to know, and they said no. But I remember making a note that it was a boy." She smiled, feeling relieved that she could help them.

"Thank you...." Austin got up, satisfied with her answer. Thomas following him but stopped when something caught his eye. Thomas smirked as he walked back to the table, glaring at Dr. Barry.

He rested his fists on her table, leaning in close to her. He wanted to be able to read her thoroughly.

"Where is Amelia hiding with my niece?"

Chapter 19

Thomas glared at Dr. Barry before he nodded at Austin to look at the box behind the door. Austin walked over to the package picking up the document raising his brow, and walking back to the table.

"What.... How...." Dr. Barry shook her head, looking back at Thomas and Austin. "I have no idea what you are talking about."

"Then how do you explain this...." Austin handed the birth certificate to Thomas.

"This is a birth certificate for Jemma Davis, father Brad Davis, and Mother Amelia Davis." Thomas held the birth certificate up, showing Dr. Barry. She swallowed hard with fear. The birth certificate indicates that Jemma was born on the day Erina was attacked.

"I don't have to answer to you...." Before she could say anything, Thomas grabbed her by the coat and pulled her against him.

"WHERE.... THE.... FUCK.... IS.... MY.... NIECE...." Thomas spoke loudly and slowly to make sure she took in every word.

"She's dead..." Dr. Barry spat out, glaring up at Thomas. He moved his hand around her neck, squeezing hard as she tried to remove his hand. "Take.... Your.... Hands.... Off.... of me."

She tried to gasps for air, her face turning red as she tried to breathe, but Thomas's grip is too tight, and she can feel the need for air burning in her chest. She scratched against Thomas's hand, trying to get free.

"Thomas….." Austin tried to pull him off the doctor, knowing they need her to get Amelia. "Thomas…. Let's get Brad." Austin pulled Thomas back as he let go of Dr. Barry. She panted, trying to breathe in some fresh air.

"You stay with her. I will go get Brad." Thomas turned, giving Austin a knowing look. "And you better hope Brad is in a forgiving mood. Because what I did is nothing compared to what he will do to you." Thomas laughed though there was no joy in it, more of hate towards the doctor.

*****

Brad froze as he heard all the alarms going of seeing the doctors and nurses scramble to help his wife. He felt his heart being torn apart, catching her just lying there. He could swear he heard her say that it's a girl. He would do anything to hear her voice only one more time.

"Damon, phone Thomas telling him it's a girl," Brad asked Damon as Brad stood there watching them work on his wife.

"I'm on it." Damon stepped out of the room to phone Thomas when he saw Thomas running towards them. He could see on his face that something was wrong. "I was just…."

"Where's Brad…. I need him now…." Thomas interrupted Damon before he could say anything more.

"He's in there." He pointed to Erina's room as Thomas walked in. "He wanted me to tell you it's a girl," Damon said in a whisper as Thomas closed the door. He wasn't even able to follow Thomas when the door swung open again, Brad and Thomas rushing out of the room.

"Damon, stay with Erina. I'm going to get my daughter." Damon nodded, watching Brad and Thomas running down the

196

hall before they disappeared around the corner. He didn't know what was going on. All he knew was that if Brad needed him to stay with Bryan, he would stay with her.

Damon stood against the wall, waiting for some news on Erina, he wasn't standing there long, but it felt like he was standing there for hours when the doctor came walking out.

"How is she?" He walked closer to the doctor, hoping with everything in him that she was doing alright.

"Why don't you ask her yourself." The doctor smiled as he patted Damon's shoulder as Damon rushed into the room, seeing Erina laying there with her eyes open, watching the nurse as she moved around her. He wanted to move out of the room to get Brad. He just didn't know where Brad went.

"Damon...." Erina whispered as he walked over to her. He could see the tears dancing in her eyes as she tried her best not to cry due to the pain and the fact that she was scared shitless.

"Bryan.... It's so good to see you awake." He walked over to her, giving her a hug making sure not to hurt her. "You gave us one hell of a scare." He said as he pulled away from her, taking the seat next to her.

Erina closed her eyes, taking a deep breath as she tried to calm this quell she felt deep in her heart. She had to ask him. She had to know. "Where is she?" Erina finally said the words she wasn't sure she wanted to know the answer to.

Damon looked up, feeling this guilt deep down, feeling that he might have saved them both if he didn't take his time to get to her. "We don't know.... Brad is doing everything to find her." Erina could only nod as tears streamed down her face.

"I.... I want Brad...." She choked out, holding a pillow to her midsection like the nurse told her to.

"I will get him for you." Damon got up, heading to the door. He turned around, seeing her lay down looking out the window. He could see her shoulders shaking as she tried to minimize her crying.

*****

Brad and Thomas entered Dr. Barry's office. Thomas telling Brad everything they learned and what he and Austin saw. Brad was furious when he entered the office. The doctor he trusted with his wife, the doctor he thought was a family friend, betrayed them and fed Amelia information during the pregnancy.

Dr. Barry's eyes shot up as she saw Brad. She could see the rage in his eyes. It was as if his whole body was glowing with anger. She gave Austin a pleading look, silently asking him not to let Brad near her.

"Where....is....my.....daughter?" Brad asked with each step he took closer to her. Austin smirked as he stepped aside to let Brad get to Dr. Barry.

"I don't know." Dr. Barry didn't break eye contact with Brad, too afraid of what he might do.

Brad slammed his fist against the wall right next to Dr. Barry's face. "I am going to ask you again. Where the *fuck* is my daughter." Brad's voice was raised, and he was at his breaking point.

"I don't know…. A courier was coming to collect that." She pointed to the box on the floor. As if on cue, there was a knock at the door. When it opened, revealing a courier guy and an out of breath Damon.

Brad motioned for them both to come in. Damon could feel the tension in the room. "Where are you delivering this package?" Brad asked the courier guy as he held the forms out for Brad to sign.

"I am not allowed to give that information out. I am just here to pick up the package. Could you please close it?" The guy stood there with a smug look on his face as Dr. Barry walked over to the package, closing it with duck tape.

Brad lunged forward, grabbing the guy by the front of his shirt pinning him against the wall, the guy tried to push Brad back, but it didn't help. Thomas and Austin sat on the edge of

Dr. Barry's desk with their arms crossed over their chests, watching Brad have at it with the courier. They knew better than to try and stop him. He wanted answers, and he knew just how to get it. Before Brad could stop himself, he pulled his arm back before his fist connected with the courier's nose.

"Fuck, who the hell do you think you are?" He spat out as he held his nose, blood dripping through his fingers.

"I AM YOUR WORST NIGHTMARE.... That is who I am..... YOU WILL TELL ME WHERE THAT PARCEL IS GOING." His voice got louder, the more he talked. He let go of the guy motioning for Austin to come closer. "If you don't...." He nodded at Austin, who stepped forward with his handcuffs. "I will have you arrested as an accomplice in the kidnapping and attempted murder of my daughter and wife." Austin waved the cuffs as the courier guy's eyes grew wide.

"I will tell you. It has to be delivered to a small cottage just outside of Manhattan." Both Brad and Austin looked at each other with confusion.

"Manhattan?" They said in unison. The guy nodded, handing them his tablet with the details on.

"That's what it says right here." Austin took the tablet putting the address into his phone.

"You won't be doing this delivery," Brad said as he took the tablet and held it out to Damon. "He will be doing it." Damon nodded, taking the tablet. "Austin, make sure Dr. Barry and this guy doesn't leave this room. No contact with anyone. We need to find my daughter." Austin nodded at Brad, Thomas, and Damon as they leave the room.

"Brad...." Damon almost shouted as he remembered why he was there.

Brad raised his brow at Damon, his heart sinking to his stomach. Damon was supposed to stay with Erina, and if he's here, something might have happened. Brad was so upset about everything that happened. He just wanted to find their daughter.

"What's wrong?" Brad asked as his voice betrayed him.

"Erina is asking for you." Damon smiled as he saw the tears appearing in Brad's eyes as he turned around, running in the direction of Erina's room.

Thomas chuckled, watching Brad run away from them. He had seen Brad run more today than any other day. "Damon, you have the best timing. Let's go see what his plan is after he has time to see his wife" Thomas clapped Damon on the shoulder as they both walk down the hall towards Erina's room. Damon taking out his phone to let Conner know that Erina has woken up.

*****

Brad stood in front of Erina's door, trying to calm his breathing and his heart. He wanted to see her, but he also knew that they will have to have a very emotional conversation. Brad finally opened the door seeing Erina lying on the bed looking out the window. She didn't even turn to see who was at the door. "Love…." She turned her head, smiling as she saw Brad's face. Brad rushed over to the bed, he felt his feet move, but it was as if he couldn't get to Erina's side fast enough.

"Brad…. I….I…." He cupped her face kissing her before she could say anything, the tears falling down both of their faces. He pulled back, looked into her baby blue eyes, and saw the pain, hurt, and uncertainty in her eyes.

"I'm so sorry I wasn't there." He brushed his hand over her cheek. "Almost losing you killed me inside." She cupped Brad's cheek as he leaned into her touch. "I am so sorry…. If… If… You never…. met….." Brad's breath hitched as he tried to talk, but his emotions took over.

"No…. Do not say that. This isn't your fault. Amelia is a psychotic bitch. You did not do this." She pulled Brad down, so his face was resting in her neck as she rubbed her one hand up and down his back and the other hand she placed on his head, running her fingers through his hair as she tried to calm him. It broke her heart to see her husband like this. He was hurt more than when he lost the twins. She hated the fact that Amelia had caused him this much pain. She had taken everything from Brad. And now she almost took his wife.

Brad stood up after calming down. He wiped his face with a towel as he turned towards Erina again. "We will find her, and I will make sure she pays for what she has done to you and our daughter."

"I know you will find her, and you will bring our daughter back to us." She gave him a reassuring smile. Brad helped her move a little to the side for him to fit into bed next to her. He laid on his side, laying his arm out for Erina to snuggle in the nook of his arm. She still held the pillow over her midsection as she laid there in Brad's arms. He told her everything they had found out, about Amelia and the people helping her. He told her that they got the maid and also that Dr. Barry was working with Amelia. He told her about the birth certificate and the fact that Amelia put her name down as the mother. He told her about how observant Thomas was and saw the evidence that helped them catch Dr. Barry. Erina felt her heart thundering in her chest just thinking of what Amelia was doing to her baby, then she remembered something Amelia said.

"I hate to think about what Amelia will do to our baby," Brad said as he combed his fingers through her hair.

"She won't hurt her." Brad looked at Erina with a confused look in his eyes. "Just before she did the procedure, she told me she was taking what should have been hers. I believe that she wants your baby...." She closed her eyes, taking a deep breath before she opened them again.

"She has an obsession with you, an unhealthy obsession. I think she was at some point in love with you, but that turned into an obsession because you never returned her feelings. She needs help, and as angry and hateful as I feel towards her, I really think she should get the help that she needs." Brad nodded as he considered what Erina was saying. All the signs were there. He just never paid attention to it. Her trying everything for

Brad to just be near her. At that moment, he felt guilty that he didn't see it sooner and didn't do something about it sooner.

"I will try my best not to lose it when I see her." Erina nodded, understanding where Brad was coming from. She held the same hate for Amelia as Brad did. Amelia had scarred her for life.

Erina rubbed her hand over her stomach, she wanted to ask Brad, but she was too afraid to hear what he would say.

"Babe…. I have to know." Brad turned to look her in the eye, telling her to ask him anything. "Will I be able to have more children." He could see her lip quivering as she tried not to cry when she saw the tears well up in his eyes.

"Dr. Sloan said that due to the trauma your body went through, he would recommend we wait for a few years before we think about having more children. They won't know if you will be able to carry the baby full term until you are pregnant. He said that there isn't too much scar tissue, but you never know what will happen." Erina nodded, taking everything in. Being a doctor herself, she knew what they meant. She had a 50/50 chance of having any more children. She didn't know if she wanted to try only to lose the baby. But she also didn't want fear to stop her from having the big family she and Brad wanted. They have talked about it since they became official. Brad wanted to be a better father than his father, and Erina wanted more than one child because she loved children and was an only child. She didn't want her child to be lonely like she was.

"Right now, we need to find our baby." She smiled up at Brad as she cuddled closer to his side.

"We will find her. Damon is out there right now, a step closer to finding her." Erina nodded as she rested her head on his chest. She just wanted to lay with him, not wanting him to leave her.

*****

202

A few hours after Erina woke up, Damon sat in the courier truck heading towards the cabin outside of Manhattan, where Dr. Barry sent the supplies. After Erina fell asleep in Brad's arms, Thomas and Damon entered the room to find out what Brad wanted them to do.

They all decided that Damon would take the supplies, but he was to take one of the junior guards with him. The guard was to take the parcel to the door and find out if the baby was in the cabin. If she was, he would head back as if nothing was wrong, and then they would send in more guards.

Damon pulled up near the cabin, letting the guard get out. Damon watched as he walked up to the cabin, seeing an older lady opening the door singing for the parcel. Damon saw the guard shake his head, motioning to the inside of the cabin. The lady nodded as she stepped aside for the guard to enter. After a few minutes, the guard came out, smiling at the old lady before he headed back to the truck.

"Well?" Damon raised his brow, taking the guard in.

"She's not here.... I think this is a halfway house for everything... The lady only speaks Greek, and she can barely see anything. She did, however, say that someone comes to collect the parcels early in the mornings." The guard said as he took his seat on the passenger side.

"I guess this just turned into a stakeout." Damon smiled as he moved the truck to a hideout. He took out his phone, letting Brad and Austin know about what happened. Austin agreed that they should sit and wait. He told Damon that he would send some more guards to help them.

Damon agreed to keep them informed of everything that happens. He just wanted to find the baby, knowing that Brad had been through enough. Damon had been there with Brad through everything, how Brad wanted to be with Erina but couldn't because of the twins, how Brad lost the twins. He had even been there since before everything. He had seen how all of this has been breaking Brad. When Brad thought he was losing Erina, Damon saw what it did to him and what it is still doing to him.

All Damon wanted was for everything to be back to normal. For Erina and Brad to be reunited with their baby girl.

*****

Thomas sat in Brad's office after returning to the mansion. He had told Brad that he would see if he couldn't figure out where Amelia might be. Mia met him there, and they were sitting going through some documents Amelia left behind when she left.

"This is hopeless... We need to start searching," Mia huffed as she threw the documents on the table. She raised her brow after not hearing a response from Thomas. "Thomas...." He lifted his head, giving her a knowing look.

He got up, walking to a map of New York. "I just saw something in that file." Thomas moved his finger along the map.

Mia took the file, her eyes going wide as she dropped it looking back at Thomas. "Do you know what this means?" She asked, concern in her eyes.

"Yes.... we have been blind this whole time." He pressed his finger on the map. "She has been under our noses this whole time. Manhattan is just a diversion. Get Brad and Austin. I know where she's holding his daughter."

Chapter 20

Brad sat in an SUV with Thomas, Mia, and Austin on their way to the place they believed Amelia to be hiding with the princess. Brad was furious to be betrayed by his board members like this. Conner had opted to stay with Erina, Brad didn't want to leave her alone, and Conner also didn't want her on her own. Erina wanted Brad to bring their daughter home. She wanted him to be there when they find her.

Brad's leg bounced up and down as the anxiety became too much for him. He was afraid that this was again a dead end. He hated thinking of going back to the hospital without their baby. It had been a week since the birth, and Erina was worried that they won't be able to bond with the baby.

*****

Thomas and Mia rushed to the hospital after getting what they needed. They had a location Thomas was sure Amelia was hiding. All the signs were pointing to it. As they entered

Erina's room, they saw Brad and Erina on the bed. Brad was staring out the window while Erina was asleep on his chest.

"Uh Um...." Thomas cleared his throat, causing Brad to turn and look at him. He moved towards the bed with Mia in tow.

"What brings you here? Did you hear anything from Damon?" Brad asked in a tired voice. Brad hadn't slept since this whole ordeal happened. Thomas could see that this is taking its toll on his brother. He had black bags under his eyes from the stress and being tired.

"We know where Amelia is. The courier was just a diversion. She isn't even near Manhattan." Brad raised his brow, motioning for Thomas to continue. "Look at this." Thomas took out a document handing it to Brad.

"This is a signed document to keep an undeveloped area of New Haven, Connecticut, from being developed. It was approved by Amelia." Brad looked back up as he read what this is about. "How does this proof where she is?"

"I know for a fact that there is a cottage there on that piece of land. Neville, built it years ago, thinking that Amelia would one day be his. That would have been their weekend getaway. He never told anyone about that cottage except for Amelia, and she wanted me to go there with her just after you were married." Brad took in what his brother said. If she was there, it would mean that she has been right under their noses the whole time. He shudders thinking of the time he and Erina were in New Haven, now knowing that Amelia could also have been there.

"Thomas.... You are the best." Brad smiled as he tried to wake Erina up. He didn't want to give her hope, but he wanted her to know what they knew. Erina's eyes fluttered open just as Dr. Sloan also entered the room. Erina looked between Brad and Thomas before her eyes landed on Dr. Sloan.

Brad told her what Thomas had found out. He explained that they might know where Amelia was hiding, leaving out the detail of where it is, not wanting to compromise anyone tipping

Amelia off. Erina's eyes sparkled as she moved on the bed to sit up with the help of Brad. Dr. Sloan shook his head at her eagerness.

"I'm sorry, Mrs. Davis, you can not go with them." Erina gave Brad a pleading look. "Mrs. Davis can't help you with this, you had major abdominal surgery, and you need to heal. If you ever want to be able to have children again, you need to do as I say." Brad and Thomas shared a look knowing Erina wanted to be with their daughter as much as Brad wanted to get to her.

"Fine...." Erina huffed as she laid back down slowly. "Brad, you have to go with them. You need to bring our daughter back. She needs her father to be with her." Brad took Erina's hand, bringing it up to his lips, kissing the back of it.

They sat talking about what their plans were after Dr. Sloan left the room. Brad and the others would meet Damon, who was halfway to the cottage already at the entrance of the cottage. Conner had arrived, offering to stay with Erina, not wanting her to be alone while they were all trying to get to her daughter.

*****

Conner walked over to Erina with a cup of tea in his hands. "How are you feeling?" Conner asked as he handed her the cup; as she reached out to take it, she doesn't meet his eyes.

"I'm alright.... Where is Christian? I haven't seen him since I have been awake." She took a sip looking over towards Conner, seeing him shift uncomfortably. She could remember Amelia saying she did something to Christian and his wife. She just didn't understand why no one has said anything about it yet.

Conner rubbed the back of his neck, trying to find a way to tell her about what happened. "He's.... Uh Um..... He's in the ICU. There was an accident at his house.... They were able to save him, but his wife and daughter didn't make it." Hearing this, Erina gasped, her hand going to her mouth as she tried to keep the tears at bay. Christian lost his family because Amelia didn't want someone to find her before stealing the baby.

"I want to see him." Erina placed the cup in her other hand down on the table next to her bed. She was determined to see her friend. She needed to know that he was safe and doing good. She needed him to be alive.

Conner looked back towards the door, his brow arching. "I don't think you are allowed to leave the room."

"I am married to Brad, one of the board members of this hospital. I am allowed to do what I want, and right now, I want to see my friend." Conner chuckled, seeing the look in Erina's eyes.

He walked towards the door, asking a nurse for a wheelchair. "Fine, but if Brad asked why you are out of bed, you will be explaining it to him." Erina nodded, completely willing to take the blame. She just needed to see Christian. Conner walked back with the wheelchair. He helped Erina out of bed, easing her into the wheelchair.

Heading for the door, they were stopped by Dr. Sloan and one of Brad's Guards. "And where do you think you are going?" Dr. Sloan asked, quirking his brow at Erina, before turning to look at Conner.

"I want to go see Christian in ICU." Erina stared at Dr. Sloan as he smirked. Conner moved protectively in front of Erina, squaring his shoulders as he stared at the Doctor in front of him. The guard noticed Conner's demeanor changing. Putting his hand on his sidearm, he looked between Conner and the Doctor.

"I'm sorry I can't let you do that. You see, I need to keep you here until I know where Mr. Davis is heading." He smirked as he took out a needle and, in a swift motion, injected the guard next to him. He crumbled into Dr. Sloan's arms. While he was distracted by trying to let the guard down, Conner took this opportunity to rushed with his shoulder into Dr. Sloan's middle, causing him to fall down. As he struggled to get up, Conner kicked him in the face. As he laid there unconscious, Conner ran back over to Erina. He pushed her out of the room and down the hall towards the elevator.

"Conner…. What the hell. We need to get out of here." Erina could feel her heart thundering in her chest. They didn't know who they could trust anymore. Conner nodded, pushing her into the elevator.

"Are you alright?" Conner crouched down in front of Erina. He took her hands into his own, trying to stop them from trembling. He could see the tears in her eyes as she looked at him.

"I…. I'm fine….," her breath hitched, trying to calm herself. She kept thinking of what could have happened had Conner not been there.

"We will go to Christian. Brad has guards with him as well." Erina nodded, knowing that they should be safe once they get the word out about Dr. Sloan, but still not sure who they could trust.

*****

Austin pulled up outside the gravel road leading to the cottage seeing Damon parked behind some bushes. Damon had arrived about 20 minutes before them, making sure that everything was secure.

Austin parked next to Damon, making sure that the SUV's would not be seen by anyone passing by.

"We will have to go on foot from here," Austin whispered to the group. "You four will have to stand guard. You do not let anyone in or out." He pointed to four of the guards, they nod walking to find a place to see anyone coming in or going out.

"We need to make sure that we go in fast and quiet. We don't know what Amelia is planning." Brad said in a serious tone. He didn't know what he would do if he was to see Amelia, all the anger that he felt for her coursing through him at that moment. Everything she has done, to him, to the twins, and to

Erina. He wanted her to pay. He wanted her to endure the same pain his wife had gone through.

"We will all need a weapon, just in case." Austin handed Thomas and Brad a gun, just to be safe. "Sir, please follow my lead. I can't risk your safety, you are only here to get the princess, and I need you both to be safe." Brad nodded, knowing that Austin will have his back no matter what. "And Thomas, Don't make me regret bringing you alone." Austin side-eyed Thomas, who just smirked at him.

Thomas didn't want to be in the way. All he wanted was for his brother to get his daughter to safety. And for Amelia to pay for what she had done to his brother and his sister in law. Thomas liked Erina. He felt that she was precisely what Brad needed. And with everything Amelia put Brad through, he wanted Brad to be happy and have the family he always wanted. After briefing everyone on what they were doing, the group made their way towards the cottage. Thomas was leading the group as he was the only one that knew the location of the cottage. As they approached the cottage, they saw Neville walking out of the cottage.

"I will have the plane ready for you in half an hour." He shouted towards the door before walking to the car and getting into it, and driving off. Austin radioed the guards at the entrance, letting them know that Neville was on his way.

"He must have been here before I got here," Damon said in a hushed tone, all watching the cottage waiting for the right time to strike.

"Alright…. we all head towards the cottage and see if there is a way in. We get the baby, and then Brad and Thomas leave while we arrest Amelia." Austin stated as they start to move towards the house.

Brad looked through the one window. It looked like a bedroom. There was a bed on the one side, and then he saw the crib with the baby in it. She was fussing, and he wanted to get to her. Before Brad could do anything, he saw Amelia walk into the room.

210

"Shhh…. It's going to be alright. We are going to take a trip. We just have to wait for someone to get me your father." She walked over to the crib lifting the baby out of the crib, cradling her close to her chest.

Brad waited to see what she was going to do. He watched as she walked over to the changing table, changing the baby's nappy before she walked over to a rocker opening her shirt taking out her breast. The baby was fussing, pulling her face away from the breast. "Come now. You need to take it sooner or later." Amelia said in a low voice, but the baby kept crying, pulling away from the breast. "My breasts are sore. You need to eat." Brad felt the anger boiling in him as he watched Amelia try and breastfeed his child. How could Amelia try and feed her when her mother is in the hospital.

After a while and the baby still not drinking from her breast, he watched as she rocked her gently before laying her back down. "I just have to pack a few things. You take a little nap, and mommy will be right back to get you ready." She walked out of the room, closing the door behind her. Brad noticed everything that she did and every sound in the room.

Austin and Thomas joined Brad to tell him they found a way in. Damon and Mia were securing it for them to enter. Heading over to the door they could enter from, Brad couldn't help but wonder why Amelia was acting like this with his and Erina's baby, but she killed her own. Erina's words running through his mind at that moment. *"She has an obsession with you, an unhealthy obsession. I think she was at some point in love with you, but that turned into an obsession because you never returned her feelings."* Why did he never notice it? Was he that blind.

Brad, Thomas, and Austin made their way towards the room where Brad saw the baby. Damon and Mia both went in separate directions trying to find Amelia.

Brad opened the door slowly, knowing that it had a little squeak, Austin and Thomas keeping an eye out to make sure that

Amelia didn't hear it. They knew that no matter what, they were between Amelia and the baby.

Brad walked in, seeing his daughter for the first time. He stopped to stare at her as he felt the lump in his throat. She looked just like her mother. She had brown hair and a little button nose. He felt his heart swell knowing that this was his daughter, this was the daughter that he shared with the love of his life.

The baby started fussing, stretching her tiny hands above her head. She was already a week old and was about to meet her father for the first time. Brad felt his eyes sting as he watched her let out a little yawn. His breath hitched as she opened her eyes, ocean blue eyes locking on ocean blue eyes.

"Hey princess, Don't worry, daddy's got you." He reached into the crib, lifting his daughter to his chest. He kissed the top of her head as he held her head against his chest. Her small hands grabbed his shirt, holding onto him as if never to let him go again. She was small against Brad. His hands almost covered her completely.

Thomas watched as his brother, for the first time, hold his daughter. He saw the tears run down his cheeks as he held her against him. Thomas felt the tears welling up in his own eyes at sight before him.

Brad, Thomas, and Austin snapped their heads towards the door as they heard fighting and screaming. Thomas and Austin rushed towards the door to see what was happening. Brad grabbed a blanket to cover his daughter before following Thomas and Austin.

Austin saw Mia and Amelia fighting. Mia had Amelia pinned against the floor before Amelia kicked Mia off her. Mia lunged at Amelia again, tackling her to the floor. Amelia fell backward, hitting her head against the floor with a loud thud. Austin rushed forward to pull Mia off of Amelia. They needed to arrest her and take her to the police station to have her prosecuted.

"Let me go. That bitch killed Brett." Mia tried to get out of Austin's grip.

Amelia smirked as she pulled a knife from her back, her eyes set on Thomas and Brad on the one side. "Noooo….." Thomas shouted as he saw Amelia lunging towards Brad.

Brad watched as Amelia came for him. He looked down at his daughter. "I love you…." He whispered before he turned his back towards Amelia, keeping his daughter safely cradled in his arms before closing his eyes, waiting for the impact.

Chapter 21

Austin and Mia turned just in time to see Amelia lunges towards Brad. Austin ran to position himself between Brad and Amelia, Just as Amelia pushed the knife into Austin's side. Mia pulled one of her daggers out from her top, first slicing Amelia on the inside of her thigh before she stabbed her just under her arm. Amelia staggered back, clutching her thigh as the blood poured out between her fingers. Mia knew precisely where to cut and stab to cause the most damage. "That's for Brett," Mia spat out, wiping the blade on her pants, before turning around to help Thomas with Austin.

Brad turned around, seeing Austin and Amelia lying on the floor. Amelia was losing blood way too fast. "Brad….. Please…. You know you love me…." Amelia reached for him with her bloody hand. He looked down at her hand, taking a step back from her. "Brad…. Don't do this…. I did this for you…. Erina had poisoned you against me….." Amelia coughed, feeling light-headed. "Save me, please…"

Brad handed his daughter to Damon, taking a step towards Amelia but still staying out of reach from her. "I have never loved you…. What you did was not for me." He leaned down to look her in the eyes. "Erina is the woman I love and will always love. I am taking my daughter back to her mother…. And you will rot in hell for what you have done to my wife, my daughter, and my friends." Brad glared at her with so much hate in his eyes. "And for what you did to your own children."

Austin took a step closer to Brad clutching his side. "Sir, should I call for help?" Brad turned, seeing the blood on Austin's hand. He got up, putting his hand on Austin's shoulder.

"Thomas, get Austin some help." Brad turned, walking towards Damon taking his daughter from him. "There we go, baby girl. Let's go see your mommy." He kissed the top of her head.

"What about Amelia?" Austin asked, looking at Brad confused as Thomas tried to lead him out of the room. Brad froze at the door. He turned to look at Austin, his eyes burning with fury.

"Damon and Mia will stay and wait for emergency services. I will send them when I get to the hospital." Brad's voice was clear, with no emotions.

"I will be dead by then," Amelia said in a soft whimper. She could feel the life draining out of her. She knew she didn't have much time.

"You should have thought about that the day you decided to cut my wife open and steal our baby. The day you left my wife for dead." Brad could feel the anger in his veins. "You will feel what she felt. And no one is going to save you. That is an order from *ME*," Brad spat out, glaring at everyone in the room. They all gave him a nod in understanding where he was coming from. With that, he left the cottage, ready to take his daughter home.

*****

Arriving back at the hospital, Brad got out of the car with his daughter in his arms. He couldn't wait to get to Erina, for her to be able to hold their baby for the first time since she was born.

Brad and Thomas walked into the hospital together, heading to Erina's room. Damon and Mia stayed at the cottage to wait for emergency services. While two of the other guards took Austin to get medical attention. Austin was lucky that Amelia was only able to stab his side and missed all the fatal organs.

As Brad neared Erina's room, he saw a few doctors and nurses standing by the door. As he approached, Dr. Sloan came walking out of the room.

"Dr. Sloan, what happened?" Brad asked with concern in his voice, holding his daughter safely in his arms. He tried to see what was going on in the room, all he could see was that Erina was not in the room. "Where's my wife?"

"Mr. Davis.... I don't know how to say this.... Conner..... He... He attacked us, and he took your wife. No one has been able to find them." Dr. Sloan rubbed the back of his neck, nervously. Brad stood there, taking in the way Dr. Sloan was not able to meet Brad's eyes. Being able to read people, Brad knew that Dr. Sloan was hiding something.

"Bro...." Thomas held out his phone to Brad. He had gotten a message from Conner telling him they were with Christian and not to trust Dr. Sloan. Brad looked back at Dr. Sloan before handing the baby over to Thomas. Thomas took his niece, walking a few steps back, knowing that Brad has been through so much already in the last week, Dr. Sloan was going to feel the wrath of a Davis today.

Brad took a few steps toward Dr. Sloan. He stopped right in front of him. "Why would Conner say not to trust you?" Brad asked calmly. Brad was at least half a foot taller than Dr. Sloan.

"I have no idea... He took your wife after I tried to stop him. He knocked me unconscious along with your guard." Dr. Sloan stood there confidently, knowing that he had to play the part.

"Do Not Lie to me." Brad towered over the doctor, his hands bowling into fists. "I know where my wife and Conner are. So let's try this again. Why should I not trust you?" Brad felt the anger rising in him. He was about to strangle the doctor but needed to stay calm.

"You can trust me, Mr. Davis. I have no idea what has gotten into Conner." Dr. Sloan said professionally. Thomas quirked his brow, knowing exactly what his brother was about to do.

"You might want to close your eyes, sweetheart. Your daddy is about to hurt someone." Thomas smiled down at his niece as he spoke to her.

Brad grabbed Dr. Sloan by his white coat, slamming him into the wall. "You better tell me who you are working for." Brad spat out, holding the doctor against the wall.

Dr. Sloan grabbed Brad's arms, trying to escape from his grip. "You have nothing on me." Dr. Sloan smirked, his eyes burning through Brad.

Brad pulled him away from the wall before slamming him back against the wall harder than the first time. "I will have you arrested for attempted murder. I don't need to know who you are working for. What I do know is that you placed my wife's life in danger. And for that, I can have you locked up for life." Brad glared at Dr. Sloan before turning towards the guards motioning for them to arrest him.

"Wait, I will tell you everything." Dr. Sloan pleaded as he watched Brad take the baby from Thomas.

"You had your chance." Brad turned around, heading to the elevator wanting to get to Erina. He could still hear Dr. Sloan pleading with him to listen to him, but Brad felt at ease. They had Neville, Dr. Barry, Dr. Sloan, and some of the others in custody. He would have his friend at the police interrogate them once his family was settled at home.

Brad knew what he wanted to do with all of them. They had caused a great deal of pain for his friends and family, but he would leave the sentencing up to the judge.

After arriving on the floor of the ICU, Brad felt his heartbeat out of his chest. He didn't know what to expect, he wanted Erina to see their daughter, but this would also be the first time they would see Christian since the accident. He knew that Damon and Conner had visited Christian since the accident, but Brad had been by Erina's side the whole time. Christian had woken up a few days ago. Luckily he had no long term injuries. Conner took it upon himself to tell Christian about his wife's death and what happened to Erina.

"Mr. Davis, we can't let you take the baby into the ICU."
A nurse walked up to Brad, stopping him from entering. Brad
gave her a confused look, not knowing why she would want to
stop him. "Sir, there are sick people in the ICU, and I do not
want the baby to get infected. I can take you to Mrs. Davis if
that is who you need to see."

"Yes, please. Sorry I wasn't thinking about that. I just
need to see my wife" She nodded, understanding how he felt.
She had heard about everything that happened and knew that
Erina had yet to meet her daughter. She motioned for him and
Thomas to follow her.

Brad stood in the room door that was separate from the
other rooms in the ICU, watching Christian and Erina laugh at
something Conner had said. He could see her eyes sparkling as
she spoke to her two best friends. He was grateful for both the
men sitting with his wife. If it wasn't for them, he would not
have been married to her or have her as part of his life. They
moved another bed into the room for Erina at Conner's request
after telling them what happened.

The baby lets out a wail just as Erina said something as if
she recognized her mother's voice. Erina stopped talking as she
slowly turned her head around, seeing Brad standing in the door
with a baby. Her eyes filled with tears as she took in her
husband holding their baby protectively in his arms. She couldn't
stop the tears from running down her cheeks.

"Sweetheart, do you want to meet your mommy?" Brad
whispered as he watched Erina on the bed. He was moving
towards her, his gaze set on hers. He felt the warm tears run
down his face as he watched her hold out her arms as he got
close to her. Brad placed the baby softly in Erina's arms before
kissing the top of her head.

"Brad…. You…. Found her." Erina choked out, holding
her close. The baby snuggled into Erina's chest, calming down
instantly. Conner and Christian watched Erina with the little girl
knowing how hard it was to not know where her daughter was.

A lump forming in Christian's throat, knowing he will never get to meet his daughter.

"She's perfect..." Erina smiled down at her. Brad sat down next to her on the bed, wrapping one arm around Erina and placing his other one under the baby.

"She is.... She's as beautiful as her mother." Brad rubbed his thumb over the baby's cheek. "Now, I believe our little girl needs a name." Erina nodded as she turned to look Brad in the eyes.

"What do you have in mind?" She smirked, knowing he had a name from the day they found out she was pregnant.

"I love the name, Eleanor." He smiled warmly at his two girls.

"Eleanor Christi Davis," Erina said. The baby stretched as if she agreed.

"I think that is perfect." Brad kissed Erina first before kissing the baby on the forehead.

Everyone got a chance to hold Eleanor while Thomas and Brad told them what happened at the cottage. He told them how Amelia had tried to stab Brad, and in the end, Mia stabbed her, and he was almost sure that she did not survive, but they would hear from Damon and Mia when they get back. Conner told Brad about Dr. Sloan and what he tried to do. Christian also told them that he had a suspicion that Dr. Barry and Dr. Sloan was up to something. He told them about another doctor that was always with them. Brad made a note of it to find the doctor and question him as well.

*****

A few days after Eleanor was found, Erina was discharged and heading home. They had confirmation that Amelia did, in fact die before emergency services got to her. Erina didn't know how she felt about her passing. All she did know is that what Amelia did almost cost her, her life, and her family. She was relieved that Amelia would not be a threat to them anymore.

Austin did not stay in the hospital as they only needed to give him a few stitches. He was back at the mansion before Brad and Erina. He had interviewed each staff member, even those who've worked for Brad for years. He was not about to make any mistakes. He felt guilty for everything that has happened to Brad and Erina. If he had been more aware, he would have seen the danger signs.

Brad laid on the bed with Erina and Eleanor. Both his girls had fallen asleep when there was a knock at the door. Brad got up, covering Erina with a blanket as he walking to the door to open it, finding Thomas and Austin on the other side.

"Sir, they are ready." Austin voiced.

"Thank you, Austin. I will be down shortly. I am just waiting for Damon and Conner." Brad smiled, stepping aside to let Thomas in. Austin nodded as he pulled the door close.

"Who's staying with Erina and Eleanor?" Thomas asked, knowing that Brad wouldn't want them to be alone while he questions the accused. Brad sat next to Thomas, brushing his hands down his face.

"Damon will be staying with them. Conner is needed down there, and so are you." Thomas nodded. He had a feeling Brad was going to need them.

"I hope they know that I will not be lenient towards any of them," Thomas smirked as Brad nodded, knowing what Thomas meant by that. Thomas had asked for special privilege from the NYPD to be head of the investigation. His LAPD captain agreed to give him time to handle the case, and so did the Captain of NYPD. Thomas had then decided to have Brad ask some questions and be there for the interrogations. They needed to find out what each of them did to help Amelia, but they also needed to be smart about it. None of them knew that Amelia had died. And Brad was going to use that to his advantage.

Chapter 22

Brad walked down the hall towards the cells, Thomas and Conner trailing behind him. Thomas could see that Brad was trying to hold it together, clenching and unclenching his fists. None of them were sure what to expect down there.

Austin stopped in front of one of the doors turning towards Brad. "Sir, Neville is in the room. Where do you want to start?" Austin waited for Brad as he looked at the other doors.

"I want to start with Dr. Barry." Austin nodded, leading the group to the third door on the left. "I would like to go in alone." Brad stopped in front of the door seeing the concern on everyone's faces. "It's not a request." They all nodded, knowing he was not going to listen to any of them.

Brad walked in, seeing Dr. Barry sitting at the table. She glanced at him as he entered, taking the seat across from her. He had a smirk on his face taking in the way the doctor looked. She doesn't know how long they sat staring at each other, Brad not saying a word. He only watched as she shifted uncomfortably.

"Mr. Davis, Please say something." Dr. Barry finally said in a broken voice. Her hands trembling as she waited for what Brad has to say.

"I don't have to say anything. Amelia has told us everything." He smirked as he got up from the chair, turning towards the door. He stopped with his back towards Dr. Barry. "Unless you have something to say." Brad looked at her over his shoulder.

"Yes, I will tell you everything." She motioned for him to sit down. He smiled, thinking that this was easy. "Could I ask for you to consider a lesser sentence for what I am about to tell you?" She looked at him with pleading eyes.

"I could consider it. It will depend on what you have to say." Brad nodded for her to continue as he settled back into the chair.

Dr. Barry looks down at her hands before she started to speak. "Amelia came to me just after you got divorced and offered me a considerable sum of money to help her with any info regarding Erina. You two weren't even dating at that stage, and I thought it would be easy money. I had no idea what she was planning until you proposed to Erina. That's when I found out about the head of the hospital and Dr. Sloan working with her. Dr. Sloan was never meant to save her the day she was brought in, but he wasn't the lead doctor, and he had hoped that she would die after the surgery. But when she pulled through, he was supposed to overdose her. And like all the other plans that didn't work either." Brad nodded at her listening to everything she told him. He could feel the anger rising in him with hearing everything they had planned to do to Erina.

"I want to know, how did Amelia know what to do during a C - section?" Brad raised his brow as he sat forward, resting his elbows on his knee. He tried his best to keep it together.

"I…. I showed her how to do it. By the time Erina got pregnant, I was in too deep, she asked me, and I agreed." Brad stood up, resting his hands on the table, not wanting to hear anymore.

"YOU….. We trusted you." Brad glared at her before standing up straight, pulling on his jacket before squaring his shoulders. "I will make sure you are charged with attempted murder, conspiracy, and kidnapping." With that, Brad turned around, walking out of the room, not even listening to Dr. Barry protesting.

Thomas and Conner were standing outside as Brad walked out, hearing her shouting at him. "Dr. Barry needs to be charged with murder, conspiracy, and kidnapping." Conner nodded as he made a note of it. Knowing that he would have to find out what has been said. "Austin arrest the head of the hospital, Mr. Greyson. He is the other missing link." Austin nodded, telling two guards to stay with Brad while he deals with the head of the hospital. Brad turned, going to the door where Dr. Sloan was. Not caring to hear anything from him, he decided just to charge him.

Brad walked into the room as Dr. Sloan sat at the table waiting. "Mr. Davis, please. I have to get out of here." Dr. Sloan gave Brad a pleading look.

"Dr. Sloan, you will be charged with attempted murder." Brad turned, walking out of the room as Conner made a note. Thomas could see that Brad was trying not to fiscally attack any of these people. Which made his job so much easier. He would help Conner talk to the DA about the charges.

Brad walked out of that room, heading towards Neville's room. He already knew what he was going to say to Neville. He just hoped that it would work, knowing Neville he would sing even before Brad would have to say anything. Brad just wanted to know what his involvement was with all of this. If he was only one of her pawns or with her all the way in this.

Brad explained to Thomas and Conner what he was about to do with Neville telling them to back him up. Both Conner and Thomas agreed that this would be the best way to approach Neville.

223

Brad walked into the room where Neville was being kept. Neville raised his head to meet Brad's gaze. "What's the meaning of this?" Neville growled, holding up his wrists where the handcuffs were on his hands.

"Neville, it has come to my understanding that you are an enemy of Davis International, and I want to know why?" Brad said with a bit of a bite as he took the seat in front of Neville. Conner and Thomas standing behind Brad with their arms crossed over their chests, glaring at Neville.

"What.... No.... I.... Would never....." Neville choked on his words as he realized what Brad had just said. And if he doesn't do something about it, he might end up in jail for a very long time.

"We have spoken to Amelia, and she told us this was all your idea. That you had planned everything and blackmailed her into stealing my daughter and killing my wife," Thomas took a step forward as he spoke to Neville, his eyes never leaving his.

"That's a lie..... I never did any of that. Amelia came to me and told me that she and her daughter needed help and a place to stay. I told her about the place I build, and then she told me just before I was arrested that she needed to get out of the country for the safety of her and her daughter's life. I made all the arrangements to help her." Brad slammed his hands down onto the table in front of them.

"Do you want to tell me that you were not aware of the bounty on Amelia's head or the fact that she stole Brad's daughter? Which was known to everyone." Thomas asked the question everyone wanted to know the answer to.

"I knew you were looking for her because of what she did to the twins, but I wasn't aware that she stole your child or attacked your wife. I thought she had a baby with someone and just wanted to get away from them. I was only trying to help. You all know that I don't pay attention to anything that goes on in the news unless it has something to do with my golf course." Brad and Thomas nodded at each other, they believed what

Neville was saying, and they were convinced that he was only trying to help Amelia because he had some obsession with her.

"Please make a note that even though Neville is guilty of trying to help her get out of the country, he was not a part of Amelia's plan to get rid of the Erina." Conner gave Brad a nod as he made the note, knowing there will still be consistences and Neville will not like what was coming to him. "Neville, thank you for your co-operations." Brad walked out of the room, Thomas and Conner following him. Not one of them saying anything, waiting until they got back to Brad's house.

Brad walked into his office and straight to his table. He stood with his back to Thomas and Conner. They could see his shoulders rising and falling as he took a few deep breaths. Brad turned around to face them after a few minutes, they were met with the anger and hate in his eyes.

"I want each of them that had a part to play in this charged and sentenced with the worst sentence possible. Thomas, I am counting on you to see that justice is served." Brad said with confidence and anger. Hearing what they had planned and knowing what they had done all along was too much for him.

"I will make sure that each of them gets what they deserved. I still need to do a few interrogations and find out more facts, but we could start the trial by next week if it would suit you." Thomas waited for Brad's answer, knowing that they will have to have Erina present for the day. She needs to give them the details as she could remember them.

"Actually, we can have Erina give her statement in front of you, me, and the judge. And the other interrogations can also be done at the police station. Where we will go over them with the DA, Austin just needs to record all of what is being said." Conner said, hoping that this would be some relief to Brad and Erina.

"I agree with what Conner is saying. And I want this done as soon as possible." Both Thomas and Conner agreed with Brad. They wanted this to be over. For Brad and Erina to be able to move on from this, they all wanted to move on from this. They wanted to return to as normal as possible after everything they have been through.

*****

Brad laid in bed next to Erina and Eleanor. Erina had Eleanor wrapped in a blanket between her and Brad. Both their hands were resting on Eleanor as they watched her sleep. This was Brad's favorite pass time to watch his girls just being there. He was so close to losing them that he never wanted to take anything for granted.

"I love you." Erina looked up, seeing the sparkle in Brad's eyes. She smiled as she leaned over, giving him a lingering kiss.

"I love you too." Brad reached out, cupping her face as he pulled her into another kiss.
It had been a week since Brad had spoken to everyone involved in the attack on Erina and everything else that happened. Erina had given her statement telling them everything she could remember about the day she was attacked and Eleanor stolen. She had told them that Amelia had an unhealthy obsession with Brad and believed that having Brad's baby would bring Brad back to her.

Christian also gave his statement about what happened at the house when he lost his wife and daughter. He explained that they hadn't used gas for a few days and knew there was no gas leak.

Thomas later confirmed that the doctors involved had helped Amelia with the attacks on everyone else. Dr. Sloan had planted the bomb and jammed the cell phone signals where Brad was, and also had cut the gas pipes in Christian's house and damaged his car to make sure he wouldn't be able to get to Erina in time. Dr. Sloan never meant for anyone other than Erina to get hurt.

Dr. Barry was the one that arranged for the summit where Conner was supposed to be to get the fish that was slightly off, making sure everyone got food poisoning. She didn't know that Conner never went to the summit.

Dr. Greyson had used his son to poison the horses knowing if Damon was busy with the horses, then he would not answer his phone. He just didn't realize that Damon had a ringtone just for Brad and would answer it as soon as he would phone, knowing that Erina was close to her due date.

With everything that had gotten out, Brad felt relieved that everything was almost behind them. The last thing to do was to be at the sentencing that was to be later that day. Brad kissed Erina on the forehead as she held Eleanor in her arms, feeding her. Brad could not get enough of watching Erina with their daughter. Seeing her take care of her made him fall more in love with her every day.

"I'm going to get some breakfast." Brad slipped out of bed, grabbing his shirt off the chair, putting it on before walking towards the kitchen. Erina joined Brad not too long after he had gotten to the kitchen. She saw him standing in front of the stove, moving as he broke the egg into a pan.

"I could get used to this." She walked over to him slowly as she ran her hand down his back. He looked at her over his shoulder.

"I would do anything for you, my love." He kissed her before turning back to the eggs. "Now sit down. The eggs are almost done." She smiled as she walked over to the baby swing placing Eleanor down in it, switching it on.

Brad dished them both some eggs, bacon, and toast. Erina smiled as he walked back to the stove before she wrapped her arms around his waist. He turned in her arms, looking down at her. "What are you doing." She smirked as she took his hand, leading him to the table.

"I want to take care of you. You have done it for me for so long." He smirked as he pulled her down onto his lap.

"I will gladly do anything for you. You and Eleanor are my life and my world. As long as you two are safe and happy, so am I." Erina nodded as she ran her hand down his chest before settling between his legs. He grabbed her hand, giving her a knowing look. "As much as I love where this is going, we still need to wait 6 weeks." Erina nipped at his neck, hearing his breathing become faster.

"I know. But it doesn't mean that I can't take care of you." She smirked as she found his lips again. Brad wanted to get lost in her. He wanted her to take care of him, but he wanted her to be safe, and getting down on her knees isn't what's suitable for her right now.

"Baby, as good as it sounds, you can't do that right now." Brad cupped her cheeks in his hands. "I would love it if you could do it on the bed." She nodded, moving off Brad's lap taking her seat.

"Fine, but tonight I am taking care of my husband. I need to.... I can't wait another six weeks, just because someone decided to steal my baby by cutting me open." She gave him a sweet smile that made Brad realize that he never thought about how she felt about all this. They could not be intimate and needed to find a way to show him that she is still his wife in every way.

Erina had to wait an extra few weeks before she would get the go-ahead from the doctor. Because of all the internal damage that was done to her by Amelia. They were now on the six weeks wait.

*****

Thomas sat at the front of the courtroom with Conner and Mia at his sides. Brad and Erina were sitting off the side as the room filled up with the public and press. When everyone was there, Thomas motioned for guards to bring all the accused in.

Austin walked to the door opening it and leading everyone in, making them stand in the front. The trial had been going on for the past three days. All the evidence and statements were observed, and every one was found guilty. And they have finally concluded and today was their sentencing.

"Good day, everyone. I will be starting with Neville and the maid." The judge nodded to them to step forward. "It was confirmed that you two were pawns in this, but still you did help Amelia, and you did not go to the police or Austin with this information, which led to Mrs. Davis and baby Eleanor to being attacked. Neville, you are, as a result of this, sentenced to ten years in jail." Neville gasped but doesn't say anything. He knew that they could have had him put in jail for much longer.

"As for you, Miss James. You are, as a result of this, sentenced to sixteen years in prison without parole." She looked at the judge as the tears started running down her cheek. She knew what they were doing was wrong. She just thought that Amelia knew better.

Erina grabbed Brad's hand, squeezing it as she knew that the worst part was still to come. Friends of hers had betrayed her worst than what she thought possible even if she had a forgiving heart. What they had done to Brad and their daughter was unforgivable. Brad could see the worry on Erina's face as he wrapped his arm around her shoulders.

"Now, the next sentence is for the rest of you. I will not be wasting time addressing each of you as you are not worth it. What you had been apart of could have wiped out a family. You conspired and acted on it to have Mr. and Mrs. Davis killed." The Judge took a deep breath, just thinking of what might have happened had his blood boiling. "As a result of this, I sentence you to life in prison" They all gasped. The doctors look at each other with fear in their eyes. "Court is now adjourned." The judge got up, motioning for Austin and Thomas to have the guards take them back to the cells.

Brad led Erina out of the room as the tears fell from her eyes, hearing the sentence. "Love, are you alright?" Brad asked concerned, pulling her closer to him.

"I'm Fine…. It's over. It's really over." She smiled up at him as he nodded, both knowing that after this, they can start fresh and let their family flourish again. "Let's go see our daughter." Brad took her hand as they headed back to their house, where Damon had stayed with Eleanor.

Epilogue

Erina stood on the balcony of her and Brad's bedroom looking down at the gardens. Staff was preparing for the wedding that was going to be held there tomorrow. Resting her hand on her very swollen baby bump, she smiled, thinking how far they all have come.

It had been five years since Amelia had attacked Erina and stole Eleanor. It had taken Erina a long time to get over the nightmares and be able to move forward. Brad had suggested that she see someone who would help her deal with the trauma she had gone through. Erina went to every appointment and finally started feeling better and knew that the danger was over. Three years after the attack, Erina discovered she was pregnant with her and Brad's second child. Everything went well with the pregnancy until they were about 16 weeks into the pregnancy. Erina had started bleeding the morning before her 16-week appointment, and the doctor confirmed that they were losing the baby.

It broke Erina's and Brad's heart losing their little boy at such a young age, not even being able to meet him or let him feel the love that was there for him already, and in a way, Erina thought that it was her fault. She started to pull away from Brad. She would spend all her time with Eleanor. Brad had noticed the change in her personality and knew that he needed to find a way to help her heal.

He had spent his time with her and Eleanor, knowing that when she was ready to talk, she would. A few months after the miscarriage, Brad walked into their room, finding Erina on the bed crying as she held a blue blanket to her chest.

He pulled her into his arms, holding her close, and that was when she finally broke down, telling him how scared she was that she wouldn't be able to have any more children. Brad reassured her that if it was meant for them to just have one child, so be it. Eleanor would have lots of friends with Damon and Conner if they ever had children themselves.

Things were going better. Erina had seen a new doctor who had done a few tests to make sure that she would be able to have a full term pregnancy. All the test results came back to prove that she was in excellent health and could get pregnant and carry the baby to full term.

A few months after the test was done, they found out she was pregnant again. At their 12 week appointment, it was discovered that she was having twins. Brad instantly felt his chest swelling with pride as they watched the two babies move on the screen.

Erina was taking things easy as she was now a high-risk pregnancy with being pregnant with twins. Brad had requested to have some of her duties given to Mia, who helped Erina with whatever she needed. Whenever Brad couldn't go with her, he would send either Damon or Conner to go with her to make sure that she was safe.

At their 28 week scan, the doctor made a shocking discovery, unsure how they missed it. He told Erina and Brad that they were having triplets and not twins. The one baby was hiding the whole time, and with the space getting a bit cramped, there was no more hiding. Brad almost fainted at the news knowing that they would be bringing three babies home and not just two. This would make them a family of six like he and Erina had always wanted.

And now here they were at 30 weeks pregnant, and the babies were all doing great. They hoped to get her to at least 34 weeks, or as long as they could keep them in there. Erina was prepared for the babies to come a bit early, knowing that triplets rarely stayed inside full term.

Erina felt Brad's strong arms come around her waist as they rested on her baby bump, feeling his hot breath on her neck. "Good Morning, husband." She looked back, smiling at him.

"Good Morning, my queen" He kissed her cheek, resting his chin on her shoulder. "How are you feeling?" He rubbed his hands over her stomach feeling the babies move under his hands.

"I am uncomfortable but excited for tomorrow." She leaned into Brad's chest feeling his heat as he tightened his grip on her.

"Mommy…. Daddy…." Erina and Brad turn to see Eleanor running into their room, smiling as her kitten Whiskey followed her. Brad leaned down, picking his princess up as she wrapped her arms around his neck. "Do I get to put my dress on today?" She asked Erina, her eyes sparkling with excitement.

"No, sweetie, only tomorrow." Erina gave her a hug while they stand and look out over the garden. Eleanor was excited to be the flower girl for the wedding tomorrow and just wanted to wear her dress.

*****

The next morning Erina stood in front of Eleanor, busy curling her hair, before pining them away from her face. Erina heard a knock at the door, telling Eleanor to sit still while she opened the door.

Walking over to the door and opening it, Erina found her friend standing on the other side.

"Good Morning." She squealed as she hugged Erina before walking in.

"Good Morning. Are you ready for today, or should I sneak you out?" Erina raised her brow.

"I am so ready for this. I will not let that man slip out of my hands." Erina laughed as they walk back to Eleanor. "Look how pretty you look." She leaned in, giving Eleanor a kiss on the cheek.

"Are you going to put on your dress now?" Eleanor smiled as she watched her walk over to the closet where her dress was hanging.

"Yes, I am." She smiled warmly at the little girl. "Do you think Uncle Conner will like it?" She asked as Eleanor shook her head back and forth.

"I heard daddy say that uncle Conner will love the dress, but then Uncle Conner said he can't wait to see you out of the dress….."

"Eleanor…." Both the ladies blushed, hearing what Eleanor said. "Were you listening to grown-up talk again?" Erina gave her a knowing look.

"I'm sorry, mommy." Eleanor hugged her mommy, pouting as she looked at her.

*****

Conner stood at the front of the aisle, waiting for his bride. He had never thought that he would meet the love of his life, but three years ago, when he took Erina to one of her appointments, he met the most amazing, beautiful, loving woman he had ever seen.

At first, he thought that Gen wasn't interested, as she paid him no mind at all, but the next visit Erina had, he went with her again. She told him that if he wanted to impress Gen, he should take her a cup of coffee, which Conner had done. And he was sure it was love at first sip. He wasn't sure what she liked most, the coffee or him, but he wasn't about to complain.

They had dated for a year and a half before he finally asked her to move in with him. And after living with her for only three months. He realized that he didn't want to spend his life without her. He wanted her to be his wife, his family, the one he spends the rest of his life with.

Erina had helped him with the proposal, all too excited that her best friend had finally found love and that his soon to be fiance was also her best friend now. He took Gen out to the marina where Erina had a table set up for them on a small island just off the shore. Conner had waited until after dinner to finally get down on one knee and asked Gen to marry him. At first, she just stared at him with this smirk on her face before finally saying yes.

And here he was, standing at the front of the aisle waiting for her to become his wife. This was a day he gets to spend with all his friends and family, a day that he thought never would come with everything that was going on five years ago.

"Are you ready?" Brad asked as he took his place on the dais. Conner smiled, giving Brad a nod as he pulled on his suit jacket, making sure that he looked perfect. "Then, I will let the ladies know." Brad smiled, sending a quick text to Erina, letting her know they were ready.

All the guests had arrived, taking their seats. Conner and Genevieve had decided to have the wedding in the backyard of Brad and Erina's mansion, the first place they kissed and officially became official.

Damon and Christian were Conner's groomsman and best man, while Erina and one of Gen's friends were her bride's maid and maid of honor. Gen's brother's son was the ring barrier, and Eleanor was the flower girl.

Brad cleared his throat, letting everyone know they were about to start. Conner turned as Damon and Christian patted his shoulders before standing next to him to wait for the ceremony to begin.

*****

"They are ready." Erina turned as she handed Gen's flowers to her.

"I'm ready as I'll ever be," Genevieve smirked, wiggling her brows. Erina knowing what she meant by it. She was happy for Conner and Gen. They were perfect for each other.
Erina bent down, telling Ash to walk first as soon as the music started. He nodded and waited for the music to start.

As soon as the music started, Conner lifted his head, looking at the back where he saw Ash walking in with the rings. A few moments later, Eleanor came walking down in her pink princess style dress, her long brown hair hanging in curls on her shoulder. She had the same tiara on her head as what Gen had.

"Daddy...." She ran over to Brad as soon as she saw him. Conner chuckled, seeing her run to Brad and forget everything else. She was a real daddy's girl, but she also couldn't be without her mom for more than an hour.

Erina and Sam came down the aisle next. Sam didn't want Erina to walk on her own, being as heavily pregnant as she was. Both Erina and Sam had long flowing pink dresses on, their hair hanging over their shoulders in curls framing their faces.

Gen came down the aisle in her mermaid style dress that hugged every curve. Conner could not take his eyes off her. She was more beautiful than he had ever seen. She had a glow that made him fall in love even more than he already was.

As she made it up to him, he took her hands before kissing her cheek. "You look.... Breathtaking." He whispered as he pulled away from her.

"You don't look too bad yourself." She winked at him as they both turned towards Brad as he began the ceremony.

Conner and Gen gave their vows, both of them making the other cry a little with their beautiful words. Conner stared into Gen's eyes as Brad continues the ceremony.

"Now I pronounce you husband and wife!" Brad smiled at them. "You may now kiss the bride." Conner pulled her close, capturing her lips in a passionate kiss. Pulling apart, he could not believe that she was finally his wife. She was now his family.

*****

A few weeks after the wedding, Erina stood on the balcony of her and Brad's quarters swaying side to side with her baby girl in her arms.

The triplets were born at 37 weeks, not needing to go to NICU. The doctor was surprised that Erina could carry them until 37 weeks, he was sure she would have gone into labor much sooner, but the babies had other plans.

Erina gave birth to identical boys and a little girl. The boys both had dark hair and blue eyes. While the little girl was the spitting image of Brad, with blond hair and blue eyes. Erina and Brad couldn't believe how lucky they were to have their babies healthy and discharged only a few days after they were born.

"Shhh... Little one." Erina calmed the baby as she swayed, trying to get her to sleep. Just as her eyes closed, Erina felt Brad's arm sneak around her waist as he stood next to her with a sleeping Eleanor in his arms. Damon appeared next to Brad on the other side with one of the boys in his arms. Gen and Conner stood next to Erina with the other boy in Gen's arms.

"Have you decided on names for these beauty's yet?" Damon asked as he cradled the baby in his gigantic arms.

"We have, we would like you all to meet, Jackson Christian Davis." Brad motioned to the boy Gen was holding. "We will be calling him Tristan." They all agreed that it's perfect.

"And this is Reagan Catherine Davis." Erina held up the baby girl. Gen smiled as she gave Erina a one-arm hug.

"Hello, Reagan.... It's perfect for her." Gen smiled, thinking of the time they were throwing names around. Reagan was the one name they all adored.

"And this little man is Thomas Alexander Davis." Brad motioned to the one Damon was holding.

"Please tell me he will not be a Thomas?" Damon looked at him with pleading eyes. Brad lets out a hearty laugh, Erina side-eyeing him, knowing what he was planning.

"No, he will be Xander," Erina smirked, knowing Brad wanted to have fun with Damon.
They all laugh as they stand together, looking out over the garden.

Five years later, and finally, everything was as it should be. Brad and Erina had the family they always wanted, and everything was perfect.

END

SPECIAL THANKS

I would like to thank the following people that have been there for me.

My husband and kids - Thank you for helping me and supporting me. My 12 year old son read the first version of this and helped me changed some of the things. Love you all.

My Sister In Law - Simone Olivier - Thanks for encouraging me and for being my support. Love you.

To my Family - Thank for being there for me. Love you all.

My Bestie - Elsebe Luyt - Thanks for being my right hand, for always having my back. And listening to all my crazy ideas. Love you.

To my Arc reader - you guys are amazing. Thank you for taking the time to read this for me.

My fellow author - Melony Ann - (She has an amazing series of the Crane family. Please check it out on Amazon.) Thank you for your insight and help. Love you.

To TabyFairies - Thank you for my amazing book cover and always offering to help. I love you.

To my Tumblr Family - Without you I would have never had the courage to do this. Love you all.

To everyone else that has always been there for me. Thank you all. This wouldn't have been possible without each and everyone of you. Love you all.

Made in the USA
Coppell, TX
09 February 2021

49552053R00134